DON'T FORGET ME

DON'T FORGET ME

DON'T FORGET ME

REA FREY

Published by Thomas & Mercer, Seattle

www.apub.com

Amazon, the Amazon logo, and Thomas & Mercer are trademarks of Amazon.com, Inc., or its affiliates.

ISBN-13: 9781662513237 (paperback)
ISBN-13: 9781662513220 (digital)

Cover design by Damon Freeman
Cover image: © [Credit] / [Stock House]; © [Credit] / [Stock House] [TK]

Printed in the United States of America

For my readers, always

Kill a man, one is a murderer.
Kill a million, a conqueror.
Kill them all, a god.
—Jean Rostand

1

The body floated to the lake's surface during my morning row.

I was on my last half mile back to the dock when it shuddered to the top. It bounced once, then settled, like a buoy. I glanced around, frozen breath spilling from my open mouth, then rowed closer, the oars trembling in my hands. I peered over the lip of the boat. The damp cold, fueled by fear, seeped into my bones and made them ache.

Only bits of the body were visible, as a plastic tarp had evaporated in several spots, revealing chunks of skin and bone: the crest of a nose, the bulk of a forearm, the patchwork of forked veins on a bare, decomposing foot.

I floundered then and sucked in audible breaths as I gauged the community behind me. Tall, wide, nearly identical black-and-white houses perched in the distance, each tiny yard manicured and maintained according to the strict community rules.

It was early, just after sunrise, and I knew the rhythms of this town by now—enough to know that no one would be near the lake except me. It was why I came out so early, because it was quiet and I could be alone, a strange fact I was still getting used to after living so long with other people.

I fumbled in my parka for my cell phone. My fingers stabbed the smooth screen, and I waited for the call to connect. When the 911 dispatcher asked what my emergency was, I glanced at the corpse.

"I found a body," I said. "In the lake." I breathed into my cupped palms, my phone cradled between my cheek and shoulder. I didn't know the exact address but told them I was in Cottage Grove, behind the community pool. There was a dock that jutted into the lake. I would meet the cops there. The dispatcher asked for my name, and I hesitated, recently having returned to my maiden name. "Ruby Knight." *No more Ruby Winslow. I am Ruby Knight.*

Before I hung up, a thought occurred to me. "Do I drag the body with me back to shore?" If the dispatcher said yes, I wasn't sure how to manage.

"No, ma'am. Leave the body where it is. Do not touch it. Officers will meet you at the dock."

I knew that in a matter of moments, our calm neighborhood would erupt to life as the flashing blue-and-red lights disturbed the peace. The quiet was partly why I liked it here. After I'd spent nearly twenty years as a trauma nurse in the inner city, Tom had relocated us out here, none of us knowing how definitively our lives would blow up from that one decision.

Now, I was bobbing next to a dead body. From the looks of it, it had been here awhile. I dug my oar back into the icy water and churned the boat toward the dock. I attempted to steady my heartbeat, which flickered beneath my sweater like a tiny light frantically being switched on and off.

I craned my neck to make sure the body was still there. I wondered how it had surfaced. Had it been shoddily tied down? Had something gnawed through a rope and set it free?

I immediately thought about his or her loved ones. As a trauma nurse, I'd experienced endless bad news over the years, which was one of the reasons I'd left. There was nothing like staring into the eyes of a family member who still clung to hope and then watching as their face crumpled and their heart broke.

No.

I did not envy the police or what would happen next, how our sleepy community would become riddled with crime tape and endless questioning.

I especially didn't envy what poor family would receive the horrible news that someone they loved was dead.

2

I made it back to the dock in record time.

I tied up my boat, secured the oars, and climbed to the surface on shaky legs. This far in the country, I realized it would take a while for the blistering sirens to disrupt the silence. My eyes scanned the body again, paranoid it would sink or disappear and the police would think I had imagined it.

My neighbor Ralph emerged from his back patio with a steaming cup of coffee in hand. The squeak of his door made me jump, and I turned, heart pounding, to issue a wave.

Ralph was tall and wellspoken and had spent the last thirty years as a judge, mostly for petty crimes and a few death-penalty cases. Until last year, we'd been friendly acquaintances, but a crisis had tipped us into allies . . . secret keepers, even. He stood in his magenta bath-robe—which reached only his dark shins, revealing two shockingly long ankles—and nodded my way.

"Morning, Ruby."

"Morning, Ralph." I practically sprinted toward him so he wouldn't come closer, wouldn't scan his eyes across the lake and spot the corpse. Though I'd seen countless dead bodies, it was in the confines of a hos-pital. Now, I imagined Ralph's eyes widening in disbelief as he located it, how he'd insist on getting closer, maybe grabbing a pair of binoculars or demanding I take the boat back out. I didn't want to disturb his morning any sooner than I had to. "You're up early."

"Big day in court." He didn't discuss his cases, of course, but on occasion, I could get him talking, and we would swap war stories about the worst things we had ever seen. In some ways, our professions were similar, though sentencing someone to death and saving people from that same fate was always the dividing line between us.

"Oh yeah?" I bobbed on my toes in an attempt to keep warm, the heat I'd worked up during my row already gone.

"You okay?" He cocked his head and slurped a long sip of coffee, then gestured to his mug. "Care for a cup?"

"That's okay. I—"

The blast of a siren shocked us both as it wailed down the main road and whined louder.

Ralph turned, one of his slippers snagging on the edge of the patio. A bit of his coffee sloshed over his cup and splashed onto the tile. "What in the world?"

I ignored the impulse to jump to action. That sound had been my *go* signal at work as ambulances barreled into the emergency room drop-off, where I'd be waiting to meet the EMTs. My adrenaline surged now as a reminder of just how many years sirens served as the warning bell to get focused for what lay ahead. Maybe the same was true now.

"Ralph."

He turned to gauge me, concern etched in the fine lines of his handsome face.

"I called them."

He stepped closer and surveyed the landscape of my body, then finally nodded as he assessed I wasn't hurt. The sirens intensified as they snaked toward the dock, probably waking every child and adult along the way. The horses in the pasture neighed and stampeded toward their barn, and guilt spread through my body, thick and warm.

5

"Why? Is it . . ." He trailed off as he looked me over one more time. I stabbed a frozen hand toward the lake, and he shuffled closer, squinting into the distance. "I don't see . . ." Again, his voice faded before he inhaled sharply, choking on his own spit. "Is that a *body?*"

I nodded, curt. "I saw it when I was rowing. It was just . . . there. Floating."

He looked from me to the lake and back to me again. "Are you okay? That must have been terrifying, especially after everything you've been through these last few months."

I swallowed the last part of that sentence, burying it with all the other trauma, and focused on what was at stake now, in the moment. Suddenly, I whipped back to the lake. "Ralph, if there's a body in our lake, then that means someone put it there." Though it wasn't a question, he nodded, seeming to make an instantaneous judgment.

"Maybe. But we have to figure out the facts first."

This couldn't have been an accidental drowning. Not when the body was wrapped up like that. I thought of Cottage Grove's obsession with true crime. There were thriller book clubs and "whodunnit" crime nights, where we "solved" cold murder cases in under three hours. We called ourselves the Murderlings. At first, I'd been hesitant to join, but once I solved my first case, I was hooked. Now, with a murder in our own backyard, they were going to have a field day with this.

Finally, two cop cars and an ambulance ground to a halt near the dock, chewing up grass and spitting gravel into the air. Ralph grunted, as we both knew how meticulous the landscaper was with his work.

A man and a woman exited their cop cars, one in uniform and one in plain clothes.

"Mrs. Knight?" the woman asked.

I raised a hand, nodding. "Yes, I'm Ms. Knight," I corrected. "I'm the one who called."

"I'm Detective Ellis," she said. "Katherine." She was smartly dressed in jeans, a white T-shirt, and a black blazer. Her brown hair stopped right at her shoulders and was stick straight. "This is Officer Dent." She offered a tight-lipped smile and motioned to the other officer, who raked a pudgy hand down his ruddy face. "Must have given you quite the scare this morning."

I swallowed. "It was definitely the most unusual thing I've seen during a row, yes," I confirmed.

She scoured the water, her ice-blue eyes snagging on the drifting form, before turning back to me. "It's going to take some time to get forensics down here, get the body out. Can you give me your address, and I'll swing by to ask you some questions? No need to stand out here in the cold."

I rattled off my address and eyed Ralph, who was taking it all in. He introduced himself, then said he had to get to court but would be available this evening for questioning, if needed.

I told Ralph goodbye and began the short walk back to my house. A few of the neighbors were out on their back decks or patios, straining to see what all the commotion was about. Avoiding eye contact, I rushed inside my house, hurried upstairs, and took a scalding shower. The morning's events replayed in my head, and I was appalled but curious to know who was in our lake.

After I could feel my fingers and toes again, I quickly dressed and padded downstairs to make some coffee. Ever since I'd left nursing, I'd yet to pick up another job. I had decent savings, thanks to the home I'd sold prior to purchasing this one. Tom had refused to let me put my own money toward the down payment. Looking back, I could see that was just one of the many ways he'd controlled the narrative of our relationship—one of the ways he'd chosen to control me.

I remembered when he found Cottage Grove, a roughly open spot on the map about an hour outside Nashville. At the time, it was nothing but sprawling farmland, and the developers were in phase one of building. He said it was going to be the hottest commodity once word got out and wanted to build the house of our dreams.

I wasn't sure. When I thought about moving from my urban life and cozy home, with all its flaws and quirks, building exactly what I wanted sounded more overwhelming than enticing. I'd never wanted to pick out my own windows or cabinets, to hem and haw over kitchen pulls or a soaking tub. Even as I told him my reservations, I could tell his mind was already made up. Tom was a lawyer, after all; he could talk his way into, or out of, anything.

I assessed the kitchen and dining room now, as if a stranger might. Everything was perfectly appointed. Pops of color in the art and throw pillows, everything streamlined and sensible. My eyes lingered on the dining room table Tom and I bought at the start of our relationship, full of nicks and scratches from so many years of use. I'd considered getting a new one, but this table had history and looked rustic in our giant modern dining room. Something old to offset all the new. I frowned. Sometimes I worried this house had no charm, that it was soulless, that I had become soulless.

I shook away the ridiculous thought and remembered we had a body in the lake. That was what mattered now. Why was I thinking about my house? I topped off my coffee. I'd been on edge lately, not sleeping, super wound up. In a few minutes, the caffeine would kick in, and the fog would lift.

I stared down into my coffee cup, knowing I needed to give this stuff up. It made my heart race and heightened my anxiety. I downed what was left and turned in a circle, a crushing loneliness meeting me when I stopped.

Sometimes, it took me so off guard, I couldn't breathe. I used to get like that sometimes in the ER, when the last rush had come through and my adrenaline had worn off. I'd be cleaning up for the day, excited to go home and draw myself a bath, and something dark would hit me—a memory, maybe, of before.

Before I'd become a nurse. Before I'd become Tom's wife or a mother. Before my mother had died. Before I . . .

I shook away the thoughts and marched to the living room to check my emails. I had no time to think about before.

Before was dangerous.

As I waited for them to load, I could feel the itch to *do*, to save, that loneliness working its way up my body like vines around a tree. Now that the house screamed back at me in its wicked silence, a reminder of what I no longer had, I realized, sadly, there was no one left to face—or save—but myself.

COTTAGE GROVE FORUM

a forum for Cottage Grove residents to share, connect, and explore our bustling community!

NOTE: We do not tolerate HATRED OR CYBER-BUL-LYING of any kind!!!

hippiemama23: have you guys heard what's happening? Someone found a body in our lake!?!?

lettucehead4life: I told the board that a manmade lake was a terrible idea. My cousin told me once about an entire family of deer that had been slaughtered and drowned in their lake. Their TODDLER found them. Can you imagine?

nashvegasart: We are talking about a human, not deer.

lettucehead4life: Well I'm partial to animals. That's why I'm a vegetarian.

nashvegasart: Your right. Deer are delicious.

lettucehead4life: wow. At least you know the difference between your and you're.

nashvegasart: At least I know where to get protein.

crystallover: Who is it? Do they know?
shianna: WTF?! We moved from L.A. to get away
from crime!!!!!!! How is this happening???????
Do you think it happened before they built these
homes???? Do you think we're safe?
hippiemama23: I think one of the neighbors found
the body. can your imagine?
crystallover: She probably did it. I've heard the
rumors . . .
hippiemama23: *you not your
lettucehead4life: Rumors about WHAT? Who is she?
crystallover: Ruby
softatheart: She used to be a nurse.
crystallover: I heard she went nuts after her kid died.
Or went missing or whatever? Then her husband
left her. Maybe she lost it and killed someone???
That's like some made-for-TV shit, right there.
dahmernotjeffrey: it's always the wife.
nashvegasart: i think you mean it's always the husband, but yeah, maybe in this case, the wife???
though we don't even know who's in the lake.
dahmernotjeffrey: still, everyone's a suspect
shianna: My brother is a producer. Maybe I should
get him out here! Ha! Sidenote: Does anyone know
if the pool is heated? We miss the water!!!!
hippiemama23: It is totally heated. Open year-
round! I'm sure it's fine!
shianna: Oh yay! Or should we not go, since there's,
like, a dead body??????
hippiemama23: I think it's okay. They'll let us know
if we need to worry about anything.
nashvegasart has left the conversation

3

NOW

Two hours later, Detective Ellis rang my doorbell.

I had fallen asleep on the couch, probably from the adrenaline dump. I stood quickly, slightly dizzy, and stumbled toward the door.

"Ms. Knight? May I come in?" Her voice was muffled from the other side.

I opened the door. The detective clocked the expensive furniture and art. "Lovely home you have here."

"Thanks." I closed the door as she stepped inside. "Coffee?"

"That'd be great. Thanks."

I walked to the kitchen, and she took her time trailing behind me. "Tidy."

"Easy when you live alone," I said.

"You live alone?" I could hear the surprise in her voice.

"Not initially." I filled the pot and shook some coffee grounds into the filter. There was an awkward silence as the coffee spit into the pot. "Cream? Sugar?"

"Black's fine."

I poured the coffee into a mug and slid it across the island. She chose not to sit on the barstool, so I stood across from her, waiting.

"Thank you."

I suppressed a bit of annoyance, ready for her to just get to the point. "Do you know who it is yet?"

"No, ma'am. No identification on him."

"Him?" Though I'd assumed it was a man, I couldn't quite tell.

"Yes." She examined the room again and pointed to a large abstract piece above the fireplace. "Great piece."

"Thanks." I didn't bother telling her I painted it, that I'd taken up painting when I couldn't sleep. My eyes lingered over the canvas. Painting made me think of Ryan, and I needed to stay focused. "So what can I help you with?"

"Ah, yes." She set her coffee down and patted her pocket before pulling out a small pad of paper and a pen. "If you could walk me through what happened this morning, that would be great."

I recalled my typical morning routine, the daily row, what I'd found, and that I called 911 immediately.

"And your neighbors . . . anyone missing recently? Any issues or domestic disputes you're aware of?"

"I . . . no, I don't think so." On the word *missing*, my heart clenched. "I only moved here a little over a year ago. I know most of the neighbors but obviously not all of them. Do you think it's someone who lived here?"

"No way to know yet. The body could have been moved from somewhere else. Water makes it difficult to determine the time of death," she added, "but that's what forensics is for." She took a loud slurp of coffee. "You said you live alone now. What about when you first moved in?"

I hesitated. "My husband, Tom, left me. Us. He left several months ago." I cleared my throat, suddenly uncomfortable.

"I'm sorry to hear that." I waited for her to press for more. "You said *us*. Do you have kids?"

I closed my eyes as the emotion brimmed once again, then opened them and steadied my gaze on the detective. "A daughter. Just started college in the fall." It felt like a betrayal to say that Lily was at college.

She wasn't. But it was easier than telling the truth. I wanted to believe she was out there somewhere, but teenage girls who went missing usually didn't turn back up.

"Where?"

"MIT."

She nodded, impressed. "Must get lonely here."

Electricity buzzed in my chest, a saw hacking through heart and bone. *What once was mine . . .* I shrugged. "Sometimes."

Silence bloomed between us. The refrigerator hummed, and the ice maker kicked cubes into the bucket. The detective snapped to attention then, as if remembering why she was really here.

"Today must have been quite the event for you."

I busied myself topping off her coffee. "I was a trauma nurse. I'm good with unexpected situations." *Except when it's happening directly to me.*

"Trauma nurse." She jotted something down. "Not a lot of hospitals nearby, are there?"

"I retired."

She smirked. "Aren't you a little young to retire?"

"Not after twenty years in the ER. Ages you." I cocked one shoulder and let it drop. "I'll move on to something else eventually. Just haven't found what I want to do yet."

"That's fair. We don't take enough breaks in life, do we?"

She asked a few more questions and then said she'd circle back around with any follow-ups. I walked her out and collapsed against the large oak door, suddenly drained from mentioning Tom and Lily.

I stepped into the foyer and assessed the house as the detective must have. There were no family photos displayed, nothing too personal to remind me of all that I'd lost. Instead, I had chosen nondescript furniture, loud art that would be a conversation starter, and clean, stiff furniture that didn't invite people to linger.

Exhausted, I tried to figure out what I wanted to do today. My fingers yearned to create, to tear into a canvas or work in the garden. But it was too cold for that. After shrugging on my coat and slipping into my boots, I headed out for a walk.

The street crackled with uncertainty as neighbors walked their dogs, whispered into cell phones, or huddled on porches with steaming mugs in hand. I wasn't sure what I was looking for or expected to find, but I wanted to know who this person was and if I should be worried.

I pulled my jacket tighter as the cold air stole my breath. I needed to gather wood for a fire later, maybe make some chicken soup. As happened so often, that deep guttural ache edged its way into my heart. Without the fast pace of my job, the busyness of raising a child, or the familiarity of having a husband, I was still gaining my footing around what it meant to be completely alone.

"Ruby!"

Cassie, one of my acquaintances in the neighborhood, rushed across her manicured lawn and fell into step beside me. As an interior designer, she was always on the go, but this morning, she looked disheveled, still in pajamas.

"Can you believe this?" she asked in a hushed whisper. "I mean, a *dead* body, here, in Cottage Grove?" I knew what she was insinuating. People paid astronomical prices to build their homes here, as if by paying more, we could edge crime out.

"I can believe it," I said. "Because I'm the one who found him."

"*No.*" She squeezed my forearm so tightly I feared she might leave a bruise. "How awful for you." She looked toward the cluster of official vehicles by the dock, her eyes registering something she would not say. "Do they know who it is yet?"

"I don't think so." I shivered again as I walked closer to the dock. "But it certainly seems whoever dumped that body had no intention of it ever resurfacing."

Cassie shuddered. "I don't know how you ever worked in the ER. Seeing all those people . . ."

It was a common refrain I heard often, but much like for a mortician or doctor, the grotesque became ordinary after a while. While I knew this situation was different, something about it *hadn't* rattled me to my core, and I worried that my job, my past, and my recent losses had made me more desensitized than I would have liked.

"God, wait until the Murderlings get a whiff of this," she joked.

I'd already thought about what fodder this would be for our next meetup. Part of me wondered if this wasn't some sick joke. What if the body wasn't even real and this was just an elaborately staged fake crime?

We stopped at the lip of the dock while bodies in protective equipment fussed around the area. I searched for Detective Ellis but didn't see her and suddenly felt like I was intruding.

"Have they questioned you yet?" I asked.

"Questioned me? No, of course not. Why? Are they going to?" Cassie's brown eyes were wild and worried, her usually smooth hair whipping manically in the wind. She went to grip her pearls but realized she wasn't wearing them and let her hand drop.

I opened my mouth to explain that they would be questioning everyone, especially since he had been found in the neighborhood, but I didn't want to give her anything else to be nervous about. "I'm sure it's standard. They'll need to talk to everyone once they find out who he is."

We observed the commotion as a million thoughts clashed for space in my brain. I wondered what would happen next, of course, but mostly, worry dug into my skin like claws, as though there was something very important I'd forgotten.

4

"Lily, you're going to be late!"

I checked the time as I poured my third cup of coffee. If it wasn't for me, Lily would never get to school on time. I used to help her lay everything out the night before, as if she were still a child. Sometimes Lily struggled with making decisions, and I found that creating a plan and staying organized helped ease her anxiety.

She had finals today, and I wanted to make sure she was up, fed, and out the door on time, especially since we now lived so much farther away.

Everything was still in boxes, and the house was a mess, but I could see how lovely it would all eventually be. This was Tom's dream home, and he'd sunk his entire savings into it. A forever home, all before the age of forty. He'd told me multiple times how lucky we were and how I shouldn't take even one second of it for granted. Though I had my doubts, I knew better than to second-guess any of his decisions.

Lily finally bounded down the stairs, shrugging her backpack on. "Do you know how long it takes to get to school now?" She reached for my coffee cup and took a swig, looking so much older than seventeen.

"It's almost summer," I reminded her. "So hopefully you can find things to do closer to Cottage Grove."

She rolled her eyes. Dark circles, imprinted from years of fitful sleep, marred the flesh beneath her lower lash line. "There's nothing to do around here."

I decided not to remind her she had a new Bronco to go with her brand-new commute, an early birthday present before she turned eighteen, but she was already deep into her phone, smirking as she fired off a text.

"You need to eat." I shoved a smoothie into her hands.

Finally, she lowered the phone with a dramatic sigh and sipped. She made a face and stared into the glass. "What is this?"

"Nutritious," I said, wiping a rag over a glob of smoothie that had dripped from the blender. I never tired of looking at Lily. With wild red hair, bright-green eyes, and a dusting of freckles across her nose, she stood out wherever she went. "Do you feel ready for your tests today?"

She chugged the smoothie, made another painful face, and smeared the back of her hand across her mouth. "Debatable."

I grabbed the glass from her, posing my next question carefully. "How have you been sleeping?" Lily had struggled with sleep her whole life, riddled with insomnia, sleepwalking, and night terrors. Finally, we'd had to medicate her for a stretch of time, on top of her other meds, as she was so exhausted she would fall asleep during class. She seemed better, but how did I *really* know if she was sleeping through the night?

She shrugged and walked around the massive island, already lost in her phone. I stopped her. "Hey, look at me."

She sighed again but looked up and offered a fake smile. A blueberry skin hugged her front tooth, and I motioned toward it, which made me laugh. How quickly she had grown up. Soon, she would be gone. She fingered the skin free, studied it, and then flicked it into the air. "I'm good, Mom. I promise. I need to go, okay?"

After moving past me, she didn't even wave goodbye as the large front door opened and shut. Before I could descend into worry, Tom appeared, smoothing down his tie as he grabbed a banana and chomped it in two greedy bites.

His dark hair was still damp from the shower, and he smelled clean and sharp. He swallowed and smiled. His green eyes—Lily's eyes—crinkled at the corners as he assessed me.

"Your first official day *off* the job," he said. He whistled as he tossed the peel into the compost bin. "How does it feel?"

I stared around the massive kitchen with its sage-green cabinets and pearly white countertops, then toward the back wall made entirely of glass. Our patio lay beyond with a firepit and heavy Adirondacks. "Strange," I finally said. "Like I'm playing hooky."

"Well," he said as he adjusted his tie. "If anyone deserves to play hooky, it's you." He gathered his papers in his briefcase and clicked it shut. "I've got a meeting with Stan tonight." He rolled his eyes. "Downtown. Don't wait up."

I leaned a hip against the island and crossed my arms. "Downtown? Are you going to hop on one of those pedal pubs with all the bachelorettes after dinner?"

He grinned. "Oh, definitely."

I smacked his arm playfully with a dish towel. *This feels good,* I realized. We hadn't been light or playful with each other in so long. Maybe this move would be good for all of us; maybe it would help repair some of the cracks in our marriage.

He patted his pockets to make sure he had everything. As a criminal defense attorney, Tom was a team player, especially when his boss was in town. He rushed toward the front door, then scooped his keys from the porcelain bowl on the entry table. The door slammed shut, and the silence descended as swiftly as an unexpected storm.

There was something strange about my family continuing on with their daily routines, rushing through their mornings, hustling to get places on time now that we were so much farther from the city. Normally, I'd be gone before both of them, happy to take my shift before the sun was even up, never knowing what I'd find. My entire career, I'd lived in fight or flight, and now?

Now, I stared at the piles of boxes to unpack, a massive house to furnish and decorate. *Did I choose this life?*

My eyes lingered on the island. Lily had left her physics textbook and her homework. Groaning, I grabbed them and thought about texting her but knew she wouldn't have time to turn around and retrieve them without being late. The last thing I wanted to do was add more stress to her day. Lily loathed taking tests, mostly because she always agonized over her answers, even though she was one of the smartest kids I knew.

I finished my coffee, swiped my keys, and drove as fast as I could through thick, stagnant traffic to get to her high school. I searched for her car in the lot and spotted it almost immediately. It was still a good ten minutes before the first bell, and kids were clumped outside, chatting, listening to music, or arching over their phones, completely antisocial.

My eyes panned the manicured stretch of lawn, but I didn't see her. I scooped her book and homework under my arm, trying to remember what she had first period. At the edge of the lot, behind a cypress, I heard yelling. I stopped, angled back, and took a few steps toward the commotion.

To my horror, a boy was gripping Lily's elbow, rattling it like a stick. He was wiry and thin, but he loomed over her. Everything in my body tensed as he dropped his voice and hissed something into her face.

"Hey!" My voice commanded attention as I stalked over, all my limbs finally moving as they should. The boy turned, the rage still apparent on his face, and Lily's eyes widened, then filled with tears as she saw me.

The boy dropped her arm and ran a hand through his greasy, unkempt hair. Up close, he had dark circles under his eyes, too, and a gnarly scar above his eyebrow.

"What's going on?" I looked between them but really more at Lily. She squeezed her elbows, caving in on herself, closing up. I knew that gesture all too well. I'd probably taught it to her. Before the boy could answer, I steered Lily out of earshot. "Are you okay? What was that about?"

I couldn't ask her more than that, couldn't overwhelm her already crammed brain. Doctors had explained early on that we had to approach Lily gently if we didn't want her to shut down. *Kid gloves*, one psychiatrist had said.

"It was nothing." She stared at her boots. "Just a misunderstanding."

The boy stalked off, muttering under his breath. In my head, I was already talking to the principal about this child and getting him kicked out of school. "What's his name?"

"Andrew," she spat. "Andrew Tarver."

"And Andrew is . . . what? A friend? A boyfriend?"

"God, no." She rubbed her hands along her sweater and looked nervously behind me. "Mom, can we talk about this later?" Finally, her eyes refocused on me. "Wait, why are you here? Is it Dad?" Worry etched in again, tiny little cracks almost visible on her skin.

"No, sweetie, nothing like that. You forgot this." I handed over her book and homework, and I could see confusion on her face. She always packed her backpack the night before, so how had she left these behind?

"I didn't take these out of my bag," she confirmed.

I shrugged. "They were on the island. Maybe they fell out?"

Such a tiny thing, a book and homework being left behind, but not for Lily. Never for Lily.

"No." I could see she was getting riled up, even more so than the spat with Andrew.

"Honey, it's fine. Why don't you get inside, okay? Try to have a good day." I squeezed her arm, not daring to give her a hug, which would be the equivalent of teenage social suicide.

Once the bell rang and the kids were gone, I marched inside to talk to her principal about Andrew Tarver and make sure nothing like this ever happened again.

\~ \~ \~

Once I was back, rather than unpack, I decided to take a lap around the neighborhood.

We'd not met anyone yet, and I was curious to see what types of neighbors we'd chosen with our forever home.

Part of me worried we'd made a rash decision moving so far, but Tom had secured the land over two years ago without much of a conversation, and with the rising cost of lumber and the explosive Nashville real estate market, the build had stalled. After endless delays, it was finally done, and here we were, in a house he'd wanted, nothing but time stretching before me.

I slipped on my tennis shoes and headed out. The summer sun was strong, even this early. Half-erected houses reminded me that this was still an up-and-coming neighborhood and that it would be noisy with construction for the foreseeable future. Our block was mostly done, thankfully, but I'd seen the plans. This place, once complete, would be its own little community with shops, a grocery store, cafés, and tailored amenities to basically ensure you never had to leave if you didn't want to.

I was used to the grit of East Nashville. When Tom and I met, I was living in a small bungalow I'd bought in the early 2000s, when that side of town was still riddled with crime and the prices were reasonable. When I'd sold it, for nearly a million dollars, I was floored and also sad to say goodbye to a neighborhood I'd seen rise from the ashes. In contrast, Cottage Grove felt pristine, so fundamentally perfect, so preplanned that I wasn't sure how I'd fit in.

I knew that Tom wanted to get out of the hustle and bustle of Nashville, with its endless traffic and new properties being built on every square inch of land. He wanted peace and quiet, especially knowing Lily would leave for college in the fall, and it would finally just be the two of us. After so many years as a threesome, I couldn't imagine it. For so much of my relationship with Tom, I had been gone for long erratic shifts, sleeping in my own house because it was close to the hospital. Now, without my work, I knew that Tom wanted me to get back into the domestic side of things. I loved to cook and throw dinner parties, and I hoped we could find a good group of friends in the neighborhood to entertain.

I waved at a few neighbors I saw, many with young kids, rushing off to school, presumably. I wondered where the nearest elementary school was and felt grateful we didn't have to base where we lived around what schools were best. Tom had enrolled Lily in the most prestigious high school, and the two of them already had her future mapped out. She'd been accepted to MIT to study engineering, and Tom couldn't be prouder that his daughter was picking such a reliable career. I didn't mind what she did as long as she was healthy and happy.

I curved down a long stretch of road where orange flags marked the next batch of homes to be built. Every house was purposefully close together so that you could get to know your neighbors. It was the same in East Nashville, though there, each home was a monument in and of itself: pink Victorians, blue bungalows, skinny moderns, tiny brick ranches. Such a rich tapestry of styles, but here, everything was uniform, either black or white. Tall and skinny, or fat and wide. No exposed aboveground wiring or streetlights, no parked cars on the side of the road, no noise pollution, no unsightly trash cans stacked on the curb. It was quiet—so quiet, in fact, that I could hear the breath escape in and out of my lungs as I quickened my pace.

I wound my way toward the lake, which was less than a quarter mile from our house. The lake had been a strong selling point for us, but the houses on the water were out of our price range, so we'd set-tled for something within walking distance. Now, the water glittered beautifully, clear and calm, and I walked down to the edge of the lake. I never saw anyone swimming, but there were no signs to suggest we couldn't. Behind me, the massive community pool sat empty as well. I knew it was a Tuesday, and most people had jobs, but I decided that I could seize the day and sit by the water for a while.

I pushed through the black gate and stepped inside, noticing the pristine cabanas and uniform blue-and-white-checked chairs. I removed my shoes, sat on the edge of the deep end, and let the heated salt water tingle my shins and feet. I tipped my head back to the sun and felt my body relax, despite an undercurrent of guilt, almost like I was on extended vacation. I'd been working so hard for so long this newfound freedom was as unfamiliar as Cottage Grove.

I knew I would find something to do, something to harness my passions. But for now, I could enjoy myself, get the house set up, and learn more about our neighborhood. The thoughts continued to come and go, drifting back to Lily and that boy, Andrew. The principal said he would keep an eye on things and to have Lily come to him if there was a problem. But I knew she wouldn't. I debated on whether to tell Tom, because I knew how easily he could embarrass Lily or make her life miserable at school. *What he didn't know . . .*

The clank of the gate disrupted my downward spiral. I opened my eyes to see a very fit, shirtless guy, not older than thirty, saunter in and place his towel on one of the chairs. He waved, and I waved back as he secured goggles over his eyes and dropped easily into the water to begin laps.

I couldn't take my eyes off him as he found his rhythm and sliced through the water with ease. After ten straight minutes, I eased my feet out of the water and claimed shade inside the cover of a cabana. I'd just about drifted off when the stranger approached, ripping his goggles off and shaking the excess water from his hair.

"New to the hood?" he asked.

He was startlingly handsome and had a crooked smile that somehow made him even more endearing. I sat up. "I am," I said. "You?"

"Ish," he replied. "Moved here about four months ago. Still getting used to it."

I nodded. "It's a different way to live, right?" I scratched my arm. "Do you do laps every day?"

"I do. I'm an artist and work from home, so I find that this clears my mind."

I perked up. "What kind of art?"

"Abstract, mostly."

"I love to paint," I found myself admitting. No one, not even Tom, knew I enjoyed painting, but I'd adored it as a child. It had become a way to escape, a way to release, a way to *forget*.

"Is that right?" He ripped a hand through his hair, which was slightly longer and curled against his neck. "You still paint?"

"No, not for years." I wanted to say more but didn't.

He smirked. "So what do you do for fun, then?"

To my surprise, I laughed. "Fun?" I shifted into a cross-legged position and tilted my head. "I do not know what this fun is that you speak of."

"Well, a few of the neighbors have started these insane true-crime nights. We have food, drinks, and try to solve murders. I thought it was ridiculous at first, but it turns out murder can be a great way to bond with other people."

"I'm learning so much about my new neighborhood," I joked.

"Seriously, you should come. There's one tomorrow night, in fact. Give me your phone. I'll put in my number."

I hesitated. Did I really want some hot guy's number in my phone? I thought of Tom, about his insane jealous streak and how it had caused endless fights in our marriage. I reminded myself that we'd been good lately, especially since the move.

And shouldn't Tom want me to make friends and get to know my neighbors? *Yes.* I fished my phone from my pocket and handed it over. "I don't even know your name," I said.

"Ryan Fisher. And you are?"

"Ruby Winslow."

He extended his muscled arm, his skin still damp with salt water. I slid my palm into his, and an electric charge throttled up my forearm. His eyes locked with mine as he shook my hand.

"Pleasure to meet you, Ruby."

"You too."

He waved and was gone in a flash. I told myself it was perfectly reasonable to think someone was attractive. I was married, not dead. I'm sure Tom saw attractive women all the time. In a moment, my phone dinged with a text.

I really hope you'll come tomorrow. You should have some fun in your life, Ruby.

Warning bells chimed in my head, but I typed back a quick response. I'll be there.

I closed my eyes, then snapped them open and changed Ryan's name in my phone to a woman's. I wasn't doing anything wrong, but I didn't want to add any fuel to Tom's jealous streak.

Before I knew what I was doing, I shimmied out of my shorts and top and stood in my sports bra and panties. I slipped into the pool and let the water consume me until I grew weightless and began to float.

5

The neighborhood stayed on high alert the entire day and night.

I kept peeking out my front window, watching the detective make her rounds to other people's houses. She would go in, stay for a bit, and emerge, gazing up at the houses, seemingly lost in thought before traipsing to the next one.

I was on pins and needles wondering who the man was and what everyone was saying. Would our neighborhood become an active crime scene? And if so, would we be allowed to come and go as we pleased?

I knew a thing or two about how crimes were investigated, how victims sometimes became suspects. Tom and I never discussed the morality of his job as a criminal defense lawyer, but sometimes the truth sat between us as he got criminals off based on technicalities. Ralph had tried many of his cases, and the two had a healthy dose of respect and friendly ball busting. But to hear about cases was a different thing entirely than witnessing the effects of a probable homicide. This was happening *here*, in Cottage Grove, and someone *out there* was responsible.

I sat outside by the fire after dinner, contemplating the man in the lake and all the months leading up to today. Ryan flashed through my mind again and the piece of art Detective Ellis had commented on.

He'd given me lessons to paint that piece, a secret I'd kept from Tom for months.

Until it wasn't.

I knocked back the rest of the wine, then refilled it with the half-empty bottle on the teak side table. I had been drinking more and more lately, drowning my sorrows with too many glasses after dinner. But drinking felt easier than missing Lily or thinking about Tom, easier than facing the truth of my life, of all that it had become.

The doorbell rang, startling me, and I sloshed a bit of wine from my glass. "Shit." I sat up, slightly tipsy, and dabbed the edge of my sweater. "Just a minute!" I called. I went inside and walked to the front, wondering if it was Cassie coming to dish on what she'd heard. I flipped on the porch light and squinted through the peephole. I'd opted not to get a Ring doorbell like everyone else. I was surprised to see Detective Ellis standing on the other side.

I opened the door and smiled. "Back so soon?"

She offered me a pensive stare. "May I come in again, Ruby?"

"Sure."

This time, she didn't linger or make idle chitchat. She got right to the point, her words slicing straight to the heart of the matter. "We've talked to most of your neighbors and showed them photos of the man in question."

I blinked, wondering why I hadn't seen a photo. She fished something out of her cross-body bag and turned it over. "Do you recognize this man?"

The plastic tarp had been cut away to reveal a face somewhat intact. The hair was gone. The eyes were closed and bloated, the mouth stretched in a horrid, gaping O. His other features were bulbous and bleached of color, the skin of his hands wrinkled like crumpled tracing paper. I forced my eyes back up to his face. *Maybe a man in his forties?* I shook my head. "I'm sorry, no."

Detective Ellis opened her mouth to speak, then pointed to the living room. "May we sit?"

"Of course." I followed behind, my head becoming sharper and more focused with every passing minute. "Do you know who it is?"

"The teeth have been pulled, fingertips scrubbed, hair removed, but we've got forensics working on it."

Jesus. "Okay. Do they know the cause of death?"

"His throat was slit." She smoothed the photo on the coffee table, and I stared at it again, a small shiver traversing my skin.

"Did he live in the neighborhood?" Several seconds passed, and I tried again. "Like I said before, I don't know everyone here, but he doesn't look like any neighbor I've met."

The detective sat back and crossed her arms over her blazer. "Here's the thing, Ruby. We talked to your neighbors at length, and several of them recognized this man."

Shock jolted my system as I sat up straighter. "What? They did?" I snatched the photo again, searching for anything familiar. The face was distorted, like a Halloween mask, a dark, jagged line puckered at the front of the corpse's neck where someone had taken his life with a blade. I shuffled through memories of parties and get-togethers in my head, but nothing sprang to mind. I didn't understand why she was being so cryptic, especially if I didn't know him. Should I, for some reason?

"Ruby . . ." She said my name as if scolding me. She locked eyes with me, and I struggled not to look away. "Your neighbors insist this is your missing husband, Tom Winslow. They identified him." She tapped a blunt, manicured nail on the photo and sat back, recrossing her arms.

I laughed, a sharp bark that died instantly. I met her gaze and registered that she was serious. I looked from her to the picture and back again. "First of all, my husband isn't *missing*. He left. There's a difference. And don't you think if this was Tom, I'd be the first to tell you? I haven't seen him in months. But *this* man"—I stabbed the photo—"is most definitely not my husband, Detective. I am one hundred percent positive."

The detective's brow creased as she searched for what to say. "When's the last time you spoke to your husband?"

I opened my mouth to respond, then snapped it shut. She took my silence as permission to continue.

"So you can't verify that your husband is alive?"

"Of course he's alive," I said. "He packed a bag, took some cash, and left. I had no reason to reach out."

"Do you have any photos of Tom I could take a look at?"

I walked to the credenza, opened the bottom drawer, and rifled through the photo albums. After so many years of digital-only photos, I'd finally gotten fed up and worked for months to print out photos so that we'd have something to physically remember. Who knew that all this time later, I'd be flipping through these photos by myself? I handed her the book. She took her time with the photos, one by one, cross-referencing with the printout of the corpse.

"We'll need to obtain DNA," she said after a while. "Do you have anything of Tom's that might be relevant? A hairbrush? A toothbrush?"

I crossed my arms, suddenly sober and irate. "After he *abandoned* me with our hefty mortgage and our brand-new life? No, I don't."

"I see."

A chilly silence descended between us as I tried to work out why on earth everyone would say this was Tom when it so clearly was *not*.

"We'll need you to come down to the station tomorrow, Ruby. Clear up a few things. Can I take these?" She waved a few photos of Tom in her hand.

I shrugged, and she placed them in a file. "Is that a request or a demand?"

The detective stood and snatched the crime scene photo to stuff back in her bag. "It's a friendly request." She offered a strained smile and then pressed a card into my palm. "Let's say nine?"

I reluctantly took the card, wondering if I needed to call our lawyer. Greg and Tom had worked together for years, and we kept in touch from time to time. The detective let herself out for the second time today, and I stood there, stunned and confused. The man in the water could not be Tom. It wasn't possible. I knew my husband backward and forward, and I'd be able to identify his dead body, even if the dead body in question was almost unrecognizable.

Wouldn't I?

"It's not him," I whispered, almost in an effort to convince myself. "It's not Tom."

COTTAGE GROVE FORUM

shianna: OMG! Did the detective come to your house and, like, question you guys?

crackersmp has joined the conversation
lettucehead4life: Yep. Pretty intense.
nashvegasart: I thought it was rad.
lettucehead4life: Did you offer her some MEAT while she was there?
nashvegasart: You realize that is too easy of a joke.
crackersmp: What did everyone say?
lettucehead4life: I told the truth. Everyone knows it's that missing husband.
crystallover: What missing husband? We are kinda new to the neighborhood.
shianna: We are too! This is all so insane, y'all.
nashvegasart: i thought you were from L.A. @shianna. Why are you saying y'all?
hippiemama23: Look guys. This is serious. We could have a KILLER in our neighborhood!
dahmernotjeffrey: there are killers in every neighborhood.

softatheart: uhhhh, what neighborhood have you been living in, @dahmernotjeffrey? That's super messed up.

nashvegasart: Or pretty rad.

lettucehead4life: you need meds.

hippiemama23: should we set up a neighborhood watch? I read about that in a book somewhere.

lettucehead4life: I think we should for sure. We might go stay with our mother-in-law in Franklin.

nashvegasart: Yeah, cause nothing bad ever happens in Franklin.

crystallover: Where's Franklin?

shianna: we should have a vigil for the deceased.

nashvegasart: They don't know who it is yet.

hippiemama23: the poor guy.

dahmernotjeffrey: maybe he was a horrible person who deserved it?

shianna: @hippiemama23, i think we should definitely plan something.

hippiemama23: 👍

crystallover: can i help?

nashvegasart: let's make it a party. I'll bring the beef.

hippiemama23: gross. Anyone can pitch in. We have to support each other right now. We are at 4245 cottage grove lane. BYOB!!!!!!

crystallover: YAY!

shianna: CU SOON!!!

6

THEN

I rang the next-door neighbor's doorbell, arranging the bottle of wine under my arm.

When Ryan texted me the address, I was floored to find that the neighbor hosting the crime night lived right next door. Daisy Dominguez was the true-crime podcast host of *Death Becomes Me*, which had gone viral after she accurately solved a cold case on air. Now, she hosted weekly crime nights to solve hypothetical murders in under three hours.

Though it didn't seem feasible to solve a crime so fast—even if it was fake—I was still curious. Inside the house, I could hear a sharp explosion of laughter. I tried the handle, and the door opened. "Hello?"

Another roar of laughter descended from the back, where a glass door just like ours was thrust open and a fire roared from a stone pit. It was a mild night, and all the windows were open, allowing a warm breeze to circulate. I glanced at the decor in the foyer, the interesting black-and-white photographs and vintage, flowery furniture so different from my own. I walked toward the kitchen and stood at the precipice to the patio. If Tom had been with me, he would have announced himself loudly and held up the wine, no doubt making a witty joke. He was always the life of the party, making himself known. As a result, I often shrank in his presence, speaking only when spoken to. Now, I just stood there awkwardly, searching for Daisy. Finally, a few people turned, and Daisy rushed forward to greet me.

"You must be my new neighbor." She was a tattooed beauty, reminiscent of a curvy 1950s pinup, with green tortoise cat-eye glasses and jet-black hair cut in a severe bob. "I've been meaning to come say hello. Glad you could join us." Her bloodred lips parted into a genuine smile.

"Me too." I offered the wine. "Who doesn't love murder?"

She laughed, a twinkle in her eye. "Only my victims." She hooked her arm through mine and introduced me to my neighbors, who, to my delight, were a wildly diverse group. Instead of the typical doctors and lawyers (though there were both), it seemed this group was also full of artists, authors, musicians, real estate developers, social justice advocates, and engineers. I asked for the engineer's card so I could give it to Lily.

I attempted to remember names as I made the rounds and got myself a drink: Katy, Ronnie, Beth, Lionel, Eddie, Zoe, Lincoln. After some small talk, I walked to the edge of Daisy's property line to stare into the thick cypresses and water maples. I couldn't help but glance at my own house. Lily's room was lit up, but ours was dark, as Tom was out. I had thought about asking Lily to come tonight but wasn't sure if it was appropriate.

"Enjoying yourself?"

I turned, smiling at the familiar voice. It was Ryan. He looked stylish and comfortable in jogger pants, Vans, a fitted T-shirt, and a ball cap.

"I am now." I immediately flushed as the flirtatious words slipped from my lips. I lifted my drink to self-correct. "Because I have alcohol, I mean." I tilted my head toward the group, which was huddled around the open glass door. "And murder."

"Ah, murder. The topic that brings strangers together." His eyes flashed as he gave me that crooked grin and stuffed his hands deep into his pockets.

I took a sip and squinted at him. "You really know how to talk to a woman."

He tipped forward as if telling me a secret. "You should see what I can do when I'm not talking."

My belly clenched as I struggled to change the subject. "So what's your story?"

"What do you mean?"

I glanced at his bare ring finger. "We've established you're an artist. Are you single? Married? Do you have kids?"

He tilted his head. "Yes, no, and no. You?"

I hesitated. For some ridiculous reason, I was nervous to tell him that I was married with a daughter. I liked being able to innocently flirt for once, to feel like I was still interesting to the opposite sex when my own romantic life had long since grown stale. Before I could say anything, Daisy rang an antique dinner bell and brought everyone to attention.

"All right, Murderlings, it's time!"

The group clapped and moved inside to the massive dining room table. There were notepads, pencils, and a case file in the middle, as well as documents in a sealed envelope.

"Most of you have been here before, but for any newbies, this is how it goes. This is a kit from In Cold Blood, which is the ultimate murder-mystery game." She stabbed the file with her black-and-white acrylic nails. "We have three hours to gather as much information as possible. Your mission is to solve the case *tonight*. Whoever wins gets a point and a guest spot on my podcast, where you can shamelessly promote the fuck out of your business . . . or whatever." She paused for a few laughs. "At the end of the year, the person with the most points wins a deliciously dark prize." She smiled and stuck out her tongue to reveal a diamond stud, then continued. "Are we ready?"

I wanted to ask so many questions. *How long had they been doing this? What happened to the actual cold case she cracked? And if someone here could solve a murder in three hours, then weren't they in the wrong profession?* None of it made actual sense, but this was only a game. I removed my pragmatic nurse brain from the equation, where everything was cause and effect, right or wrong. When using outside-the-box thinking sometimes worked and other times meant life or death.

Daisy set a timer and then opened the case file and read: "Hazel Powell: Case B12-06070998. On November twelfth, the small town of Bowling Green, Kentucky was shocked by the brutal murder of one of its young citizens the night before her college graduation. The victim, Hazel Powell, was murdered in her campus parking lot after celebrating with some friends in her dorm's common area. Jerry Stevens, a local homeless person, was framed for the murder and spent over two decades behind bars despite being innocent. Your job is to prove his innocence and convict the real killer. Who killed Hazel?"

She scattered the contents of the file on the table. I studied each one: There was a headshot of Hazel, blonde, young, and smiling at the camera. Though this was fictional, my heart wrenched at the thought of something like this happening to Lily. I roamed over the suspect sheet, all the friends from the college party with their headshots and statements about what happened that night. There were fabricated newspaper clippings about Jerry, the homeless man; his fingerprints; a police report; and an outline of Hazel's body with indications of what happened. She'd been brutally stabbed fifteen times, strangled, and left behind a car. I winced as I read the report, while others hungrily started making notes and chatting with each other. There was a palpable energy that turned my stomach, but I reminded myself this wasn't real. I'd seen worse things in the ER.

I settled into my own methodical rhythm, getting the hang of it as I cross-referenced other people's notes, and we entered into a passionate debate about who it *couldn't* have been. Daisy had a giant whiteboard off to the side, where we tacked up the suspects' photos and made observations in red marker.

Something sparked in my chest as we began to laugh and get rowdy, arguing with each other. It was the first time in a while I felt purposeful and free, not constantly in my head, worrying about tomorrow or my place in the world. Instead, all that disappeared, and I lost myself to the task at hand as we crept closer to the truth.

As I studied the autopsy photos, which were wildly realistic, a distinct knowing crept up the back of my spine as the murderer jumped immediately to the front of the stack. I stared at the wounds again and checked one of the suspect's statements. The answer bubbled in my chest until I couldn't contain it. "I know who it is," I said.

Daisy's eyes flashed as she glanced at her watch and smirked. "It's only been forty-five minutes, newbie. You really want to make a guess? If you're wrong, you're out."

It was like a game of Clue, but I wasn't bluffing. I was certain.

I made my educated guess—the best friend, Danielle, who'd professed her love to Hazel and been rebuffed and embarrassed. I bit my tongue, not wanting to reveal how I'd figured it out: the stab wounds were only chest height, suggesting the murderer was short, and a man wouldn't have had to stab her so many times without killing her. Also, the strangulation marks were smaller, like a woman's hands, not a man's.

"Is that your final answer?" she joked.

"It is," I confirmed.

Daisy walked to the tiny envelope revealing the true killer and plucked out the piece of paper. She read the findings and stared at me. "Well, I'll be damned," she said.

Several people groaned and slapped the table in frustration, while Ryan gave me an impressed smile.

I shrugged. "It's easy when you pay attention to the details," I said. "Or when you understand murder," Daisy retorted.

Something twitched in my gut, but I smiled and downed the rest of my drink. With the night cut short, wineglasses were refilled, and there was a renewed enthusiasm about learning more about me and my background. It seemed I'd proven myself worthy of their company. I had won the game.

As I relaxed into the conversation, an ear-piercing scream erupted from my house next door. Heart in my throat, I leaped up.

Lily.

Without a word to anyone, I took off toward my house.

7

NOW

I pulled up to the police station right before nine.

Chapel Hill Police Department shared a wall with the fire department and was situated on a busy block of auto shops, cafés, and local boutiques about twenty minutes from Cottage Grove. I hadn't slept at all last night, going over and over what the detective said. *Your neighbors insist this is your missing husband, Tom Winslow.* I'd wanted to call Daisy or Ralph and ask what the hell was going on, but I figured it was better not to talk to anyone yet.

Instead, I called our lawyer, who said he'd meet me at the station. I wasn't sure it was necessary, but I wanted to cover all my bases. I searched for Greg's Mercedes but didn't see it and wondered if I should wait to go in.

I sighed and walked to the front of the police station and stared up at the nondescript brick building. I pushed through the door. Inside, people shuffled around. Burnt coffee and antiseptic filled my nostrils as I approached the front desk.

"I'm here to see Detective Ellis," I said.

An older man with a handlebar mustache under a nose like a flattened mushroom nodded and picked up a phone and barked into the receiver. "Got a visitor." He motioned to the wooden bench attached to the brick wall. "Pop a squat."

I'd been to a few police stations in my life—once when Lily had gotten herself in trouble with some friends from school and was arrested for public drunkenness. Another time when Tom had officially reported her missing. I thought of my father then, with his bushy beard and mean eyes. He'd been arrested multiple times for DUIs, and though my mom had bailed him out every time, she'd always made me wait in the car.

"Ruby." Detective Ellis stood in the hall in slim-fitting jeans and a turtleneck. She looked as tired as I felt. "Follow me."

"My lawyer, Greg Goodard, is meeting me here."

She nodded. "Brant, make sure Mr. Goodard finds us, will you?"

He raised one meaty paw, then dropped it. "Roger that."

The detective skipped the niceties, just as she had last night, and ushered me to a small room with a desk and one window. She motioned for me to sit in the spare metal chair. "As I mentioned, we just have a few more questions about your husband."

I chewed the inside of my cheek, my heart already in my throat. "I'd like to wait until Greg is here."

Detective Ellis sat across from me, folded her hands together, and leveled me with her startling eyes. She ignored my request and launched right in. "When your husband left, did you report him missing?"

The question threw me off. I opened my mouth, closed it. "No."

"But it was out of the ordinary for him to just leave without telling you, wasn't it?"

I shrugged. "We were having marital problems. I assumed he left."

She inched closer to me, sniffing out the truth. "And why would you assume that?"

"Because . . ." *Because I wanted a divorce. Because I'd been lying to him. Because he was a monster. Because of what I did.* "Like I said, our marriage wasn't in a good place at that time."

"So you thought he would just leave? Leave his new house and his wife?"

"Isn't that what I just said?"

"Ruby." Detective Ellis cleared her throat and recrossed her legs. "We are trying to understand where your husband went. You said he packed a bag and took some cash. Did he ever try to contact you? Didn't his parents or colleagues find it suspicious that he just left?"

I thought back to what happened before he left, the threats I'd made. He would have been a fool to return, but I knew why he left. Instead of going to the police, I'd gone to Daisy. The truth was I hadn't wanted the police involved.

"I knew his family filed a police report right away, though I told them his luggage was missing, as well as some of his personal items. His safe had been cleaned out. He kept a large sum of cash in there, which I figured he took so I couldn't track him by his credit cards. I tried to tell them he wasn't missing, but they were convinced otherwise."

"His parents said nothing ever came of the police report."

So they've already talked to Tom's family? "Well, Tom is an adult. Sometimes adults just leave." I didn't mention that his boss, friends, and colleagues had hounded me relentlessly for a couple of weeks. It wasn't like Tom to just abandon his work or his cases. Just like when Lily disappeared, there were search parties and pleas plastered all over social media. But I didn't want him found. I didn't want him back.

"How do you support yourself? Without his income?"

The personal nature of her question shocked me. "I don't think I have to answer that." The proceeds of my house had been squirreled away in several investment accounts. Though I wasn't rich, I was comfortable and loved not needing his money anymore. I glanced toward the door, practically willing Greg to walk through it.

I hadn't purposefully thought about Tom leaving in so long. Lily was gone at that point, and Tom had been in a downward spiral. He was angry and hurt. I'd known something bad was coming, could feel the rush of doom, swift and cruel. One day, he was there. The next, he wasn't. I should have been more shocked, but every moment leading up to that day suggested an end of some sort. The end of him. The end of me. The end of us.

I explained as much to the detective, though my brain screamed for me to shut up. "Tom and I were very independent. He had a separate bank account, and I didn't have access to it online." A deep foreboding worked its way over my skin, and everything in me demanded I stop talking before I let something slip.

"And so that was that? You just assumed he was gone for good?" She clapped her hands together as if finished with something.

I gritted my teeth, suppressing a snappy remark. "My father left my mother—and me—when I was young. One day, he said he was going to pick up takeout, and he just never came back. My mother assumed the worst—that he'd gotten in a car wreck or had some other sort of tragic accident. She called hospitals for weeks, convinced he was lying dead in a ditch somewhere. She heard about a year later that he'd moved to Florida and was getting remarried. I think she was more heartbroken by the fact that he'd just left us than thinking he was dead." The lie flew easily from my lips, but I steeled my gaze and looked directly into her eyes. "I never wanted another man to hurt me the way my father hurt my mother. So yes, I let Tom go. I figured if he didn't want to be with me anymore, I certainly wasn't going to chase after him."

The door opened, and in walked Greg. His hair was slick and pushed back, his three-piece suit impeccable. He gave me an apologetic smile as he scraped a chair across the floor to sit beside me. "Greg Goodard. Sorry I'm late. Nashville traffic never ceases to astound."

"You being here is really unnecessary, Mr. Goodard. We're just asking Ruby a few questions."

"Oh, it's fine, Detective. I've made an entire career from 'unnecessary' appearances, so please." He flourished his arms wide and adjusted his Rolex. "Continue."

Detective Ellis changed gears and produced the photos of the deceased again—this time, uncovered and naked. It appeared his body had been submerged for some time, as it was unnaturally bloated in some places, so drained of color in spots the flesh was white as milk; in others, the skin had been pecked at by predators to reveal tiny bits of bone. I looked away as Greg studied the photos and then slid them back across the table.

"And you believe this man is Tom Winslow, why? Because some neighbors said so?"

She nodded. "Unfortunately, since his fingerprints aren't viable, his teeth have been pulled, and the body has been submerged, it's difficult to ascertain the exact time of death, so what the neighbors say is all we've got. But it appears he's been here for a while." She turned her attention to me. "Did Tom have any distinguishing marks? Birthmarks, scars, that sort of thing?"

I glanced again at the photo, wondering if this man suffered before he died. "No birthmarks. No scars that I can recall." *Like a ghost.* "Are you going to try and find Tom, at least?" Greg shot me a look to stay quiet, and I shrugged. "What I mean is, wouldn't that prove this man isn't him? Even though I've already told you it isn't?"

"Yes, Ruby. We will be looking for your husband until we have confirmation of the deceased."

Greg cleared his throat. "Then why is my client here? If you don't have confirmation?"

"I'm just trying to understand the events that led to Tom's departure." She motioned to the photos. "Either way, whether this is Tom or not, Ruby's husband has been missing for three months, and she's just now reporting it."

Greg snorted. "Last time I checked, it wasn't mandatory that a wife report her husband has left her."

Detective Ellis smoothed her hair behind an ear. A diamond stud caught the light and twinkled. "Maybe not. But if this man does turn out to be Tom, as everyone in your neighborhood attests to but you, things are going to get a whole lot more complicated."

I frowned, but Greg butted in. "Because you're insinuating someone wanted him dead."

Detective Ellis studied me, then flicked her gaze to Greg. "Yes. And it's our job to find out who and why."

"And what does my client have to do with that?"

The elephant in the room took one giant, heavy step.

"Wait." I sat up straighter. "You think if the man is Tom that *I* killed him?" I laughed, a hoarse, empty sound that bounced around the small room. "And what? I was able to drag him toward the lake with nobody watching, then somehow sink and secure his body to the bottom? And *then*, when he magically resurfaced, *I* called the cops to report it?" I laughed again. "That seems completely rational." My fists shook, and I held them clenched in my lap. "Are we done here, or do you have more ridiculous questions?"

A sharp knock interrupted us as a young woman stuck her head in and told Detective Ellis she was needed.

"Wait right here, please." Detective Ellis left the room, and I exhaled, turning to Greg.

"Do you believe this?"

"Ruby, you need to let me do the talking, okay?" He glanced toward the door and then down at the photos. "You're absolutely positive this isn't Tom?"

I balked. "Of course I'm sure." I stared at the photos. "Why?"

He looked away and fiddled with his watch again. "If you know it isn't Tom, then we have nothing to worry about."

I didn't press further, because I wasn't sure I wanted to know what he was thinking or what any of this meant. I was exhausted and confused and just wanted to move on. "How long will it take them to identify the body?"

He wiped his hand over his face and sighed. "Without fingerprints, teeth, or hair, it's usually blood, but in this case, I'm not sure that's applicable. You said Tom hasn't had any surgeries. Any other recent medical records to check?"

I shook my head. "He literally never went to the doctor. Healthiest guy I know."

He scratched his head, then smoothed his tie. "There's also DNA or presumptive methods. Right now, they're just going by physical attributes, which isn't scientific, to say the least."

My fingernails bit into my palms as I considered what any of this meant. "But regardless, there's a body in our neighborhood."

"I know."

"Greg . . ." There were so many things I wanted to ask. In the few months Tom had been gone, I wanted to know if he'd heard from him, if Greg was somehow keeping secrets in order to protect me.

Detective Ellis returned before I could form a question and gave us both tight-lipped smiles. "You're free to go for now."

My lawyer scoffed. "That implies she's being held, Detective, and since she hasn't been read her rights . . ." He gestured to the door.

I shook my head, annoyed. *Why did she even call me down here?*

Detective Ellis smoothed right over Greg's response. "We will identify the body and get to the bottom of what happened." She scooped the photos back into the file. "So we might be seeing a lot more of each other, Ms. Knight." She nodded at us and exited before we did. I turned to Greg, lifted my hands, and dropped them.

"You braved Nashville traffic for that?"

He snorted as we made our way to the front and then outside. The air was bitterly cold, and we could both see our breath. "Look, Ruby." He steered me toward the parking lot, out of earshot of anyone coming and going. "If they start looking into things, Lily will come up. You know that, right?"

A spark of pain ignited in my chest. "I know."

"If it comes to that, you call me, okay? I'm here for you." He squeezed my shoulder and left.

I slid into my car and sighed. We'd had to hire Greg in a lawsuit against Lily when she was fifteen. As a criminal defense attorney, he worked mostly on domestic violence, DUI, or disorderly conduct cases. As far as I knew, he'd never dealt with murder. Lily shot through my brain again. I wasn't ready to talk about her or what happened before she disappeared.

Especially because she had everything to do with why Tom left.

8

THEN

When I rushed inside the house, Lily was crumpled at the bottom of the stairs.

"Lily!" I darted over and crouched to assess. No bones at odd angles, no blood pouring from her head. She was conscious but barely. I leaned over her, and the alcohol, pungent and sharp, wafted off her breath.

Her eyes were open and unfocused. She struggled to sit up. "I fell!" Her words pushed together, and she giggled as her body betrayed her. A disappointed sigh erupted from my mouth before I could stop it.

"Those stairs are too sick. *Slick*. Sick slick." She erupted into laughter again, holding her ribs.

"Are you hurt?" Even as I asked the question, I figured she was too drunk to even register any pain. Tomorrow, we would know what bones were bruised or what she'd smacked on the way down.

"I'm *fine*." She looked around, her red curls blocking her face. Her eyes were much too sad for a seventeen-year-old, and I wanted to ask why. *Why* was she suddenly self-medicating and withdrawing again? She wasn't supposed to drink with her meds. While I knew everything with Lily could be a slippery slope, usually there was a catalyst. I thought about Andrew Tarver again, the stern way he'd grasped Lily's arm. Did that behavior have something to do with this?

I sorted through the other usual suspects in my brain—sexual trauma, relationship issues, grades, peer pressure, bullying, substance abuse, addiction—and while I didn't want to pry, I needed to get to the bottom of it. With Lily, it could spiral very quickly from normal teenage angst into something serious. Something dangerous. Now, she attempted to focus on my face, but her eyes kept sliding behind me. "Weren't you at your party thing?" She motioned next door.

"I was, yes. I heard you scream."

Her large eyes widened even more, and she hiccupped. "That's crazy."

"Come on, sweetheart. Let's get you in a cold shower and off to bed."

More and more, I'd been babysitting Lily, watching her moods and behavior. Tom had long ago made his stance known that his child was not to be medicated under any circumstances; he thought all psychiatrists were quacks and had fought me tooth and nail when I'd tried to get her real treatment. Whenever Lily went off the rails, he chalked it up to "normal" behavior, too overworked with his cases to put much stock in it. I could sense there was more going on with her, so why didn't Tom see it too?

Once the shower was warm, I helped Lily inside, but she protested it was still too cold. I helped her acclimate to the temperature and rushed to her room to grab some pajamas. As I rummaged through her top drawer, my fingers circled around something hard and long. I stopped. I didn't want to invade her privacy, but curiosity won out. I pulled out a pocketknife and exhaled. Tom had given it to her ages ago when she loved camping. She'd probably stashed it and forgotten.

I grabbed a pair of pajamas and then pulled back her sheets. Her room was clean and large, and she hadn't hung any of her art or collages on the walls yet. It was so completely devoid of her personality it didn't feel like her room.

Knowing Lily was sensitive to light, I searched her nightstand for her eye mask and stopped when I saw her meds. I palmed both bottles, which should have been close to empty. Instead, they were full.

I turned my head toward the bathroom, as if that would bring me answers. *When did Lily stop taking her meds?* Despite Tom's protestations, I'd gone to great lengths to make sure she stayed on her regimen. To suddenly go off her medication could cause all sorts of nasty side effects.

Again, I contemplated the catalyst. When had her behavior started to shift? Was it the move? We hadn't talked about how it felt to leave all her neighborhood friends in Nashville. The compromise in moving here was agreeing to stay at the same school as long as we got her a car. Lily seemed surprisingly okay about the entire thing, though she occasionally made passive-aggressive comments. But didn't this behavior suggest that she wasn't okay? That she was hiding how she really felt?

The shower cranked off, and I helped her step into a fluffy towel and gave her privacy to change. When she was all tucked in, I smoothed the hair from her face and set a glass of water on her nightstand.

"Do you feel like you're going to be sick at all?"

She shook her head. "No, I didn't drink that much."

I hesitated. "Lil, have you been taking your meds?"

She swallowed, her eyes closed. "Of course."

I sighed, not wanting to push. We could talk about it tomorrow. More importantly, I wanted to know why she was just sitting here, drinking on her own, alone? Was it that boy? A friend? Was she nervous about college? There was so much more stress being a teenager today than when I was young. I couldn't imagine the endless pressures of social media, endless text chains, and navigating the abyss of technological distraction in a filtered world. I constantly worried that we weren't doing enough for her as her parents, but Lily had always been so wildly independent. At times, I forgot that she was only seventeen and still had so much growing up to do.

I stroked her hair again, and she smiled. "That feels nice. I'm sorry I ruined your party, Mom."

An opening. "You didn't ruin anything. Look, if you don't want to talk about it, it's okay, but does what happened tonight have something to do with that boy, Andrew?"

Her body tensed, but she shook her head. "No. I just don't feel very good lately." To my surprise, she burst into tears and covered her face with her hands.

My heart ached as I rubbed her shoulder and waited for her to talk.

"I just feel discouraged." She slapped the sheets beside her, then clenched them in her fist. "I don't feel like anyone likes me, and Andrew . . ." She shook her head and smeared the tears away. "I just feel like I don't fit in anywhere, Mom."

"Oh, sweetie. I know just how that feels." I opened my arms, and she fell into them, gripping my back with her fingernails.

"Sometimes, I get so sad I'm afraid of what I'll do."

Warning bells trilled in my head. I knew what depression could do. I knew how it could clutch you in its fist and shake you until you couldn't breathe. I knew how sometimes you thought it might be better to remove yourself from this world completely. They were lies your brain told you, and they were dangerous. I'd been there before, and I'd managed to crawl my way out a thousand times.

"Do you want me to make an appointment with your doctor tomorrow? That might be nice." I smoothed her hair until she calmed and gave a tiny shrug. I handed her more water, and she gulped it down. I made sure she was situated on her side so that she didn't get sick in the night and retrieved a glass bowl just in case. I put that next to her water and sat with her, rubbing her back, until she fell asleep. Her breath deepened, and her lips parted as she sucked air in and out.

As I watched her breathe, I realized how serious this had gotten. Lily wasn't happy. Lily wasn't taking her meds. It was time to have a serious conversation with her doctor—and Tom.

I slipped out of the room and back downstairs, then booked an emergency appointment with her psychiatrist, Dr. Forrester. I could still hear the rowdiness from next door. I wanted to explain why I'd left so abruptly, but I was suddenly drained and didn't feel like socializing. After tidying the kitchen, I heard a soft knock at the front door. I opened it to find Ryan standing there, a concerned look on his face.

"You okay?"

I smiled. "Yeah. My daughter had a fall."

He glanced behind me. "Oh no. She okay?"

"She is." I didn't elaborate, and he didn't ask me to.

He brandished a bottle of wine from behind his back. "In that case, does the winner want a celebratory drink?"

There were a million reasons I should say no. I didn't know Ryan. Tom wasn't home. Lily was asleep upstairs but could get sick any moment. But something drew me to him, and even though I knew nothing could happen between us, his energy was palpable, reminding me of another life I could have possibly lived if I'd chosen art as my passion, instead of medicine. If I hadn't chosen to be Tom's wife.

"Sure." I opened the door, and he stepped inside, his ribs brushing against mine. He smelled like cedar and soap, and everything in my body crackled to life.

I shut the door, and he waited, our bodies mere inches apart. "Beautiful," he whispered.

I didn't know if he was talking about the home or me, but I felt paralyzed, rooted to the spot.

"It's a bit of a mess at the moment."

"Nonsense." His eyes trailed to my mouth, and I searched for something to say. He brushed some hair from my cheek, and I shivered. He smiled as he noticed my reaction to his touch.

"The kitchen is this way." I moved around him, my skin on fire, my body throbbing with desire. *How long has it been since Tom looked at me with anything other than spite?* I reminded myself that he'd been nicer since we'd moved here. That was something at least.

We took the wine out back, and I was surprised to see that next door had gone quiet. "What happened to the party?"

He laughed. "You won, remember? Party's over."

"Whoops." I smiled and downed my wine. Before I could protest, he refilled it to the top.

"You're full of surprises, Ruby."

"You don't even know me, Ryan."

He rolled his head toward mine, reclined in his chaise. "Oh, but I will."

Now it was my turn to laugh. "Sounds like someone is *awfully* sure of himself."

"I am . . . about things that are important, anyway."

My heart pounded as I took another sip of wine. He was definitely flirting, and I was definitely not telling him to stop.

"Well, doesn't this look cozy?"

I sat up, startled, and slapped a hand to my heart. "Jesus, Tom, you scared me."

He looked from me to Ryan and the open bottle between us. His eyes were cold, and automatically, my body tensed.

Ryan gave him a lazy smile but made no gesture to stand. "Hi, Tom. Ryan Fisher."

Tom assessed Ryan and then turned his attention back to me. "I thought you had that thing tonight."

"Oh, we did," Ryan interrupted, casting me a conspiratorial grin. "But your wife solved the murder in just forty-five minutes flat, which, if you're wondering, is a new record. Blew everyone away. Especially me."

Tom's jaw clenched. "Is that right?"

I lifted my glass, though my fingers were shaking. "Well, I *am* married to a criminal defense attorney. I know all your dirty little secrets, remember?"

"I knew you had to have some sort of unfair advantage," Ryan quipped. When he was met with an awkward silence by Tom, he scooped up his glass and motioned to the kitchen. "I'll just leave this inside and let myself out. See you later, Ruby."

"Thanks for the wine."

He let himself out, and Tom turned to me, hands on his hips. "What do you think you're doing?"

My entire body froze, but I made my mouth work. "He just dropped by to congratulate me. He's a friend."

"He's a *guy*."

"So?" I sat up, every nerve on high alert. "I'm a grown woman, Tom. I can have male friends. You don't own me." The words shot out of my mouth so fast we were both stunned into silence. I had never talked to him this way, never spoken up.

Tom loomed over me. "What did you just say?" He dropped his voice to a whisper, and everything in my body screamed *run*.

I craned around to look at him from my chair. "You heard me. Ryan is just a friend. I met a bunch of new friends tonight, in fact. I'm doing exactly what I'm supposed to be doing in our new life. Which was your idea." I clenched my glass and stood, but he grabbed my elbow hard and yanked me back into place.

"We're not finished," he growled.

"You're hurting me, Tom." My past roared into focus until I was afraid of my own rage. I closed my eyes, then opened them, and suddenly I was standing in the kitchen, alone. I turned slowly in a circle. The lights were off, and it was dark. I wasn't drunk, but I stumbled forward as if I were, smacking the light on with a trembling palm. I hoped Lily was still upstairs, asleep. My cheek pulsed, and I gently touched it. The flesh was swollen.

What just happened?

Even as I tiptoed to the guest bathroom, I already knew. It hadn't happened in a long time, but here it was: I was losing time again. I flicked on the light and squinted into the mirror. A raised red welt bloomed along my cheek. I lost time because of one thing and one thing only. How long since the last time? Six months?

I looked down at my own hands but knew I wouldn't find any defensive wounds. I never fought back, never stood up for myself, mostly because I detached from reality until it was over. The dissociation began when I was little and trickled into my marriage when the bruises started.

I'd told Tom I would leave him after the last time, that I would ruin him professionally. I'd been bluffing at the time, but he'd seemed to believe me, and the random acts of violence had stopped. Mostly because I'd removed all the triggers: no male friends, no locked phone, no secrets to hide.

Except the ones he doesn't know.

I couldn't believe I was repeating the same patterns from childhood. But wasn't I better off than my mother? I removed my phone from my back pocket to see what time it was. Late. I scrolled through my texts and realized I had a message from Ryan, which I'd programmed into my phone as Lacey Sumner so Tom wouldn't know.

I've been thinking . . .

Despite the late hour, I typed back. About?

I want to paint you.

My heart pounded wickedly beneath my T-shirt as I read those words. I glanced upstairs, as if Tom could see what I was writing.

I thought you were an abstract painter, I typed back. Am I going to be a red splat across the canvas?

I do portraits too. Will you sit for me?

My head screamed no. I'd be playing with fire. I'd be giving Tom new ammunition. But before I could stop myself, I typed back yes.

He asked if next week was good, and I told him I would get back to him. I deleted the text chain, stuffed my phone back into my pocket, and stared at myself once more in the mirror. My long brown hair was wild and wavy, my cheek angry and sore. Who was I becoming? Was I so unhappy I was distracting myself with a hot young painter? I was too smart to fall for such a ridiculous cliché. And I knew what would happen if Tom found out.

I flipped off the lights and let my thoughts wander. Upstairs, I checked on Lily, who was still asleep on her side. I knew her behavior was a sharp cry for help.

You're the one who needs help, I thought.

Upstairs, I slipped silently into bed beside Tom, and he rolled over, startling me. "Babe, come here. I'm so sorry. I didn't mean for that to happen." His eyes were inky, the shadows playing tricks on his face. He traced my cheek and then pulled me into his bare chest. My body went rigid beneath his touch, but he held tight. "You know I just get so jealous sometimes. You're such a beautiful woman. It won't happen again, okay? I promise. I've been doing better, haven't I?" These words used to have an effect on me. I used to believe his apologies, believe he'd change.

Now *I* understood. He would never get better. And as long as I stayed with him, nothing would change. I would be trapped. Hurt. *Wounded.*

There would be no escape.

9

Back at home, my mind worked overtime.

I needed to understand why everyone thought the dead man was Tom and, more importantly, why Detective Ellis was looking directly at me as the prime suspect. I knew my mind played tricks on me sometimes. Was there something I just couldn't see—or remember—because my brain was trying to keep me safe? I dropped my belongings inside my house and ran over to Cassie's and knocked on the door.

She opened it immediately, almost as if she'd been expecting me. She searched behind me and then yanked me inside. "God, are you okay?" She looked me over head to toe, as if I'd been in an accident.

I jerked my arm free. "No, I'm not okay. Apparently, everyone in this neighborhood thinks the man in the lake is Tom. Even you?"

Cassie opened her mouth, eyes darting around the room nervously. "I mean, I only saw the photograph, but yeah. I'm pretty sure it's Tom."

I dragged a hand over my face. "Don't you think *I* would be able to tell, Cassie? He was my husband. I would know."

"But . . ." She trailed off. "It makes sense, Ruby. He disappeared without a trace, and then a dead body pops up in our lake. Who else could it be?"

"Anyone!" I screamed. "It could literally be *anyone* else."

"But after everything that happened with Lily . . . you said so yourself that he was acting strange after she was gone. Not like himself."

"So that means he ended up in the bottom of our lake?" I paced in her foyer, too antsy to sit. "Did Tom have enemies here?" *Besides me.* Not that I wanted to assume the body was Tom, but I was willing to play out the scenario just to eliminate it. I waited for Cassie to assure me that he didn't, but instead, she remained silent.

"Cas? Did Tom have enemies here?" I sorted through all the friends we'd made, all the social events, cocktail parties, and game nights. I knew who he could become behind closed doors when no one was watching. But to the outside world, he was charming, loud, affable. But once Lily had disappeared, he'd become less and less interested in anything that had to do with other people.

"Yes, Ruby." Cassie's words sliced through my shaky reasoning. "He did."

I wanted to press for more, but Cassie's phone rang, and she excused herself, whispering "Client emergency" to me on the way to her study. I paced toward the living room, which was on the opposite side of the house as ours. Everything was beautifully appointed with rich, warm textures, funky vases, and pops of color everywhere. I always joked that Cassie had never met a throw pillow she didn't like, and true to form, there were about ten stacked on her sectional. I sank down into the cushions and let my eyes roam over the evidence of Cassie's life. She was married, had a great career, and a beautiful home. She had everything most of us wanted. She had everything I'd lost.

I glanced at her bookcase and stood to study the spines. Cassie had eclectic reading tastes, as demonstrated by the book clubs she threw. I scanned some familiar titles and stopped at a book that looked wildly familiar. It was *The War of Art*, by Steven Pressfield. I grabbed the copy. Tom had one just like it, as it was one of his favorite books. He'd once told me the book was about resistance, not just being a creative. It was a metaphor for life. I flipped through the worn pages and stopped cold as I glimpsed inside the back cover, which had messy, jumbled writing clustered across every inch. In Tom's copy, he'd written all kinds of notes to himself too. I flipped through it again, his familiar handwriting scrawled throughout. This *was* Tom's copy.

"Sorry about that," Cassie said, entering the living room and smoothing her blouse.

I turned and gestured at the book. "Why do you have this?"

She cocked her head, walked over, and then flipped through the book. "I don't know. Must be Charlie's."

"No, this is Tom's," I said, almost accusatory.

"Okay, well, I don't know. Maybe it got mixed up somehow when I was helping you decorate." She handed it back.

I clutched it to my chest. "This is Tom's favorite book. He never even let *me* borrow it. Why is it here?" I remember he'd given me the silent treatment for days after it had been taken from his nightstand and put on the bookshelf without his permission. My voice was rising, but I couldn't seem to stop myself. Tom would never loan this copy out. He carried it with him, like a secret, like a journal.

"Ruby, calm down. It's just a book. I'll ask Charlie when he gets back in town, okay? I'm sure there's some sort of explanation." She motioned for me to sit. "Why don't I make us some tea, and we can talk. Let's get your head clear."

I slumped onto the couch. Nothing made sense. Everyone but me thought that dead man was Tom, and I had no way to prove otherwise. And now his favorite book was here. Did it mean nothing? Or was it pointing me toward something? I racked my brain to think back to those last months before he'd disappeared, trying to sort through his erratic behavior and strange absences.

I thought he'd just been obsessed with finding Lily, but what if that wasn't all?

What if he had known where Lily was and told someone like Cassie? What if he'd written clues in this book and brought it here? My heart pounded. I knew I was being dramatic, probably so entrenched in our true-crime nights that I was spinning a tiny, nothing detail into something improbable.

Cassie walked back in a few minutes later with a flowered ceramic teapot, two matching cups and saucers, a plate of lemon shortbread cookies, and a pot of cream. Always the perfect hostess.

I stared at the book beside me, feeling like it was a clue.

What am I not remembering?

"Okay, let's just work through some of this, okay?" Cassie offered me a cup, and I took it with trembling hands.

As she talked, I started to wonder how well I really knew Cassie. Could she be hiding something? Could Charlie?

I sipped the tea and let her talk while I only half listened. If I wanted to prove the man in the water wasn't Tom, then first I had to know what my neighbors knew . . . and to get to the bottom of why they were so quick to claim it was my husband in the water.

10

"Okay, which ones do you like?" Cassie fanned a plethora of fabric swatches and tile samples across my kitchen island.

She smoothed them carefully, arranging everything with an interior designer's precision.

"Well, let's see." I studied the samples, but nothing jumped out at me. We'd been in our house officially for a month, and everything was still a plain white box. While I was essentially okay with that, so used to the sterile environment of the ER, Tom exclaimed he didn't want to live inside what looked like an insane asylum. Everything was *still* in boxes. I could feel his rage that I wasn't pulling my weight, that I wasn't morphing into an obedient housewife. It was inconceivable to me how I had once worked so diligently without complaint, and now I couldn't even unpack some boxes and get my home in order. It was not a skill set I readily possessed, as most of my adult life had been dedicated to time outside the home.

My East Nashville bungalow had been cozy and well lived in, but most of the furniture was vintage or collected from yard sales. Tom loved new things, expensive things. He wanted his home to be the envy of all our friends.

Absently, I fingered the fading bruise on my cheek that I'd covered with makeup. True to his word, Tom hadn't touched me since the night after the Murderlings gathering, but like always, I knew it was just a matter of time.

I tried to retrain my focus on the task at hand, which was studying samples. Since Cassie had been so friendly when we'd first met, she'd offered me the "friends and family" discount to help decorate. Perhaps she suspected how lost I was, being in this rich neighborhood with a bunch of strangers. Or perhaps she just wanted a project.

I had a headache. Design so wasn't my thing, and already, I felt decision fatigue. While I thought I'd simply pick out some curtains and paint samples, Cassie had an entirely different agenda. I poured myself another cup of coffee in a desperate attempt to match Cassie's natural energy. "Tell me what you think."

Cassie rolled her eyes. "It doesn't matter what *I* think, silly. This is your home. You have to live with it."

"Um." I flexed my palm around the mug and randomly pointed to a fabric swatch. "Maybe that one?" And then a herringbone tile sample. "And that?"

"No, no, those don't work together." Cassie clucked her tongue and gathered the materials to deposit back in her bag. "Look. I know you have a lot on your plate, but I just don't want you to make these decisions and then regret them later, you know?"

I nodded, but I didn't know how to tell Cassie that no, I didn't have a lot on my plate, nor did I care enough about aesthetics to regret anything. But I supposed anyone who would spend a million dollars on a home should care about the details. And be grateful. And fall into their new role as housewife with utter ease. "I trust you."

Cassie lit up like a Christmas tree. She straightened and nodded. "Then say no more. I'm going to make this perfect for you, Ruby. Absolutely perfect. You'll see." She glanced around. "Do you mind if I take some measurements?"

"Knock yourself out."

I nursed my coffee, but what I really wanted was a drink. I'd been shifting happy hour up by increments until I'd started to think about having a glass of wine at noon. It was a coping mechanism, of course, a way to numb myself to the detritus of my marriage.

As I yawned and stared at the literal blank canvas that was my life, the front door opened and slammed shut. I froze, adrenaline spiking and heart ratcheting into my throat. "Tom?"

"No, Mom. It's me."

Lily walked into the kitchen, breathless. She'd gone on a long run with some girls from school, as they had the day off for teacher in-service. Her cheeks were beet red, but her eyes looked clear, focused. Exercise had always been a great way for her to move old, stagnant energy and work out some of her demons on the trails.

"Good run?" I offered her a bottle of water.

"Really good. We discovered a new trail. I'm getting faster."

"That's great, sweetie. How are the girls?" I held my tongue as I wanted to ask why she hadn't resumed cross-country. She'd loved it for a while and then let it slip, like so many things.

"Good." She tapped her fingers on the glass and looked away.

Her three closest friends—Hannah, Kristen, and Bree—used to come over often, but they hadn't been to the new house yet. I figured it was just because of the distance, but now I wondered if it was something else. "Do they want to come by for lunch? Or a movie night? I'd love to see them."

She picked at the bottle's label with her stubby fingernails. Her cuticles were mangled and bloody from ceaseless gnawing, a nasty habit from childhood she'd never been able to break. "Maybe." She motioned upstairs. "Who's here?"

"A designer. She's helping me figure out what to do with all this." I motioned around us. "This isn't my thing."

She cracked a grin. "Oh, I know." I waited for her to say something more, but she didn't. "I'm going to shower."

"Hey, Lil?"

She turned at the bottom of the stairs.

"You know I'm always here if you want to talk, right? You can come to me with anything. I mean it. Nothing too big or small." What I wanted to tell her was that I was just like her. I understood her in ways Tom couldn't. I'd often debated about how much to tell Lily about my own life, if it would help or potentially harm her.

"I know, Mom. Thanks." She opened her mouth to say more, then refrained before jogging upstairs.

When she was out of sight, the front door opened and shut again. I frowned and checked the time. It wasn't even eleven o'clock. Tom was supposed to be in court all day. Fear shot through my system, enhanced by so much coffee. *What if he's been fired?* Quickly, that fear twisted to hope. *That would mean I'd have to go back to work.* Maybe not medicine, but even the possibility of another job felt like a gift.

Tom entered the kitchen smiling, then saw my panic-stricken face. "You okay?"

I plastered on a fake smile. "Fine. You scared me." I offered a perfunctory peck on his lips, which were chapped. "Why are you home?"

He grinned. "We settled out of court, so I'm free for the day and thought I could take my lovely girls to lunch. Lily back yet?"

I searched for the appropriate response. A husband who came home to take his family for lunch should make me feel grateful. Instead, there was only dread. "She's showering, but Cassie's here taking some measurements. Maybe after she's done?"

"Oh?" He adjusted his belt and flicked his eyes upstairs. "She pick out anything good yet?"

I shrugged. "I don't know. I just kind of told her to do whatever she wants."

His eyes narrowed. "But it's our house, Ruby."

But I don't care! I wanted to shout. Suddenly, this house had changed our entire lives, and I resented it in a way that scared me. I missed my old life, my old routine, my old neighborhood, my own home that Tom had practically forced me to sell. What had I been thinking, leaving everything that was safe and familiar? I, more than anyone, knew what that could do to a person.

I flicked my wrist toward the stairs. "Go tell her what you want, then."

He nodded in affirmation and practically sprinted up to the second floor, probably afraid that Cassie would make everything frilly or pink. Sometimes Tom was so clueless about how "modern women" functioned outside the traditional paradigm his parents had modeled for him when it came to marriage. Even though Tom claimed to be a feminist, I knew what he really wanted: Stability. Clearly defined roles. Everyone fitting firmly in their place. *Me* firmly fitting in my place.

I downed the last of the coffee and searched for something to eat, already deciding that I didn't feel like getting dressed to go out for lunch, but I wasn't sure if it was worth the fight. Upstairs, Cassie laughed and then fell quiet.

Eager to check on Lily, I walked silently up the stairs but hesitated as I turned the corner and paused outside the guest room. Beyond the cracked door, I could hear hushed whispers. Why would Cassie and Tom be whispering? They were practically strangers.

My hackles went up as I moved closer and strained to hear.

"You know I would, but . . ." Something muffled was said, but I couldn't hear without stepping fully into the room. The ensuing silence was so loud it practically fizzed in my ears. Before I could stop myself, I pushed inside the room, and the two of them jumped apart, clearly startled.

"Ruby! We were just looking at this catalog." Cassie waved the thick, fat catalog in the air. "Tom has so many ideas. Who knew he had such an eye for design?"

"Certainly not me," I said, my voice dripping with sarcasm. I searched both their faces for guilt but saw none. If this had been me and a man, Tom would have dragged me by my hair from room to room. He would have humiliated me, hurt me, made me pay.

Instead, I felt like the intruder, the idiot wife, as they slipped right back into their conversation. Is that why they'd been standing so close and gotten so quiet? Because they were simply looking through a catalog?

I left them to it and padded down the hall to Lily's room, wondering how I'd feel if they'd been flirting. Would I care? The thought of Tom having an affair had crossed my mind plenty of times. At our lowest, I'd actually prayed that he'd meet someone else and divorce me. I'd even fantasized about him dead.

I knocked lightly on her door.

"Come in!"

Inside, she was already dressed and piling her unruly hair on top of her head in a sloppy bun.

"Dad wants to take us to lunch," I said. "He settled out of court."

"Okay." She opened her nightstand, stared at her meds, downed them, and then slammed the drawer shut again.

I sat on the edge of her bed and motioned for her to join. "Lil, we need to talk about this." After our emergency meeting with Dr. Forrester, he'd encouraged her to resume her protocol until we could create a new plan.

Her back was to me, but she sighed, sank beside me, and rested her head on my shoulder. "They make me feel numb, Mom. I go from feeling everything to feeling nothing at all. I'd rather feel unglued than feel nothing." She lifted her head and stared at me. "I want to learn to manage without them."

I didn't know what to say. I understood the desire, but she didn't yet have the tools to manage all her symptoms, and she certainly couldn't do it with alcohol. "We can talk about it again with Dr. Forrester, okay?

We can create a tapering process. But you can't just quit cold turkey again. It's dangerous."

She rolled her large eyes. "But I don't want to take them!" Her voice boomed across the room and shocked us both. Lily rarely raised her voice, rarely lost her temper anymore. When she was younger, her moods had ping-ponged all over the place, reminding me of Tom. I worried that his rage was genetic, passed down to her. And I knew if she couldn't manage her emotions, couldn't find someone to hurt, then she would hurt herself.

Rather than reprimand her, I changed tactics. "Hey, I have an idea if you're not too tired?"

"I'm not tired."

"You know that if you want to manage your symptoms without medication, exercise is one of the best ways to do it, just like Dr. Forrester said, right?"

She nodded.

"Well, when I was younger, I found rowing, which really helped me. Would you like to try?"

Her eyes lit up. We used to go kayaking all the time, but she'd never shown much interest in rowing. "Can we go now?"

I thought about Tom in the other room, flirting with Cassie. I thought about his anger if we refused his lunch invitation. But I didn't want to go to lunch. I wanted to spend time with my daughter, on the water, helping her.

"Sure."

We walked downstairs bypassed the kitchen, and I grabbed my shoes by the door. Being on the water soothed me in a way nothing else could. People often asked if I'd rowed in college. I told them yes because it was easier than telling the truth. Yes, the water calmed me, but there was a reason why I needed it.

A reason I worked very hard to make sure no one ever found out.

11

"We were having an affair." Cassie placed her cup in her saucer with a delicate clatter.

My head snapped up. "Excuse me?"

She actually had the audacity to roll her eyes. "Ruby, don't act like you're so innocent. Everyone knows you were screwing Ryan."

My throat constricted as I searched for what to say. "Ryan and I weren't having an affair." The word *affair* sounded dirty in my mouth. Of course I'd thought about it, especially as Tom and I had grown further apart, but I knew affairs never fixed anything. They ended, or they didn't. But they usually destroyed lives and left carnage in their wake. And if Tom had ever found out, he would have killed me.

She huffed and crossed her arms, gauging if I was telling the truth. "I really cared for him, you know," she said. "He was going to leave you."

Instead of the words landing with an icy punch, they bounced right off. Despite the situation, I laughed. Cassie's face fell.

"Is that so hard to believe?" she asked. She crossed her legs and stared uncertainly into her teacup. I assessed her, my neighbor, my friend. Blonde hair cut in a perfect bob, face full of makeup, expensive clothes, leather flats.

As if deciding something, I nodded. "Yes, it is," I said. Tom was many things, but he would never leave me. If he left me, then he couldn't control me. When Lily had disappeared, I figured he'd simply vanished to find her. That, as punishment for what I'd done, he was hiding Lily from me, keeping her away. The fact that he hadn't come back and that the whole neighborhood thought he was the dead man in the lake . . . well, I didn't want to think too deeply about what that meant.

"When did it start?" I racked my brain for signs. Cassie flirted with everyone, even Ryan. The more I had gotten to know her, the more I'd sensed it was a harmless reaction to her lonely marriage instead of anything real. Charlie was always traveling for work, perpetually away, and despite trying for years, they'd never been able to have children.

"It doesn't matter when it started. We ended it before he disappeared." She sniffed. "I told him I couldn't leave Charlie."

Somehow, I didn't quite believe that. "Does Charlie know?"

"Of course he knows." Her cheeks flushed as she raised her eyes to mine. "We have an open marriage."

"What?" My head was spinning. Did I know *anyone*, really? What went on behind closed doors? I counted how long we'd been friends, how many conversations we'd had over wine, at her house or mine. Not once had that ever come up.

"So you thought because you have an open marriage, you could fuck with mine?"

"No, it wasn't like that." She pinched an invisible piece of lint off her navy slacks and stared at the bookcase. "It was Charlie's idea in the first place. To have an open marriage. I was resistant at first but then decided, why not?" She shrugged, her eyes glassy and vacant. "Everyone knows sex with a long-term partner doesn't set your soul on fire, so it seemed like a safe, fun way to explore while still coming home to the man I love. But then Charlie got jealous of Tom. He could tell it was serious, for both of us. He made me choose."

Motive shot through my brain, clear and obvious. "Did Charlie ever confront Tom?"

She nodded. "He did."

I clutched the *War of Art* book again, Steven Pressfield's kind, wrinkled face staring back at me from his author photo. Were there obvious clues I was missing? "Then what happened?"

"Nothing. They're guys. They have a code or something. They worked it out. Never brought it up again." She sighed and crossed her arms. Had she wanted them to fight over her?

"Just like that?"

Cassie offered a sad smile. "Just like that."

I replayed all our time together again, our many conversations. I'd confided in her about my marriage, about how it was falling apart, how *I* was falling apart. She'd sat there, pretending to be my friend, when really, she'd been screwing my husband.

"I have to go."

"Ruby, wait." She rushed toward me and placed a hand on my arm. "I'm sorry. We shouldn't have gone behind your back like that. I know we shouldn't have. Things just got out of hand."

I shook her hand off me and opened the front door. "Stay away from me, Cassie." I slammed the door behind me and shielded my eyes from the sun.

Though the affair was a shock, it still didn't get me closer to understanding what had happened to Tom. I knew for the sake of this investigation, I needed to play along; pretend it was Tom in the water. And if it was, I had to find out who put him there.

As I walked down the block, I waited for grief to wrap its arms around me, but I just couldn't get there. I'd seen so many dead bodies over the years that a kind of desensitization had occurred, as if all my empathetic sensors had been burned away. But this was Tom we were talking about.

A dark thought floated through my head as I took a sharp right back toward the lake. Hadn't I wished, on more than one occasion, that something bad would happen to Tom? That it would be easier than telling him the marriage was over because of what he might do? I shook away the thought as I realized where I was headed: not to the lake but to Ralph's.

If anyone could help me make sense of this, lay it out logically like a case, it was Ralph. He was about the only person I trusted in this community. Before I made it there, someone called my name. I turned, startled.

Ryan jogged to catch up and placed a hand on my shoulder. "Hey. I've been trying to reach you."

His fingers burned into my skin, but I didn't shake him off. I thought about what Cassie had said. Did everyone really think we were sleeping together? And if they did, what did it matter now?

"Do you know what everyone is saying?" I hissed, looking around. No one was out on their porches. The street was still and quiet, most people tucked behind their doors, waiting for a verdict.

"I do. But hey, I'm on your side." He squeezed my shoulder.

"On my side for *what*?" Finally I came to my senses and shrugged him off. He looked wounded by the sudden movement.

He slipped his hands into his pockets and rocked back on his heels. I remember how often he used to do that when studying art, whether it was his own work or someone else's. "About what people are saying."

"About Tom? Trust me—I know. I'm trying to get to the bottom of it." I turned to go, but he reached for me again. His fingers slid easily around my wrist, and suddenly, a montage of images flashed through my head: *A bruised wrist. A crumpled body. Blood.*

He shook his head. "No, not about Tom. About what they're saying about you."

"About me?" I racked my brain. Other than not believing it was Tom in the water, what could they be saying?

"They think you did it, Ruby." He lowered his voice and leaned back in. "They think you killed Tom."

COTTAGE GROVE FORUM

hippiemama23: Okay, y'all. Things just got
real!!!!!!!

nashvegasart: they make pills for that.
crackersmp: What's up?
hippiemama23: I KNOW WHO KILLED TOM!
crackersmp: OMG, OMG! WHO?
shianna: Oooh, dish girl, dish!
hippiemama23: his cray-cray ex-wife. I heard she's
like a junkie or something.
nashvegasart: i heard she was banging that hot
painter.
lettucehead4life: how do we know YOU'RE not the
hot painter?
nashvegasart: you don't
crystallover: oh god, are they swingers? I had a
friend who did that and she got chlamydia
softatheart: swinging can be healthy.
hippiemama23: i heard she got fired from being a
nurse.
dahmernotjeffrey: i heard her kid got addicted to
pills too before she disappeared

lettucehead4life: DUH! Because she's a junkie!!!!!!!
Probably stealing meds. Or giving them to her
daughter, may she rest in peace.
crackersmp: or because she's into MURDER!
lettucehead4life: OH MY GOD! I just realized! She's
part of The Murderlings!!!!! She solved that first
murder in like two seconds. Remember that????
crackersmp: UM, prolly because she's so good at
killing people.
crystallover: OMG! Do we think she killed her
daughter too?!?!?!?
crystallover: 💀💀💀💀💀💀💀
nashvegasart: you guys really need professional
help.
lettucehead4life: i think you're the only guy on this
thread.
dahmernotjeffrey: because this handle is such a
FEMALE name?
nashvegasart: how do you know i'm a guy?
lettucehead4life: because you're a dick.
shianna: what do we do now, guys? there's an actual
MURDERER among us.
hippiemama23: we need to set up a neighborhood
watch. For real.
crackersmp: I'm down!
crystallover: Me 2
shianna: me 3
lettucehead4life: me 4
hippiemama23: okay, i'll work on deets. WOW. I'm
sharking. I mean SHAKING.
crackersmp: its soooooooo wild
dahmernotjeffrey: it's not that wild

shianna: i wonder if they'll make this into a MOVIE?
nashvegasart: if they do, i hope all your characters die.
lettucehead4life: not unless you die first.
dahmernotjeffrey: now we're talking

12

THEN

I knocked on the door and smoothed my sweaty palms over my jeans.

I hadn't told Tom where I was going this morning, for obvious reasons. But I was interested in art. I used to love to paint but had given it up as an adult.

Before I could think too much more about why I was doing this, the door jerked open, and Ryan gave me a crooked smile. He had a face for film: leading actor, bright hazel eyes, a small dimple in his left cheek. He was wearing paint-splattered overalls and wiped his hands on a dappled rag. His feet were bare, and a glob of black paint marred the top of his foot.

"I didn't know if you'd come."

"The narcissist in me won," I joked, stepping inside. The only thing I knew about modeling for art was that it usually involved being nude. I'd taken one of those classes in college and blushed the entire time. I'd vowed that I could never be that brave, could never offer my body to someone for that sort of *looking*. It was the most vulnerable I could ever imagine being.

He laughed and stepped around me. "Water? Tea?"

"Wine?" I blurted out, even though it was only ten in the morning.

"Coming up." He grabbed a fistful of brushes sticking out of a paint can and motioned to head to the kitchen. His walls were covered in art, wild, abstract, portraiture, sketches. His furniture was minimal and all in muted colors to let the art sing.

"You're quite the collector."

"Part of the job. Red or white?" He fisted two unopened bottles.

"Red."

He nodded, uncorked the bottle, and poured me a healthy glass. "Nervous?"

I thought about lying or brushing it off. Instead, I nodded. "Terrified."

"Don't be. I'm doing a series of heads, so I'll only be painting you from the shoulders up. You will be fully clothed. I should have said that earlier."

Something like disappointment throttled through me, swift and unexpected. Had I *wanted* to be naked for a total stranger? I took a giant gulp. "Sad you won't get to see my toe ring. Or my tramp stamp. I was very excited to show them off."

His eyes roamed slowly from my face down to my toes and back up. Heat hit me right between the legs. "That is a shame," he whispered. He leaned forward, elbows on the island. I suddenly felt more awake than I had in years. Every nerve was firing with possibility. Not that I would ever cross a physical line. I wasn't interested in an affair, but being looked at and seen? Every woman deserved that type of consensual longing.

"This way, madam." He ushered me past his sunroom and outside, where a separate studio sat on a tidy patch of grass, a smaller replica of his beautiful home. I stepped inside and was smacked with the scent of palo santo. A soft beige tarp covered the floor. The walls had been painted white, and two-by-fours had been nailed everywhere, where canvases, in all states, hung or perched. He had a chaise in one corner and three different easels stacked against one wall. His brushes and paints were all organized in empty paint cans on homemade shelves.

"This is perfect." And I meant it. There was nothing pretentious here. It was the space of a serious artist, and I immediately felt my nerves ease. I walked slowly from painting to painting, trying to nail down his style. It was slippery, shifting dramatically from one canvas to the next, so I couldn't get a grasp on how to label him. "You're extremely talented. In many areas," I added.

He was arranging his canvas and easel, plucking what colors he wanted and smearing them onto a wide wooden palette. "Thank you." He didn't ask me what I liked about his work. He didn't search for compliments. Finally, he gestured for a place to sit, a comfortable chair with soft lighting behind it.

I'd been instructed to wear something I could easily slip from my shoulders. Now, facing him, I settled my glass on a side table and eased into the chair.

He approached me and squatted down to eye level. "May I?" he asked.

I didn't know what he was asking permission for, but I was in instant agreement. Tenderly, he pressed his paint-splattered fingers against my body, arranging my left shoulder, my right hip, the tilt of my chin. My skin burned with every touch. When he had me arranged to his liking, his fingers slipped to the base of my neck and spread to my shoulders, where he tugged down the fabric of my shirt, achingly slow, until it hovered near the top of my breasts. I wondered if he could feel my heartbeat, erratic and hard. He pushed back a few errant hairs from my shoulders, then ran a finger across my cheekbone, which still had a hint of the bruise. My skin erupted into goose flesh.

"What happened here?"

I couldn't breathe, couldn't move, couldn't think. "Tennis. I got a backhand with my doubles partner right to the cheek." The lies always came easily, just as they had for my mother. On the water the other day with Lily, she'd asked the same thing. "What happened to your face, Mom?" Her eyes had been fearful of my response. Once I said it out loud, it made it true. Her father was a monster, which meant she could be a monster. I wasn't ready to hand that off to her. It was too big.

He seemed to consider the answer, then stepped back and resumed his position behind the easel. "Ready?"

No, I was not ready. I wanted him closer—I wanted him to keep touching me—but I nodded.

"If you need to move, just move, then try and position yourself as close to where you are now, okay?"

"Okay."

I watched him paint, fascinated by every stroke. I memorized the way his brow furrowed, how he bit his lower lip and seemed to stop breathing as he leaned in close to work on certain details. After a couple of hours, we took a break for a light cheese-and-fruit plate and more wine. I was drunk on watching him, drunk from being watched and studied, like a book.

"You have an incredibly symmetrical face," he said before he bit into a fat strawberry. Pink juice dribbled down his chin, and I wanted to lean in and suck it up.

"What?"

"Your face." He motioned to me. "It's really beautiful. Perfect for portraits."

"I'll be sure to thank my mother." Even saying the word *mother* shot me right back to a reality I wanted to forget. A sick feeling formed in the pit of my stomach at the mere thought of her. People used to say we could be twins.

"You okay?"

"I'm fine." I racked my brain to change the subject. I didn't want him to ask me about my mother or my family. It was part of my past I had chosen to tuck away, like a bad first marriage. Another life entirely. "Didn't realize how much it takes to sit still."

"Right?" He stretched, and his shoulder muscles flexed. "No one sits still anymore."

We walked back into the studio, and I settled back into my pose.

After another hour, he told me we were done, and I felt gutted. I didn't want it to be over. I didn't want to go home. I liked being stared at. I liked feeling useful, even if I was just sitting in a chair. "Can I see?" I adjusted my shirt and stood, my body stiff from perfect posture.

"It's not done yet, but sure."

I walked around, our elbows touching, and I audibly gasped. "Ryan, my God. This is . . . this is exceptional." And it truly was. He'd captured something in me—a sadness in my eyes, an entire world of secrets behind them, a vulnerability in the quiver of my mouth. A face that was a result of so many broken promises—a total exposure no one else had ever snapped in a photograph. It was like he'd ripped away the exterior and burrowed right into my soul. "It's *me*." *The real me.* I turned to him, tears in my eyes. "How did you do that?"

"It's what I do." His eyes searched my face, clearly sensing the emotion there. "I'm glad you approve."

We were inches apart. It would be so easy to lean in, to kiss him and give in to the moment. Before I could make a bad decision, he stepped back. "So tell me about your mom." He swirled a few brushes in water and tapped them dry.

I was thrown by the topic. "What?"

"Earlier, when you mentioned her, your whole demeanor changed."

"She's dead." The words were flat leaving my lips because I'd long ago buried that pain. *She's dead. She's gone. She's no longer with us.*

"I'm sorry." He arranged his paints and wiped his hands on the same rag. "And your dad?"

"Also dead." I almost choked on the word. The memory was so clearly etched into my mind, even now, it stole my breath.

Seeming to sense I didn't want to say more, he nodded. "Want to stay for a proper lunch?"

I did want to stay, but I didn't trust myself not to tell him everything. He had that way about him, getting people to open up and spill all their secrets over sandwiches and wine. "Thanks, but I need to get back." The desire I'd felt before had fizzled, and now, there was just an aching void. I let myself out and walked numbly back to my house. I stared at the front door, thinking of another front door. My mother's front door. The last night my father was alive. All the lies and secrets between us.

It had been so long since I'd thought about either of them, and I didn't want to start now. I didn't want to think about what I'd done or what it had cost me.

13

They think you did it, Ruby. They think you killed Tom.

Ryan's words reverberated in my head. I wobbled on the sidewalk, and he reached out to steady me. His touch didn't deliver that same electric current it used to. So much had happened. So much had changed.

"That's ridiculous." My voice was shaky. I cleared my throat and tried again. "I didn't kill anyone." I blinked up at him, and he studied me as he had that day in his studio, probing, searching. *What is he seeing that I'm not?*

"Look." He moved in closer and lowered his voice. "Regardless of who's in that water, you and I both know Tom wasn't a good guy. And you had plenty of reason to—"

I lifted a hand, cutting him off. "Stop talking. Please."

I made my legs move again, and he fell into step beside me. His strides were long and easy, whereas mine were short and jerky. Despite the blinding sun, my breath escaped in a tiny cloud in front of my face, and I shivered beneath my coat.

"I'm on your side, Ruby, okay?"

"You don't even know me, Ryan. I don't need you to be on my side."

The words wounded him, just as I'd intended. I wanted him away from me, away from this mess. It was for his own good.

As if in surrender, he lifted his hands. "Fine. I don't know you. Whatever you say, Ruby." He turned. I watched him go, a bit of my heart going with him. I buried that old, sad residue and turned back to the task at hand: talk to Ralph. I checked the time, wondering if he'd even be home. It seemed the entire neighborhood was on pause as we all waited to see what the detective came up with next.

While I walked, I became more enraged. When had my community decided behind my back that the dead man was my husband and that *I* was the murderer?

I ignored the few sets of eyes that watched me walk, arriving at Ralph's in five minutes flat. His Lexus was in the driveway, and I sagged in relief. Ralph didn't have a wife. They'd divorced ages ago, and his kids were grown, so I hoped he'd be alone. I knocked, and he opened the door almost immediately.

The last time I'd seen him, he'd been in his robe. Now, he was smartly dressed, and I wondered if he was on his way to court.

"Ruby? Everything okay?" He looked behind him, as if expecting a cavalry.

"May I come in?" I didn't wait for his reply. I pushed past him into the foyer and glanced around. Ralph's house had been the first built here. It was warm and dark, full of masculine furniture made of leather. Stale cigar smoke clung to the air.

He cleared his throat as he stepped into the foyer behind me. "I'm assuming that's a no?"

I turned, confused. "What's a no?"

"That everything's okay?" His warm brown eyes regarded me carefully. "Would you like to sit down?"

I nodded and entered his den, which was crammed with books, throw blankets, and a fireplace with wild orange flames licking the black grate around it, as if desperately reaching for escape.

"Cup of tea?"

"No thanks." I sat and smoothed my hands on my thighs. "Did you know Tom and Cassie were having an affair?"

I could tell that I'd caught him off guard by the sudden question, but his lack of surprise told me that yes, he knew. He sighed and sat across from me in his old recliner, crossing his long legs. "I heard the rumors."

If there were rumors about Tom's affair, were there also rumors that he was abusive? I'd had plenty of opportunities to air his dirty laundry since he'd left, but I hadn't. It had been such a gift when he vanished that I thought I should leave it alone. Though in the back of my mind, I always feared his return. "What am I missing, Ralph?"

He scratched his head and lifted his hands before dropping them heavily against his slacks. "This is a small town. People talk."

"You mean *Cassie* talks." I glanced at the fire. "She told me that he was going to leave me for her."

Ralph chuckled. "Well, I don't think that's true, but consider your source."

"That's what I said." I attempted to gather my thoughts, which were zigzagging all over the place. "As you know, everything changed after Lily disappeared." I held his gaze for a moment, remembering that time and the monumental secret between us. We still didn't talk about it even now, as if by not talking about it, what we'd done had never happened. "Tom became more detached," I continued, "but I assumed he finally went off on his own to find Lily, since the police kept coming up empty. Now I learn that he's been screwing our neighbor probably since day one, so how do I know Charlie didn't threaten him? Or maybe he left to get away from everyone? Not just me but Cassie, the neighborhood, all of it? Did someone at work find out about them?"

The words were spewing out of me rapid fire, but Ralph was used to making sense of quick and difficult questions. However, this wasn't his courtroom, and no one was on trial. At least not yet.

Rea Frey

"Take a breath." He leaned back in his recliner. The fire crackled in the silence. "You know Tom and I weren't that close outside of work, so I can't possibly know what he was thinking. But what we can start with is figuring out if that's Tom in the water and then work backwards from there."

I snorted. "Well, everyone on earth seems to think that yes, it is Tom."

"But you don't."

It wasn't a question. I shook my head. "No, I don't." I sighed. "But if everyone, including Detective Ellis, does, then what does it matter what I think? Apparently, Ryan just informed me that I'm suspect number one."

Ralph balked in surprise. "You? Why?"

Did Ryan really know what Tom was capable of? What I was capable of? I swallowed the truth and swept the emotion from my face. "Exactly. What would *my* motive be? Other than the affair, which I literally just found out about." *And him beating the shit out of me for years.*

We sat silently across from each other as one of his grandfather clocks ticked and the fire continued to burn.

"Tom had some enemies, you know." Ralph said it so softly I had to lean in to hear. "From his cases. He kept a lot of bad men out of prison."

Hadn't Cassie just said the same thing? "Ralph, I'm really getting the picture that there was this whole other life Tom was leading I knew nothing about. But I've been right here the entire time. How could I have missed it?" But I already knew the answer to that. I missed things. Chunks of time disappeared when bad things happened. Stupidly, I had thought those bad things just happened to me. I'd been so busy trying to not piss off Tom and handle Lily's downward spiral that I'd missed all the signs. Or maybe I'd just stopped caring. Either way, I didn't have the whole story.

He fiddled with a large class ring he wore on his pinkie. "We miss all kinds of things when we don't know what we're looking for. You know that better than anyone." He stared into the flames before settling his friendly eyes on my face. "How can I help, Ruby?"

"Tell me I'm not crazy. Tell me you don't think it's Tom."

He hesitated, and I knew he couldn't give me what I wanted.

"Fuck." I stood up, pacing back and forth. "What am I not seeing?" But Ralph couldn't answer that question. Only I could. I'd filed away some piece of evidence somewhere, either a clue where Tom had gone or why he was dead, and I just wasn't recognizing him. A terrifying thought seized me: Had *I* done something that I didn't remember? Did everyone think it was me for a reason? I stopped pacing. I knew it was possible. It was more than possible.

Suddenly, Ralph stood, his frame towering over me. "Let me get you some water." He walked toward his kitchen, just as my cell rang. I glanced down at it.

"It's Detective Ellis." My stomach roiled as I answered it. "Hello?"

"We need you to come down to the station." She skipped all formalities, and the urgency in her voice gave me pause.

I looked at Ralph. "Do I need my lawyer?"

She hesitated before responding. "Just get here as soon as you can."

The detective hung up, and I bit the inside of my cheek as I pocketed my phone. "She wants me to come to the station."

Ralph led me to the door. I called Greg and told him to meet me. I wasn't sure what she'd found, but something told me it wasn't good.

14

For the second Murderlings night, I brought Lily.

She'd always been a true-crime buff, and I wanted to get her out of the house. She'd been opening up to me more in the last few weeks, especially since she was back on her meds, and I wanted to keep that streak alive. Wine in hand, I vowed that there would be no sudden departures tonight. No rush to prove myself. Daisy had seemed both impressed and annoyed that I'd solved the murder so fast last time and disrupted the flow of the night. Frankly, I was relieved she'd invited me back.

Inside, I searched for Ryan in the garden but didn't see him. The disappointment stung more than I would have liked. But I wanted to see him. It was one of the main reasons I'd come. I refilled my own drink as Daisy made a beeline for me and Lily. Tonight, she was wearing red ballet flats, a bright-pink dress, and her signature red lipstick. I bristled as she approached, but I didn't know why exactly. Something about her made me nervous. As she stopped to say hello to a neighbor, I sorted through what I knew of her from my Google search that had turned into all-out digital stalking.

Daisy Dominguez had been a criminal law major, then switched to forensics. After her undergrad, she'd taken a year off for a series of odd jobs: apprentice to a mortician, crime lab technician, and cemetery worker, to name a few. The only reason I knew this was through her old blog, *Death Becomes Me*, a spoof on the 1992 movie *Death Becomes Her* with Meryl Streep and Goldie Hawn. Apparently, someone had read one of her blog posts and invited her on a podcast, and the episode had gained traction. That had given Daisy the idea to start her own podcast by the same name. Everything had blown up once she'd solved that first cold case, which made her both wildly fascinating and a bit of a local celebrity.

"Ruby. Good to see you again. I see you brought a guest?"

"This is my daughter, Lily. Quite the true-crime buff herself."

"Is that so?" She laughed and studied Lily's face. "Favorite serial killer?"

Lily laughed. "Easy. Elizabeth Báthory. Not for what she did to women and girls but for how prolific she was before she got caught."

Daisy's eyes glittered wickedly. She was clearly impressed. "Báthory. Wow. Haven't heard that name in a while. We're going deep into the history books. I'm impressed, young one. Come. You're with me." She slung an arm around her shoulder, and Lily smiled and offered me a curt wave as she was introduced to the others.

Just then, Ryan opened the front door and sauntered in, hoisting a bottle of tequila. A few people cheered at his late arrival. Happy for the distraction, I shot him a smile as he approached.

"Hey, you." Tequila in one hand, he raked a hand through his messy hair with the other.

"Didn't know if you were going to make it."

"Yeah." He set the tequila on the island to rub the back of his neck, and I noticed his fingernails were caked in paint. "I got caught up in a piece."

"Oh?"

We hadn't been in contact much since he'd painted me, though I hadn't been able to stop thinking about it. What I'd felt, sitting there, watching him. What I'd wanted to do. Part of me didn't trust myself to be around him, even now. I thought time would cool the crush, but apparently not.

"Yeah, I just got commissioned by the Frist."

"Ryan, that's fabulous." The Frist was the biggest art museum in Nashville and would be great exposure for his career. "Congratulations."

"Thanks." He cocked his head as he looked at me. "Where's the hubby?"

"Trial." I didn't say more. He'd been working a first-degree murder case and practically sleeping at the office. It felt good to have him gone, to not tiptoe around. Even Lily had noticed the difference. "But I did bring reinforcements." I motioned toward Lily, who was already part of the group, laughing about something. It did my heart good to see her smile.

"Is she as good as you?"

"You'll have to wait and see." I pushed myself away from the island as Daisy gathered everyone to tell us our new assignment.

She stood in the same place as last time, holding a glass of champagne in hand. "I don't think we have any newbies besides Ruby's daughter, Lily, who you've all just met, so let's dive right in." Everyone lifted their glasses in a silent cheers. "Tonight's case is a doozy. So buckle up." She wiggled her eyebrows, and a collective "ooh" rippled through the room. "Tonight we're working a seemingly cut-and-dry homicide. Abusive husband who was murdered by his wife. She went to prison and died there." Daisy shared the details as everyone waited for her to produce the envelope of goods. When she didn't, the neighbors sprang to attention, scrambling to memorize details. But I didn't need to listen. Her words about this case were as familiar to me as my own reflection.

I made eye contact with her, and she locked in on me as she continued talking. The room spun, and I clutched the back of a chair to keep from tumbling over. Ryan eyed me, concerned, but I pretended to listen. I didn't know what Daisy was doing, but the last thing I wanted was to show her that I was rattled by this "fake" case. She continued spouting off details and then stopped.

One of the neighbors, Phil, looked around the table. "So where's the evidence? The case file?"

"I'm getting to that." Daisy walked to a credenza and unlocked a drawer with a gold key looped around her neck. "This, my friends, is a *real* case I was able to snag. Don't ask me how, because yes, I will have to kill you." The small crowd laughed and shifted, the air fraught with excitement. This was a real case, which meant the stakes were higher.

My heart rioted dangerously in my chest as she scattered the contents on the table. Staring up at me were my mother's and father's faces, then my own. I was ten. But my name, of course, wasn't Ruby. It was Penelope Elaine Richter—Penny for short. I'd changed it after.

There, splayed on Daisy's table, was the rubble of my family, my dark secret history, that horrid past I'd worked so hard to get away from. And Daisy, for reasons unknown, had just laid it bare for the whole neighborhood to see. It was the ultimate betrayal. Whether this was some sort of punishment for ruining her last party, I didn't know. It felt bigger than that, more sinister somehow. But I wasn't about to confront her publicly, especially in front of Lily. And I sure as hell wasn't about to let everyone dig into my past, because this most certainly was not a game.

"Daisy? Can I speak to you for a second before we start?" I snatched all the papers and shoved them back into the envelope, fingers shaking, as everyone looked on, confused. "Just don't want any cheaters to get a head start!" I said, forcing my tone to sound bright. I tucked the envelope under my arm and jerked my head toward the guest bathroom around the corner. Thankfully, Daisy obliged.

"Be right back, Murderlings!" Daisy trilled.

I practically ran to the bathroom, stopping briefly to clock the worry on Lily's face, and locked the door once she was inside. "What the hell is this?" I shook the envelope at her, the contents burning my fingertips from shame.

"What?" Daisy blinked at me innocently, and though I did not know her well, I wanted to strangle her.

"This. This file. *My* file. What are you doing with it?"

Her lips quirked upward in the slightest hint of a smile. "I'm just doing my due diligence into a seemingly cut-and-dry case. Though, the more I dig, I really don't think it's a simple homicide after all. Do you?"

Dread seized my entire body, almost shocking me into paralysis. But I'd been there before, and I forced myself to breathe. *In and out. In and out.*

"What do you want?" I finally sputtered. I'd dealt with plenty of unreasonable people in my past, and it always came down to one of two things: money or power. Which did Daisy want?

"Well, that's the thing, *Ruby*." She emphasized my name, clearly knowing it wasn't my birth name. I was Penelope Elaine Richter, a name smeared through the press in 1992. Fortunately, that girl was dead.

"As you probably know, solving a case like this could go a long way for my career, especially seeing as one of the people in this case happens to be my neighbor. I mean, what are the odds?"

"What do you want?" I repeated the question, racking my brain for what I could possibly have access to that she could need. This case was water under the bridge. Both my parents were dead.

She hesitated for a moment, then crossed her arms. "I want you to come onto my show."

I looked at her dumbly. "Why?"

"It's rare I get to talk to someone who lived through a murder in her own backyard. Literally. Your mother went to prison. It might be cathartic to tell that story."

I didn't even have to think about it. "No."

"No?" She shrugged. "Fine. Then we can just talk about it tonight."

I weighed my options. Obviously, I didn't want my dirty laundry aired for some stupid podcast, but in the back of my mind, I knew there was a more serious reason for not wanting to go public with a story I needed to stay hidden. I wavered between saying something to placate her or blowing her off completely. She obviously wanted me to know she was smart, that she could dig where no one else was looking, and she knew part of my deepest, darkest secret.

But not all of it.

"Fine," I said, straightening. "Let's talk about it tonight. No one knows it's me."

She laughed, a deep belly laugh that in another setting could have been infectious. "Okay, then. After you."

I stormed out of the bathroom and attempted to keep my face blank. Lily was here, which meant she was going to try to solve this crime like everyone else. I had to play along, stay calm, and not blow my cover.

"Sorry about that, Murderlings! Had to have a brief chat with the winner from last time so she doesn't spoil it for us again. But she promised she wouldn't jump in and guess the murderer right off the bat, right, Ruby?"

Everyone's heads swiveled my way expectantly, but all I could do was nod. Lily looked at me, and I gave her a smile, but I could see the question in her eyes. Why had I pulled Daisy aside? What was I hiding?

I eyed the file, wondering if I could snatch it after everyone was done ripping apart my past. Regardless, I wasn't leaving this house without it. Knowing Daisy, I figured she'd probably made copies. I tuned her out as she spilled all the details, and my neighbors formed little excited clusters, eager to dive in. Was I surrounded by sociopaths? My eyes lifted to study Daisy again, who'd paired off with Ryan and Lionel. And was she the one at the helm?

"Earth to Mom. You ready to do this? Everyone's already started." Beth was part of our group and tapped her foot impatiently as she read through the file.

"Yep, I'm ready." I swallowed and forced myself to pretend this wasn't my story. This wasn't my pain. This wasn't a time in my life I'd tried to forget. My gaze fixed on my mother's mug shot, and a thousand memories stabbed the surface of my conscience. I missed her so much, even now. How I wished it could all be different. "I'm just going to grab a drink first. You two go ahead."

Shakily, I poured myself a drink at the kitchen island and tried to compose myself. The only person who knew I wasn't Ruby was Daisy, and I could make sure it stayed that way. As I turned, Daisy caught my gaze, raised her own tumbler, and smiled.

I raised my glass in response, debating between that and throwing it at her. The old adage *keep your friends close and your enemies closer* had never mattered more, it seemed. I didn't know what game Daisy was playing, but my past was mine. I would do whatever it took to make sure it stayed there.

15

Greg and I sat in the stuffy room, waiting to find out why I was here.

"I'm going to get right to the point, Ruby," Detective Ellis began. "Recently, some information has been brought to our attention that puts this investigation in a different light."

"Okay."

Greg shot me a stern look. I'd been strictly forbidden to say anything unless he gave permission.

"Tell me about your daughter."

Greg stiffened beside me. "You're going to have to be more specific, Detective."

Detective Ellis smiled and focused on me. "When I asked about Lily, you told me she was at college—isn't that right?"

Greg looked at me and gave me a small nod to speak. "I did, but that's only because it's easier than trying to explain the truth."

"Which is?"

I debated my options. I couldn't tell her the entire truth, of course, but I could admit part of it. "That she took off, and I think Tom went to find her."

"Did you not think that was important to mention?"

"Is this why we're here, Detective? Do you have information about Lily's whereabouts?"

She paused, and I held my breath expectantly. "No, we have not located Lily. But we have established that Ms. Knight likes to manipulate the truth." She fixed her startling eyes on me. "Can you tell me a bit about your parents?"

All the air evaporated from the room. I palmed the arms of the chair and attempted to steady my breathing. I glanced at Greg, and he eyed me uncertainly. I'd never told him about my parents. I'd never told *anyone* about my parents, not even Daisy. She'd read a version of what had happened, but no one knew the real story.

Greg unleashed a heavy sigh. "Where's this going, Detective?"

Detective Ellis sat back in her chair and folded her hands smugly over her cherry-red blazer. "We would like to know anything you think might be relevant to this investigation, for starters."

I chewed over her words. I knew what she meant, of course, but I chose to play dumb. "I don't know how anything about my parents would relate to this investigation," I blurted out. Greg gave me another sharp look to stay quiet.

The detective watched me, probably looking for tells or cracks in my demeanor. I expected her to brandish a file and spill my secrets all over the table, just like Daisy had. Instead, she leaned in and folded her hands on the table, as if leveling with me. "The last time you were here, you gave this grand story about your father leaving your mother and getting remarried. Isn't that correct?"

I swallowed. My throat was suddenly on fire. "Yes."

"But that's not what happened, is it?"

Greg butted in. "Why is any of this relevant?"

The detective scratched her head, a few hairs coming loose from her stubby ponytail. "I'm just trying to get the story straight. *Did* your father leave, or was he murdered?"

Greg let out a short dry cough, trying to cover his surprise. "Get to the point, Detective," he snapped. He cleared his throat in an attempt to pull the focus back to why we were here. "If you don't have anything specific for my client related to the John Doe in the water, then . . ."

"Oh, there's definitely something specific." She reached down to her satchel and pulled out a mug shot of my mother. "My team has been doing some digging. Your mother murdered your father in cold blood, once she'd had enough of the abuse." She tapped a nail against the photograph, then dropped her voice. "That must have been hard, living through that. And she almost got away with it too. But then she turned herself in when they found the body. Didn't even try to fight."

I fidgeted with the ends of my sweater before digging my fingernails into my palms. The sharp sting brought me back to my body, back to this room.

"My father was a terrible man. I don't like to talk about it," I said. I didn't even bother looking at Greg. I knew he just wanted me to shut up.

Detective Ellis tapped the photograph again. "But this wasn't where the abuse stopped in your life, was it? Somehow, you married a man who was *also* abusive, a man eerily like your father."

"I'm sorry, what?" Greg scoffed. "That is a ridiculous accusation."

All the color drained from my face. *How could she possibly know?*

Detective Ellis ignored Greg and stared deeply into my eyes. "I know what it's like, to be hurt by someone you love," she said. "I know that sometimes there's only one way out."

Suddenly, I couldn't breathe. I grabbed the arms of my chair again until my knuckles turned milky white.

Is this when I should finally tell the truth? I'd never told anyone what Tom had done, what a monster he was. I'd bluffed about leaving; I'd bluffed about revealing his darkest secret; I'd bluffed about calling the cops. And yet he'd finally left me. After all that time, he couldn't hurt me anymore.

"I need to confer with my client for a moment," Greg said, pushing back his chair. "Ruby, outside. Now."

"I think we're all done for now," Detective Ellis said, sliding the photograph back into a folder. "I got what I needed." On the way to the door, she turned. "We'll call you when those DNA results come in, Ruby. Don't go too far."

I shuddered as she stepped out of the room. Greg motioned once again for me to follow him down the hall, past the jangling phones and police chatter. Outside, cold wind slapped me awake. When we were alone, Greg pulled me to the side of the building.

"Was Tom abusive?" His bluntness shocked me.

I shrugged. "Sometimes."

"Jesus Christ, Ruby. This isn't good." He dragged a hand over his face and glanced at the sky, which was bleached with pearly clouds. He cocked his chin toward the station. "If our John Doe is identified as Tom, there's your motive. Angry wife who'd had enough. Repetitive pattern of abuse, just like your mother." He exhaled. "Look, we need to get your defense together. Where you were the night he disappeared, what was happening between you two. They're going to dig deep, Ruby. Find all the dirt on your marriage. When was the last time he hit you?"

I opened my mouth, then closed it. I knew exactly when it was, but I shook my head. "I don't remember."

"Well, you need to start."

I thought of our last altercation, of Lily, of Ryan, of Tom's affair with Cassie, of his enemies in the neighborhood, of his secrets. And mine. There were motives everywhere, and they were stacking up. I swallowed and looked at my boots.

He sighed again, probably because he could tell I wasn't being forthright. "Look, the next time the detective calls, let me handle it. Until they have a definitive match, stay quiet, and lay low. You hear me?"

I nodded. He gave a distracted wave as he answered another call and hurried to his expensive car to head back into the city.

I watched him drive off, back to his life in Nashville. An intense loneliness gripped me so suddenly I felt the ache in my bones. I missed my neighborhood walks, my friends, sitting in various cafés or restaurants, heading down to the greenway to walk or go see a show. Life had been easier then. I'd had a rhythm and a routine. I had known what to expect.

I sat in my car, not yet ready to return to Cottage Grove. I thought about that photograph of my mother. I remember the day she turned herself in, which had started a pattern of being bounced from foster home to foster home until I had finally been adopted. She'd thought she was doing the right thing, but really, she'd stolen the only bit of stability I'd had.

And because of it, I'd turned into someone else completely.

16

Daisy and Cassie showed up together right on time.

After the debacle with Daisy at the Murderlings, I'd decided to dig into my neighbor's motivations and see if I couldn't strike some sort of deal to keep her quiet about my past.

Though the other night had been uncomfortable, no one had guessed the truth about what really happened, not even Daisy. It was another case that simply came and went, though Lily had been awfully invested and kept talking about it for days after.

"Come in." In a lame attempt to make friends outside of Ryan, I'd decided to invite them both over, more so that Tom would get off my back. He wouldn't let me live it down that Ryan was the only person I'd warmed up to, so here I was, making an effort, even though Daisy felt more like enemy territory than a possible friend. Still, I wanted to keep her close, see if I could change the dynamic between us somehow.

Cassie and Daisy were most definitely not friends, did not run in the same circles, and stood a good six feet apart on the front porch. Where Cassie was poised and quiet, Daisy was loud and borderline obnoxious with her honesty.

"Oh, this place really sings, Ruby," Cassie said, handing me her bag as she stepped inside. "It's breathtaking."

I hung it on the rack and admired her work. "I'd say thanks, but this is all your doing."

Daisy rolled her eyes and assessed the furniture and art, smacking loudly on a piece of gum. "Looks like a design catalog threw up in here."

Despite my feelings about Daisy, I laughed. "Wine?" I steered them both toward the kitchen and then ushered us outside around the firepit. The sun had not yet set, and it was a warm night. We sank into the Adirondacks and stared at each other awkwardly as I racked my brain for what to say. I'd never been great at making female friends outside the hospital. I found digging into emotional conversation tedious, and I didn't like to gossip. Because of that, I naturally gravitated toward men. Or spending time alone.

"How's your little podcast thing going, Daisy?" Cassie asked, swirling her wine.

"Great," Daisy said, folding her gum in a tissue before knocking back half her glass in a single gulp. "We're up to almost ten million downloads." She wiped her mouth. "How's your little design thing going, Cassie?"

The insults had been launched, and Cassie's mouth fell open before she closed it. "It's going quite well, thank you."

Daisy focused on me. "So, Rubes, why don't you work anymore? You were an ER nurse, right? The commute too far or something?"

My story was that I'd retired, but for tonight, I didn't feel like telling that same tired lie. "Tom wanted me to quit so I could play house." The words shot out of my mouth so fast Cassie choked on her sip of wine, but Daisy looked intrigued.

"I don't like Tom," Daisy said. "Something about him I don't trust."

"Well, that's a terrible thing to say," Cassie snapped.

"Why?" Daisy said, gesturing between us. "We're not friends here, right? We're neighbors—acquaintances, really. Why not be honest?"

Cassie snorted. "Well, Ruby and I are friends."

Were we? She'd been friendly enough, and she'd decorated my house, but she wasn't someone I would seek out alone time with if she didn't live down the street.

"Look." Daisy leaned forward and topped off her glass. "The rich don't know how to be friends. Builders create these insulated little bubbles for millions of dollars so we can have everything at our fingertips: Amenities. Community. Safety. But what no one really has is a true connection. We get together, we get drunk, we play these ridiculous social games to show off who has the bigger, better life. It's all an illusion." She eyed me before turning her attention to Cassie. "But we don't really get to know each other beyond swinging our big shiny dicks in each other's faces. It's a class thing."

Cassie laughed. "So you're rich, then, are you?"

Daisy smacked her lips together after taking another healthy chug. "Yep."

"Well, I'm not rich," I said. "Tom is, but we keep our money separate."

Cassie wrinkled her nose, staring down into her goblet. "Why on earth would you do that?"

I shrugged. "We've always been that way. I like having clear boundaries, even while married. I don't ever want to depend on a man."

"Cheers to that." Daisy clinked her glass against mine. "Or a woman, which, if you both didn't know, is more my speed."

I eyed Daisy again, wondering what she was really after. Had she truly wanted me to come on her podcast, or was she using me to get to something else? Tom flashed through my mind . . . all the cases he'd tried, all the guilty people he'd gotten off. Was she trying to bribe me to get to him?

"Anyone special in your life?" I asked.

"No. Men may be stupid, but women are a hell of a lot more work."

Despite myself, I smiled. "God, that's true. It's why most of my friends are men."

Daisy offered a genuine smile. "Me too."

Cassie cleared her throat. "I don't think men and women can just be friends."

"Spoken by someone who has no male friends," Daisy said.

"I have male friends," Cassie said, smoothing her trousers. "But I prefer the company of women."

Daisy and Cassie lobbed passive-aggressive insults back and forth while I got progressively drunker. Before I knew it, the sun had set, and Tom and Lily came barging through the front door, pizzas in hand. They'd had a father-daughter date, their first in months, and Lily looked excited as she poked her head out back.

"Do your friends want to stay and eat?"

"Why don't you go grab some plates, sweetheart?" I said.

"There's that word again," Daisy mumbled. "Friends." Though she'd had more to drink than me, she was stone-cold sober. "And how's my little Murderling?" Daisy assessed Lily, then addressed Cassie. "You should have seen this kid the other night. A total natural. Thinks like a killer."

"Daisy," I warned.

"Who thinks like a killer? Hello, ladies." Tom flashed his bright smile, which made my stomach clench. He'd always been able to woo women, always been able to hide who he really was in most public situations, and yet Daisy saw right through him. He leaned in and kissed me on the cheek, and it took everything in me not to flinch.

"Your daughter," Daisy said, seeming to sense the tension between us. "I think she could have a profession in forensics. Or as a detective or something."

Tom laughed. "Lily is going to MIT in the fall. Majoring in engineering."

Daisy snorted. "Is that her decision or yours?"

The silence crackled, and I resisted the urge to jump in and smooth things over. Part of me admired Daisy for just going for it, for saying exactly what she meant.

"Is what my decision?" Lily reappeared behind Tom, and Cassie's gaze bounced from one person to the next—she was clearly unsure of what to say.

Daisy straightened in her chair as a muscle in Tom's jaw flexed. "Your plans for school. I told your dad I think you could have a career in criminology. The way you dissected that case the other night was impressive."

I clutched my wineglass stem a little harder, careful not to give away my facade. Tom didn't know she'd come along with me to Daisy's. Lily glanced up at Tom. Her whole life, she'd placated him, bending over backward to do as he pleased. Looking at her now, I wondered if that was a strategy so he didn't lose his temper. Maybe Lily was a lot more aware of the dynamics in our house than I gave her credit for. To my surprise, she gripped the back of an Adirondack and shrugged. "I think it would be cool to study something like that."

Tom whipped his head toward her, and Cassie shot straight up. "Tom, will you help me with the drinks in the kitchen? I just got a sudden craving for a martini. Do you have vermouth?" She ushered him out of earshot, and for a moment, I was overwhelmingly grateful for Cassie's quick thinking, even though I already knew I would pay for this later.

Lily collapsed in a chair beside Daisy, and I stared at her. "You know, you can study whatever you want," I said. "Your future isn't written in stone."

"Damn straight." Daisy slapped her on the knee. "Wait, I have an idea. Do you need a summer job?"

Lily's eyes lit up. "Yes, actually. I've already been dreading how bored I'm going to be until I leave in September."

"I've been needing an assistant forever. The last one 'quietly quit,' or whatever they're calling it these days." Daisy blew her bangs out of her eyes. "What do you say? Want to learn about the wild world of podcasting? And cold cases? And murder?"

Lily looked at me expectantly. There was one very big reason to say no, but hopefully Daisy wouldn't bring up my case file again. Plus, I wanted Lily to explore other avenues of interest, especially since she hadn't started college yet. I wanted her to have options and spread her wings before it was too late.

"It's okay with me," I said. "As long as your dad agrees."

She rolled her eyes. "He'll never agree. You just saw his reaction."

Daisy sat forward, groaning in the process. "What about if we just keep this between us? It will be our little secret. I'm good at keeping secrets. How about you?"

I ignored her remark and glanced into the kitchen through the floor-to-ceiling windows. Cassie was laughing at something Tom had said, touching his shoulder seductively. I already kept so many secrets from Tom . . . what was one more? He worked so much he wouldn't even notice if Lily was next door from time to time.

"I'm in," I said.

Daisy smirked, something like respect flashing between us.

"Really? This is so cool." Lily clapped and went inside to grab a slice of pizza.

I settled back in my chair. "How am I supposed to trust you with my daughter?"

"She's a good kid," Daisy said. "I really am just trying to help. Especially if you won't be on my podcast. This way, I get some help at a cheap price. We'll call it even."

"We'll call what even?" I said. "You trying to expose an old family wound for sport?"

"Is that what that is? A wound?" She cocked her head, and neither of us said anything. Finally, she stood. "One thing to know about me,

Ruby. I may be blunt, but I can be an ally if you let me. And trust me; you'd rather have me as an ally than your enemy."

She walked back inside, making a loud joke as she entered.

I wasn't sure if I was comfortable with Lily spending so much time with Daisy, but maybe, just as Daisy was keeping an eye on me, I would use Lily to keep an even closer eye on her.

17

Instead of going home, I decided to drive into Nashville.

I hadn't been back in a while. The day was crisp and cold, and the winding roads gave way to vast rolling hills. I remembered a friend saying how beautiful Tennessee was compared to most states: It wasn't flat, but it wasn't overrun with mountains either. Instead, we had valleys and peaks. It was all soft curves, nothing too severe.

I reveled in the beauty of the country before it opened up to the choppy, bustling city, sprawling with midrises and new construction. The sounds of city life pulsed in my ears as I stabbed my windows down. Frigid air blasted my face, but I didn't mind. I wanted to feel cold. I wanted to feel *something*.

I couldn't figure out how Detective Ellis had found out about my parents, but now that she had sunk her teeth into that narrative, she wouldn't let go, which made me her prime suspect. All the honky-tonks and tourist traps whipped by downtown as I looped past the library and toward midtown. Finally I found myself in front of Metro General. The familiar hospital, which had been the container for so much of my life, loomed in front of me. I gripped the steering wheel, debating what to do, but after a moment, I exited my car and walked toward the entrance.

The automatic doors parted, and every muscle in my body unclenched. Even with the crush of frantic patients and nurses in scrubs and the stench of antiseptic and blood, it calmed me in a way little else could. I took the elevator up to the ER, and as the doors opened, the chaos unfurled like an unexpected wave. My nervous system calmed as the sounds around me strengthened. It took everything in me not to grab a chart, roll a stretcher, or offer a hand. The woman at the front desk looked up, but I didn't know her.

It had been over a year since I'd left. Did I even have friends here anymore?

"Ruby?"

In answer to that question, I turned to find Whitney, one of my dearest coworkers, staring at me in disbelief. She was disheveled, her ponytail lank, her skin sallow, a few bloodstains marring her scrubs. *Car wreck,* I thought. By the looks of her, she'd probably been here since last night.

"Hi, Whitney." I waved my hand awkwardly as she whispered something to the front desk woman and then motioned for me to follow with a sharp jerk of her head. I walked behind her down the hall and to the nurse's hub, which was really nothing more than a converted storage closet where all the nurses could get a quick respite from the chaos. Whitney motioned to a tiny folding chair by the door.

She stayed standing and crossed her arms over her small chest. "What are you doing here?" Her voice was icy, gray eyes cold.

The harshness of her words brought me right back to another well-kept secret: I hadn't quit. I'd been fired.

"I just felt compelled to stop by."

"Why?" She scratched her wrist, a terrible habit left over from a lifetime of crippling psoriasis.

"I don't know." And it was the truth. Everything I'd done lately didn't seem to have a tether or a point of reference. I felt like I was

106

floating aboveground, looking down, desperately seeking some sort of direction or footing.

"If Rob sees you here . . ." Her voice trailed off. She didn't have to say more.

"I know." I understood what it would mean. I hesitated. "How is he?"

Her eyes flashed. "Fine."

I struggled with what to say, picking at the cuff of my jacket. "I am sorry, you know." My eyes lifted. "Lily was in a bad place, and . . ."

Whitney lifted a hand, which was dry and chapped from excessive scrubbing. "Save it. I don't want your apology now. I wanted it then." She laughed. "You know, it's been over a year, Ruby. A *year*, and this is the first time you've ever even attempted to apologize for what you did."

I looked at my lap. What could I say? "I wasn't ready then, but some things have happened that . . ."

Whitney bumped the spare chair, and the metal legs squealed over the linoleum. "Oh, I know all about the things that have happened," she said. "Everyone knows what you did last year." She crossed her arms again, this time tighter. "You need to go. Right now." Her nostrils flared, her bright eyes fixed on the door behind me.

I lifted my arms in surrender. "I'm going." I wanted to tell her it was nice to see her, that I missed this place, that I really was sorry, but if I'd learned anything over the years, it was that words didn't matter. Only actions mattered. What you did mattered, not what you said.

And what I'd done was unforgivable.

I sighed and let myself out, peeking into rooms, where all the trauma was contained. This part of my life was over, and yet I'd been drawn back like a moth to a flame. Would I ever have quit if I hadn't been fired? I doubted it.

As I was heading toward the elevator, Rob emerged from a patient's room, a stethoscope looped around his neck like a tiny snake. His hair was longer, and he looked tired, but he was still fit, still had that flash of pure joy about him. He moved with authority and purpose; that was, until he caught me jabbing the elevator button as if my life depended on it.

"Ruby?" His voice wasn't as cold as Whitney's, but as he approached, his eyes dimmed, and his mouth turned into a grim line. "What are you doing here?"

I'd been banned from ever setting foot in this hospital again. Or practicing medicine. That was my dirty little secret even Tom didn't know. I hadn't quit because I'd wanted a slower pace of life or because he'd wanted me to. I'd agreed to the move in order to *get away*.

I shrugged. "I was in the neighborhood."

His eyes raked over my face, and I could tell he wanted to say so many things. I'd put his career on the line. I'd been his most trusted nurse, and then I'd gone and ruined everything.

"Don't worry. I'm going." The doors opened, and I hesitated before I stepped inside. "You know, I did what I did because I was trying to help Lily," I finally said. I pressed one palm against the cold door as it tried to close. "I was just doing what I thought was best, as her mother, but it turned out it was all for nothing." I glanced at him briefly, and something like forgiveness crossed his face.

He stepped forward. "I heard about Lily, and I'm so sorry, Ruby. I know what you did came from a good place, but . . ." He trailed off and glanced behind him. "You can't be here, okay?"

A year ago, he would have asked me for coffee, and I would have said yes. We would have sat in a warm, sticky booth, and he would have asked me about my problems. I would have told him things, private things, and he would have really listened, maybe even offered stellar advice. Not today. Not ever again.

I studied his earnest, handsome face. Though we'd never crossed any physical lines, I'd had a healthy crush on him like all the other nurses. But he was one of the good ones, faithful, loyal to a fault, clear boundaries professionally intact. I'd had to tell Tom he was gay just so he didn't turn his jealous wrath on me. I'd ruined our professional relationship and our friendship, as if I were prewired to self-destruct.

"They think Tom is dead," I suddenly confessed. "And the police think I had something to do with it."

Rob opened his mouth to speak and then shoved a hand through his messy dark hair. "Ruby, I don't know what to say. That's awful."

"I didn't," I finally said. "I don't even think the man they found is him." I sighed. "It's complicated."

A page rumbled over the system for Dr. Hawthorne, and he took a few steps back. "I'm sorry, Ruby. I've got to go."

"I know." I waved, understanding instantly that I might not ever see him again. I wasn't sure what I wanted from him, but something nagged at me, something I needed to know. "Wait."

He turned, his sneakers squeaking on the floors. A flash of impatience wrecked his features. When a patient needed him, that was priority number one—not conversation.

"Did you know Tom was abusive?"

He looked at his shoes, then shook his head. "I had a feeling."

I bristled. "Why didn't you ever say anything?"

He scratched his jaw and let his hand drop. "I didn't want to get involved if you weren't ready for help."

I nodded, knowing better than most that abused women often weren't ready for help, even when we thought we were. Tears filled my eyes, and I stepped onto the elevator before it closed. Rob walked away as I pressed the button for the main floor. I'd never told a soul about Tom, and now four people knew: Greg, the detective, Ryan, and Rob. What did it matter now? He was gone—or possibly dead.

As I stepped back outside, I let the cool wind calm my racing mind. It was time to get to the bottom of all this before Detective Ellis did.

18

I woke to the sound of the front door being slammed shut.

I startled in bed, then moaned as I felt the bruises on my ribs. Last night slowly shifted back into focus—at least the parts I could remember.

We'd been celebrating Ryan's opening night at the Frist. What I hadn't known was that my portrait was one of the star pieces, and every one of our neighbors had seen the sad eyes, the faintly bruised cheek that could have doubled as a shadow. The title, *In Hiding*, had sparked endless conversation. Tom had been humiliated but kept his cover publicly intact. When it was time to leave, Lily had stayed to hang out with some friends because she'd driven separately.

We'd barely stepped foot inside the door before he'd exploded. I'd come to on the floor, gasping for air. Now, my ribs ached, and my throat was raw. I fingered the skin there, thinking once again of my mother.

I was at a breaking point.

I gingerly rolled over to check the time. I needed to get Lily up for school. She had only a week left before summer. Now that I knew she was back on her meds, thanks to Dr. Forrester, I was paying more attention than ever. I knew, since she was almost legal and headed to college, she'd be making her own health decisions soon, but for now, I wanted to make sure she kept her normal routine while she still lived under our roof.

Even though she seemed better, I *knew* that something was going on beneath the surface. I'd brought it up to Tom briefly before our fight, but he'd said she was fine. I'd exhausted the laundry list of possible suspects. I'd been inspecting her wrists for bruises, one of the first telltale signs of physical abuse.

I should know.

I remembered when my mother would show up for breakfast, eyes red rimmed, thin bangles or scrunchies attempting to cover the nasty bruises that encircled her wrists like handcuffs. It had started just at her wrists, then blossomed to other parts of her body: her neck, her ribs, her cheeks. She could cover most of them with clothing or makeup, but I knew. And I began waiting for my father to turn his wrath on me.

I was so young when it had started, but even in my adolescent brain, I'd thought it was somehow my fault. My father grew so distant from me, always drunk and mean, that I stopped addressing him completely. I stayed small, never asked him for anything. As a result, my mother became my whole world, and I figured he knew it. He punished her because of me.

I trampled the memories as I went to wake Lily. Regardless of what was going on with her, I knew she was doing better, but we hadn't gotten to the root of her recent issue. Andrew flashed through my mind again. She hadn't mentioned him since that day at school, but that didn't mean he wasn't still bothering her. I thought about calling a family meeting, something we hadn't done in at least a year. Tom had left for an early case at the courthouse, so I didn't know what time he'd be home, but I would send him a text about it. This was more important than a case or his rage about the portrait.

Upstairs, I knocked on Lily's door, which she had recently started locking. I couldn't very well ask her to unlock it: she was seventeen and deserved privacy, though now I wondered what she wanted privacy from. For a moment, as I stood on the other side of the door, I longed for the young girl I had raised. I missed her rumpled hair and sour morning breath, the way she would fold into my lap and tell me about her dreams. I missed the weight of her little body, arranged perfectly in my arms, the closeness we used to share.

But there were other things I didn't miss.

I twisted the knob, and it turned freely in my hand. Her room was warm and smelled like pot. I sighed as I moved toward the lump in her bed. She wasn't allowed to smoke pot in the house; she knew that. As I got closer, I realized it wasn't a human under there; it was simply pillows. A shot of worry traversed my body in an instant. Had she snuck out last night or this morning? Had I even *seen* her last night once she'd gotten home from Ryan's show?

No, I hadn't.

The last time I'd seen her was at the Frist before we'd left. Had she not come home?

I searched her room for her backpack, but it was gone. Clothes were strewed across the floor in wrinkled piles, but I didn't see her phone. I opened her closet. The clothes weren't arranged in any order—all seasons jumbled together, some of her pants having tumbled from a shelf. I couldn't tell if anything was missing. I hunted for a note and removed my phone from my back pocket. I dialed her number and heard a ringing under her bed. I dropped down to my knees and grabbed her phone.

Lily never went anywhere without her phone. She'd had it last night, so she must have come back home. I attempted to unlock her phone, but I didn't know her password. I called Tom, but it went straight to voice mail. I knew I wouldn't be able to get him all day, since he was in court.

I sat on Lily's bed, weighing my options. I didn't have any of her friends' numbers. I didn't even know if she had a boyfriend. I dropped my head in my hands. When had I stopped paying attention to what was going on in her life? I was no longer busy with my job, so what excuse did I have?

Slowing my breath, I started to calm my system. Maybe she had gone for an early-morning run. Maybe she'd slept over at a friend's or just needed some space. In the back of my head, though, I knew how unlikely that was. It was a school night. Plus, her phone.

Despite how important privacy was, I shuffled through Lily's drawers, searching for what, I wasn't sure. I turned to her nightstand and yanked it open. Her meds were gone. I stared into the empty drawer, perplexed. What did that mean? I grabbed her phone and went back downstairs. It buzzed in my palm just before I sat it on the countertop.

you got the stuff? meet in usual spot b4 class?

My breath stalled as I read the text. Obviously, Lily had planned on selling something. Drugs? I immediately thought of the meds she'd just started taking again, the meds that were now gone. Surely she wasn't selling them. I tried to log in to her phone again but stopped before I got locked out. I knew one person who could help. I scooped my keys from the table, put on my shoes, and headed out. I stopped in the driveway. Lily's car was gone, which meant she either had taken off this morning or had never come home last night.

It was a hot day, and I made the quick jaunt next door. I knocked on the oversize brass knocker, shaped like a skull, and waited.

Daisy opened it almost immediately, as if she'd been expecting me. "Well, well. To what do I owe this unexpected visit?" She was in a black dress adorned with giant red roses and a headband to match.

"Can you break into a phone?" I asked, wagging Lily's phone in the air.

Despite our differences, Daisy grinned. "One of my specialties, my dear." She opened the door wider. "Come on in."

COTTAGE GROVE FORUM

hippiemama23: Alright, guys. Theories on this guy (AKA TOM'S) murder. Go.

shianna: Ooh, this is fun. Okay, let me think . . .

crackersmp: well, i mean, we already kind of know how he died but how would anyone be able to dump him in the lake without us seeing?

dahmernotjeffrey: his throat was slit right?

lettucehead4life: where did you hear that????

crackersmp: what about the people who live RIGHT on the water????

shianna: we live right on the water!!!! wut ru saying?

nashvegasart: i thought you were all convinced it was Ruby.

hippiemama23: well, only if the guy si tom. even if it was, she'd have to have help, right???? Unless she's like a TOATL psychopath. *total

shianna: good point. what if there's more than one killer????????

dahmernotjeffrey: there's usually always more than one killer

softatheart: i just can't believe tom's really gone

dahmernotjeffrey: no one knows if it's tom

crackersmp: well lets say it IS. usually it's about money, right? Did ruby have a big insurance policy?

hippiemama23: OH YOU R GENIUS!!! I BET THAT'S WHY SHE DID IT!

nashvegasart: ☺

lettucehead4life: thats my theory to

nashvegasart: based on . . . your penchant for vegan crime shows?

shianna: no, she's write so many people murder for money its sad

nashvegasart: you know what else is sad? The grammar on this thread.

lettucehead4life: 👆

nashvegasart: is that a pc middle finger? or are you being racist and calling me yellow?

hippiemama23: YOU GUYS WE NEED TO TAKE THIS SERIOUSLY. THERE IS A MURDERER AMONG US

dahmernotjeffrey: jesus christ you people

crackersmp: we just got a new security system

nashvegasart: be sure to give everyone the passcode

lettucehead4life: Oh she will. It's 111, FUCK OFF.

nashvegasart: good one, rabbit food.

softatheart: you guys we need to come together not fight

lettucehead4life: I say we confront her. Make her confess.

crackersmp: Could we get her on video??????

crystallover joined the conversation

crystallover: WE SHOULD TOTALLY DO THIS

hippiemama23: I have a cousin who's a PI. Maybe he could help.

crystallover: PERFECT.

nashvegasart: you ladies are literally going to get yourselves killed

lettucehead4life: at least we are TAKING action, unlike YOU

nashvegasart: i don't have all the facts yet. You can't take action until you have all the facts.

dahmernotjeffrey: exactly

shianna: wow, he's kinda right. Should we get more facts?

crackersmp: 👍

hippiemama23: okay, okay, let's find more facts people!!!!!!!!!!!! WE HAVE A REAL CASE TO CRACK.

19

I drove back to Cottage Grove from Metro General, battling Nashville traffic.

My phone buzzed, and I checked it at a stoplight.

Come over. It's about Tom.

My stomach clenched. A text from Cassie. I picked up the pace and thought about my conversation with Cassie, her confession of the affair. I didn't even know how I felt about it. I was beginning to wonder if I'd ever truly loved Tom or if I'd just craved stability, a family, money, all the things I'd never had growing up. But why had I stayed after he'd shown me who he really was? There wasn't a price tag in the world worth that type of pain . . . but maybe, deep down, I felt I deserved it as some sort of punishment.

I parked in front of Cassie's and walked inside, knowing the door would be open. Most neighbors didn't lock their doors in Cottage Grove. I used to be one of them.

"Hey, Cass. It's me." I closed the door behind me, but the house was quiet. I hated that I was still calling her by her nickname, but the truth was I just didn't care that much. Maybe I should have, but I didn't.

I waited for her to appear, to offer me coffee or a snack, the ever gracious hostess. But the house was completely silent. I called out her name again and then fired off a text and heard a ding somewhere from upstairs.

Uncertain, I followed the noise, wondering if she was in the bathroom or had fallen asleep.

Cassie's house was pristine, everything in perfect order. My eyes roamed over all the ways she'd made this house into a home, and I reminded myself it was easy to maintain when you didn't have children. I passed the guest room, her work studio, and the office used by Charlie, who never seemed to be home.

Deep down, I knew Cassie was lonely. It was why most women cheated, even if her story of an open marriage was true. Women just wanted to feel seen. Women wanted desire. Women wanted love.

At her bedroom door, I knocked softly. "Cassie? It's Ruby. May I come in?"

I waited, not wanting to catch her indecent, but finally, I pushed the door open. The lights were off, the shades drawn, and I blinked, trying to focus. I could see a lump in the bed and began to step out of the room, realizing that yes, she was napping. But something stopped me.

My breath caught as I stepped closer, silently, over the plush Italian rug. "Cassie?" My breath was warm, and the room smelled of iron.

No, not iron, I realized. *Blood.*

I flipped on the bedside lamp and gasped as I stared down at Cassie. Her throat was slit; thick, dark blood had congealed on her pale neck and expensive sheets. She was in a nightgown, her face perfectly made up. She clutched something in her right hand.

"Oh my God." I scrambled backward and fumbled to find my phone. I went to call 911, then hesitated. If I made the call, it would be the second crime I'd reported. The second dead body I'd found.

I spun around. *Was this a setup?* Was someone trying to make me look guilty? I rushed back down the stairs and hesitated. Instead of going out the front door, I went out the back and peeked around the side of the house to see if anyone was walking by. The last thing I needed was a witness saying they'd seen me go into Cassie's house.

I speed-walked back to my car and tried to catch my shaky breath. What was happening? I glanced back up at her house, as if it might offer an answer. I drove quickly back home and locked myself inside.

I called Greg. "We have a major problem," I whispered. I explained what I'd found, and he told me not to call the police.

My hands were trembling as I poured myself a glass of wine up to the brim. I drank it greedily, refilling the glass nearly to the top. I assessed my big empty house. Was I safe here?

I imagined Cassie had thought she was protected in her home, that nothing bad would ever happen. And now she was dead. *Poor Cassie.*

I walked from room to room and then stopped at the bottom of the stairs. I remembered when I'd found Lily here, crumpled and drunk, how worried I'd been. I took another gulp and thought of Cassie. Did she know her killer? Could she have stopped it?

I lowered my glass and thought of the text. I reread it on my phone. *Had* she texted me, or had it been the killer? Because now, when the police found her phone . . .

Oh God. They'd know she had contacted me right before she died.

Before I could think too much more about the implications of that damaging text, I heard the very distinct groan of a heavy footstep upstairs. My breath caught. I gripped my glass.

Time slowed. My heart jabbed into my ribs.

Move, Ruby. Now.

I wasn't an idiot in some horror movie. Instead of going upstairs to inspect, I grabbed my phone and keys and ran back outside.

20

THEN

Daisy broke into Lily's phone in just ten minutes.

I exhaled a breath I didn't know I was holding. "You're a lifesaver."

She shrugged. "I owe you, right?"

Once Lily had taken the summer job with Daisy, the tension had diffused between us. Lily loved working on the podcast and digging into cold cases. Though Daisy had become a mentor, Lily had also become indispensable to Daisy's life and work. If something happened to Lily, it would affect Daisy too. I shifted and tried to hide my discomfort from my aching ribs. I hurriedly texted back a different location to meet the mystery person and showed Daisy the text. "Does this read young to you?"

She read it and laughed. "No." She deleted my message and retyped one into the phone before handing it back to me.

2 much heat. meet behind bleachers instead.

I stared at Daisy. "How do you know about the bleachers?"

She laughed. "Lily tells me things. But obviously not things like this."

I pressed send and sighed. "I'm worried." It was the first time I'd said the words out loud. My gut told me this wasn't just Lily out and about before school. Something was wrong. I could feel it.

"She's a good kid. I'm sure she's fine."

I showed myself out and drove to Lily's school. Traffic was awful, and I wondered how she was handling this commute every morning. Once again, I realized how selfish this move to Cottage Grove had been, how viciously it had uprooted everyone's lives. But Tom wanted what Tom wanted, regardless of who it hurt. I parked by the track in the back of Franklin Road Academy, the smell of synthetic rubber mingling with the freshly cut grass of the football field. I glanced around, realizing I had no idea whom I was meeting. However, I figured I'd be the only one behind the bleachers, so it seemed like a logical choice. I locked my car and glanced around, Lily's phone secured in my back pocket. I was the first there, so I decided to scroll through her phone now that it was unlocked.

I scanned her texts, not understanding the poor grammar and lingo she used with her friends. The person who had texted her today had no history between them, which meant she'd been deleting all communication. I wondered why. I searched for Andrew Tarver's contact information, but there was none. Again, my gut twisted. If she was caught up in drugs—using, selling, or both—I had to get her help immediately. No more pretending it would get better on its own.

I checked her browser history, but it had been wiped clean. Again, another bad sign. I opened her photos and scanned through, the knot twisting as I saw tons of sexual selfies taken from her bedroom.

"Oh, Lily."

Was she taking these for herself, or was she sending them to someone? Suddenly, I felt foolish that we hadn't been keeping a closer eye on her. That *I* hadn't been keeping a closer eye on her. Just because she was a good student and appeared responsible didn't mean she couldn't fall prey to the same downfalls as other kids, especially with her anxiety and depression.

I glanced up as a tall lanky boy with mussed brown hair, tight jeans, and a motorcycle helmet dangling from his fingers stood about ten feet away. I hadn't even heard him come up.

I pocketed Lily's phone and stood upright, nearly as tall as him. "Are you waiting for Lily?"

"Uhh . . ." He scratched his neck and looked around. "Is she in trouble or something?"

"I'm Lily's mother, Ruby." The words *she's missing* hovered on my lips, but I kept quiet. "When's the last time you talked to Lily? Or saw her?"

"Not sure." He was already taking a few steps backward.

"Wait, please." In my job, I'd worked with all types of people: drug addicts, the unhoused, CEOs, politicians. I'd become proficient at reading people. "I think Lily's in trouble."

His eyes darkened, and I could see it: he cared for Lily, which meant he might be willing to help.

"What kind of trouble?"

"She wasn't at home this morning. Her car's gone, but she left her phone behind." I showed him the phone, and he eyed it and then me, chewing on the inside of his cheek.

"Can you tell me what you were meeting for? Is it drugs?"

His defenses went back up, and I tried a different tact.

"Look, I don't care what your arrangement was. I just want to know where she could be right now. Do you think you could help me figure out where she might be?"

I could tell he knew something, by the way he kept shifting his gaze and his feet, eager to run.

"No one's going to get in trouble," I reassured him. "I just need to know when you saw her last."

Again, he scratched the back of his neck. "Leonard's party last night." He sighed. "She was really wasted."

Who was Leonard? Why did I know nothing about my daughter or who was in her life?

"Where does Leonard live?"

"In the city."

So Lily had gone to a party last night after the Frist.

"She left late."

"Was she drunk? Did she drive?" I knew I was asking too many questions.

"I don't know. Look, I've got to get to class, so . . ." He turned, and I jogged to catch up.

"Can you just tell me what you were meeting for?"

He eyed me again, as if I might be a cop about to bust him. Instead of producing a baggie of pills or white powder, he erected a fancy pocketknife. I thought of the similar one I'd found in Lily's drawer.

Who does she need protection from?

"A knife?"

He scoffed. "It's not just any knife. This thing can fuck you up. Best there is." He shoved it back in his pocket and began walking away.

"Were you doing a trade?" I took a few steps to reach him again.

He looked me over again and sighed. "Yeah. She gives me pills; I give her this."

"What type of pills?"

He sighed. "Antipsychotics, mood stimulators, psychostimulants." He counted them off on his fingers, then shrugged. "Whatever was on her." He straddled his motorcycle and secured his helmet.

Lily was selling all her meds; the meds I had gotten her years ago without Tom's knowledge, the meds I'd snatched from the hospital just so he wouldn't know.

He throttled the engine, preparing to take off.

"One more question," I shouted over the roar of the engine.

"Yeah?"

"What's Leonard's last name?"

"Dominguez," he yelled back before taking off toward the road. My heart hammered in my chest.

Dominguez.

Like Daisy Dominguez? I knew there could be infinite Dominguezes in Nashville, but it seemed too coincidental to be irrelevant.

New facts swirled in my head as I searched Lily's phone for a contact for Leonard. No luck. I decided to call Daisy, but she didn't answer. Maybe it was just a coincidence. Or maybe she could help me find my daughter.

After waiting past the first bell, I knew Lily wasn't showing up today. I didn't want to get hysterical, but my past made me prone to worry. On more than one occasion, my parents had disappeared on weekend binges after they'd made up, leaving me to fend for myself. As a result, I'd suffered from wild abandonment issues and had to grow up fast because of it. Once my mom went to prison, everything fell apart. I'd done everything in my power to keep Lily from feeling the same way. I'd wanted to make sure she felt safe, secure, loved. *Protected.*

And now she was gone.

I convinced myself to stay calm until I had proof that something *was* wrong. Teenagers disappeared for chunks of time, and that didn't always mean they had been kidnapped, or worse. Lily was a kid who craved space, but didn't Tom and I give her plenty of space? Now I realized that it might have been too much.

I tried to call Daisy again on the way to Tom's office, but she still didn't pick up. After navigating rush hour, I pulled into the courthouse and checked my watch. I didn't know Tom's trial schedule or when they would recess, but I decided to just sit outside the courtroom until he emerged. I kept looking through Lily's phone, trying to get to the bottom of a question I couldn't quite answer.

Inside the courthouse, I located Tom's courtroom, A-102, and sat outside the double doors on a bench, head buried in Lily's phone. I cycled through her contacts and recent texts and sent a few messages. No one replied.

I sighed and slapped her phone against my open palm. Finally, the large oak doors groaned open, and out flooded lawyers, dressed smartly in crisp suits, and spectators, who chatted excitedly. This was a first-degree murder trial and had made the local news. I didn't know if the day was over or if they were just taking a break, but I searched for Tom's face in the crowd.

He was talking intently to his cochair, and I stood dumbly a few feet behind him, desperate to get his attention but not wanting to anger him. Finally, he gave a wave to someone else and made a beeline for the exit, briefcase in hand. I jogged to catch up and grabbed his elbow when we were outside.

He spun around, instantly on guard, and didn't relax when he saw me. "Ruby? What are you doing here?" His eyes traveled toward my ribs, probably remembering what he'd done.

"I . . ." I fumbled with where to start. For a moment, I wanted him to think this was about last night, that I was finally going to expose him for what he was. But I cared more about Lily, especially right now. "Lily's missing." The words tumbled from my lips, sinister and twisted. *Is she really missing?*

He scoffed and had the audacity to check his watch. "What do you mean, Ruby? How can she be missing? We were with her last night."

I filled him in: she wasn't at home this morning, and her car was gone, but she'd left her phone. I kept out the part about selling drugs. Even now, it felt like a mistake to withhold something so big, but I knew Tom would ask too many questions. Where had Lily gotten the meds? Why did she even have them? It would all lead back to the lies I'd told, the infinite ways I'd deceived him. Even now, I wanted to keep her secrets, wanted to protect her from Tom.

"Look, I really can't deal with this right now." A muscle in his jaw twitched, a *warning*. "I'm sure she'll show up."

A colleague passed Tom and whistled for him to follow.

"I've got to go. Just keep me posted, okay?"

He squeezed my shoulder a little too hard and disappeared, leaving me truly dumbfounded. This was his *daughter*, not some random stranger.

Suddenly, I remembered one time when Lily was eight—she'd packed up her most precious belongings, slung her worn backpack over a bony shoulder, and marched to the door. She'd taken a shaky breath as she'd glanced at us. We'd been eating dinner and paused, midbite.

"Where are you going, sweetie?" I'd asked.

"I'm moving *out*." She'd stormed outside and stomped through the backyard. She'd gotten as far as the tree line before bursting into tears and running back inside.

I vacillated with who to call or what to do. I couldn't report her missing yet. It had been only a couple of hours. I tried Daisy again, and this time, she answered.

"Yo. You find her?"

"Who's Leonard?"

"Um, you're going to need to be more specific."

I shuffled impatiently from foot to foot. "Leonard Dominguez. Are you related?"

She exhaled. "He's my dipshit nephew. What's he done now?"

"Nothing. At least not that I know of. Look, Lily was at his party last night. And that's the last time any of her friends saw her. Do you know where he lives?"

"I'll text you the address."

"What's he into, Daisy?"

She sighed. "Nothing good. Keep me posted."

She ended the call. The text came through. He lived in Germantown, which wasn't too far. A sickening dread trampled my body as I thought about all the dark corners and alleys where something bad could happen to a young girl in Germantown. Though the baseball stadium had been built, as well as plenty of midrise apartments and overpriced restaurants, there were entire chunks that were still industrial. People roamed and wandered. A person could take a wrong turn, make a bad decision, and disappear.

At my car, I punched the address into my phone and stomped the gas pedal. I didn't know if I was on a wild-goose chase, but I had to do something.

I had to find Lily.

21

I ran so fast out of my house that I tripped down the front steps.

I sprinted around back, hoping I could catch a glimpse of the per-petrator through the windows, but before I could get there, I ran face first into Ryan.

I screamed, and he shot his hands up in surrender. "Whoa, it's just me. What's going on?"

I looked at him, confused, not understanding where he could have come from. Why was he in my side yard?

"There's someone in my house!" I hissed. "Upstairs."

"What? Are you sure?" A flash of concern morphed his handsome features. "Stay here." He bolted around the side as I chased after him.

"Ryan, do *not* go in there. Seriously."

But he pushed his way inside anyway to inspect. I stood there, fully expecting him to be slaughtered in the next five minutes. I'd seen those movies. I knew how they ended.

Ten minutes later, he reemerged, shaking his head. "No one's in the house, Ruby. I literally checked everywhere."

"He could have escaped while you were upstairs," I said. I looked at him, my heart pounding. "Why are you here?"

"I . . ." He glanced behind him. "I need to talk to you."

"Come in."

I yanked him inside and closed and locked the door. There was no way I could stay here tonight, not without somehow reporting Cassie's murder first. How was Greg going to figure that one out? I paced in my front foyer, clearly on edge.

"I really don't think anyone was here, Ruby. What did you hear?"

"It sounded like a footstep." I pointed upstairs. "I *know* it was a footstep."

"Okay, okay, just calm down. Breathe." He stepped toward me and rested his hands lightly on my shoulders. I stepped into a hug, and his arms tightened their grip. It reminded me of when I'd fallen apart after Lily had disappeared and how he'd been there for me every step of the way.

"I'm sorry about earlier. I'm just in a bad place."

"I know." He stroked my hair absentmindedly, and I closed my eyes, being lulled by his familiar scent. It had been so long since I'd been in his arms, so long since anyone had comforted me. I opened my eyes and stared down at his shoes. Drops of red paint clung to the top.

Or is that blood?

Every fiber in my body seized. My arms stiffened, and he felt it.

"Hey, you okay?" He pulled back. His eyes were friendly and warm, full of genuine concern.

"What did you need to tell me?" I took a shaky step back.

His eyes changed as he exhaled a breath and moved to the living room. "I don't know where to start."

I motioned for him to sit. He sank into an armchair, and I sat on the couch across from him.

"I've been doing some digging myself," he said. "About Tom."

I looked at him, confused. "What about Tom?"

"I just never trusted him. And after I knew how he treated you, I don't know . . . none of it sat right with me."

My phone dinged. I fished my phone from my pocket with trembling hands. It was from Daisy. Cassie's text sat right below it. I vacillated between telling Ryan or just letting him continue to talk.

"Ryan, first I need to tell you something."

He waited for me to continue.

"A little while ago, I got a text from Cassie to come over." I filled him in about our conversation this morning and her news about the affair. "When I got there, she wasn't answering. I went upstairs, and I found her in bed . . . with her throat slit."

He shot out of his chair in an instant. "Jesus, Ruby! Did you call the police?"

"I can't call the police. They'll think I did it."

"Wait, what?" He paced back and forth, ripping a hand through his hair. "Does that mean we have a serial killer?"

"I have no idea," I said. "The two might not be connected."

His fingers reached into his pocket, and he hurriedly dialed 911. Before I could protest, he held up a hand. "I'll leave you out of it." He talked in fragments into the phone, requesting a patrol car to check on a neighbor who wasn't answering her door.

Smart.

When he hung up, only one thought shot through my head. "I need to get her phone."

He blinked. "What?"

"Her phone. The last text someone sent was for me, luring me there. If the police find that, they'll think I killed her."

"Did you respond to the text?"

Did I? "No."

"Then you have nothing to worry about."

I didn't necessarily believe that. I collapsed back against the couch, utterly wiped out. "I just don't understand what's happening."

"Ruby." Ryan lowered himself to his knees in front of me so that he was eye level with me. He was mere inches from my body. My legs

130

parted instinctively to make room for him, and even in the midst of a murder, my body reacted to him like a teenager flooded with hormones.

His hands found the tops of my thighs, and I inhaled. *What is he doing?*

"Come home with me," he said. "I don't think it's safe for you to stay here."

My brain jumbled as I tried to make sense of his words. For a year, I'd wanted nothing more than to go home with him, and now, what was stopping me? My marriage was over. Everything was going to shit. I wanted to feel something, *anything,* other than this fear that coursed through my body like a terminal illness.

I nodded, once, and shifted away in an attempt to clear my head. He dropped his hands but still crouched there, staring at me, until a hard set of knocks made us both jump.

"Ruby, it's Detective Ellis." Her voice was muffled, but the intention was clear. "Open up."

22

I pulled up in front of a squat brick home on a sketchy block in Germantown.

It was still one of those neighborhoods that sported either million-aires or people on welfare. There wasn't an in-between. I double-checked the address and noticed a small VW bug in the driveway. I assumed Leonard would be at school, but maybe his mother was home.

I knocked on the door, and while I waited, I clocked the random items in the yard: a fat muddy tire, rusty car parts, a battered chest of drawers. I searched the grass and spotted cigarette butts and a few empty bottles.

Finally, the door wrenched open, and a shirtless guy, maybe early twenties, squinted into the light. Tattoos made a patchwork quilt across his chest and abdomen. His black hair stood on end, and he had a wispy mustache that suggested he'd never be able to grow a beard.

"Yo, what you get?" His Mexican accent was thick, and my eyes fell to his elbows, searching for tracks. When I saw the bruised, collapsed skin, I faltered and glanced back up to study his face. Was he high?

By the agitated way he looked at me, I guessed not.

"Are you Leonard Dominguez?"

"Who asking?" He tipped his chin up, tough, probably used to fighting for everything in his life. I knew the feeling.

"Lily Winslow's mother."

"Who?" He yawned and leaned against the doorframe, punching the screen door back as it attempted to slam shut.

I pulled up a recent photo of Lily, from an early college visit to MIT.

He squinted at the photo. "I don't know, man. So many girls come through here, dawg."

"Well, *dawg*," I said, stepping closer. "If you've served alcohol or drugs to minors, you can go to jail. So either tell me what happened last night, or you can get your story straight with the police." I didn't know what I was saying, but the stakes were too high to wait around for a punk kid to tell me his version of the truth.

Fear flashed in his eyes momentarily, then vanished. "What are you, a cop?"

"Where is she?"

He shrugged his bony shoulders and scratched his stomach. "I don't know, man. She was fucked up last night, though. Shoo. She knows how to party, though, yo. For real." He smiled, and I was surprised to find his teeth blindingly white and straight.

Annoyance gripped me by the throat until I wanted to shake the truth out of him. If he'd touched Lily, if he'd hurt her in any way . . .

"But she left, like, before midnight."

This unexpected piece of information cleared my head. "How do you know it was before midnight?"

"'Cause I looked at the time, yo. It was so early and shit. She said she had to be up early or something."

Lily had to be up so early because she had to leave earlier to get to school. *Tom's fault.* I turned to look at the road. If she'd left before midnight, she would have been home before one at the latest. I needed to see if any car accidents had been reported, but I knew someone would have contacted us most likely.

"Did she have her phone with her?"

"Man, I don't know. I'm not her daddy, yo."

I wanted to scream but pulled out a piece of paper and scribbled down my number. "If you think of anything else, please text me, okay?"

He shrugged. I knew he'd probably lose the paper the moment I left.

"Your aunt says to say hello, by the way," I said, pausing on the way back to my car. "Daisy?"

His face changed, and he swallowed, instantly alert. "She did?" He shifted from foot to foot.

"Yeah."

He shook his head and retreated toward the house. "Yo, that bitch is crazy. You don't even know."

He slammed the door in my face, and I let my mind focus on the task at hand. Should I call hospitals? Look up accident reports? I shot a text to Tom and asked him if he could access what we needed. She left a party last night before midnight. She was wasted. I'm worried, Tom. This is serious.

The *delivered* message turned into a read receipt, but he didn't attempt to write back. "Perfect." I started my car but didn't know where to go next.

Part of me wondered if Lily could already be at home, if she'd just gone somewhere to sleep it off, realized she didn't have her phone, and gone back to retrieve it. Because we didn't have a landline, she'd have no way to contact me.

I called Daisy on the way back. "Hey, can you see if Lily's car is in the driveway?"

"Hold, please."

I heard her groan, and after a few minutes, she returned. "Negative, but your darling husband is home."

"What?" I didn't understand. He was just in court. He'd brushed me off. How was he already home?

"Did you find Leonard?"

"Oh yeah." I laughed in spite of the situation. "He's scared shitless of you."

"Damn straight. I took him to death row one time and told him that if he kept going down the same old road, he'd end up there too."

Jesus. "Did it work?"

"Clearly not." She was quiet for a moment. "I'm sure she'll turn up, Ruby. Don't worry."

I hung up and stepped harder on the gas. I didn't understand why people always said that. Of course I was going to worry. It was my child.

After letting my mind wander to some dark places, I pulled into the driveway and practically ran inside.

"Tom?"

I didn't hear him on the main floor, but as I climbed up the stairs to our primary, I could hear the shower running. Why was he taking a shower in the middle of the day?

"Tom?"

He startled as I entered the bathroom. "You scared me to death."

"What are you doing?"

"I believe they call it showering," he snapped, cranking off the water. He grabbed a fluffy towel and dried himself off. Tom was still fit and blindingly attractive, but when I looked at him, I felt only the residue of his anger, like a phantom bruise that would never fade.

"Why are you home?" I asked. "Showering of all things?"

"Case settled. Just felt like taking a shower." He ran the towel over his hair.

"Did you get my text?"

"Yep." He slipped into comfortable clothes and padded by me to head back downstairs.

"And aren't you going to *do* anything?" His nonchalance was an outrage.

"What am I supposed to do, Ruby? She's a teenager. She'll show up eventually."

I grabbed his elbow and dug my fingernails into his flesh, then immediately dropped my arm and took a shaky step back. "Tom. This is serious. You have no idea how serious."

He glanced at his elbow where I'd touched him. I never grabbed him. It was always the other way around. For a moment, I held my breath, afraid of what he would possibly unleash. Instead, he brushed past me, ripped back the fridge door, and opened a beer. "How's that?"

I grappled with what to say but knew it was time for the truth. "Your daughter is off her meds."

He looked at me blankly. "What meds?"

I tried to figure out how to tell him what I knew. "She's been on medication for a long time, Tom. Antipsychotics and mood stabilizers."

He clamped the neck of his bottle and laughed. "No, we decided she would not be medicated under any circumstance. If my daughter were on medication, I would know. You wouldn't be able to get a prescription."

I tapped my fingernails against the table. He was connecting the dots. I was a nurse. I had access to medication that he didn't. I didn't need a prescription.

"What's going on, Ruby?"

The warning in his voice was clear, but I knew it was time to finally tell him the truth. "Lily started showing signs of erratic behavior very early, as you know. I got her diagnosed. I took care of it, even when you decided to look the other way."

He took a step closer to the island, and I visibly flinched. I was safe on the other side, the shiny marble a dividing line between us. "Diagnosed with what?"

I shrugged. "It's changed over time. She has a mood disorder, mostly."

He scoffed. "You couldn't possibly get her medication without my permission."

I opened my mouth, then closed it. He was wrong about that. "It was under control . . . but I just found out she's been selling her meds instead of taking them. I think she might be in real trouble." I climbed onto a stool, finally letting it all spill out. "Remember when she got arrested? She was off her meds then, too, but you wanted to blame it on the other girls. She promised me she'd get back on them, and she did. But now . . ." I shrugged, my voice fading.

Tom was completely still, the beer hovering near his lips.

"Look, Lily is great when she's on her meds. We just have to get her back on track, especially before college." I didn't dare tell him that I'd stolen meds from the hospital and gotten caught. That I'd looked like a liar and a thief in front of my boss. That I'd had everything ripped away from me because I wanted to get my daughter help without a prescription. I had done it because Tom didn't believe in medicating her. He thought she would be fine on her own, so I'd had to go behind his back so that she didn't become completely unglued.

"And where the fuck was I during all of this?" he exploded. "Why are you just telling me this now?" He slammed his open palm against the marble, and I flinched. I hated that he had this effect on me, that I still didn't believe I was safe in my own house.

"Because you would have never gotten her the help she needed!" I screamed. "You would have brushed it off or said she'd grow out of it." There were so many things I could tell him, awful, terrible things I'd witnessed over the years. As the words erupted out of my mouth, severe and cutting, I watched them land like a blade. He looked as though I had physically slapped him. *Good.* I wanted him to know how much I'd had to take care of on my own, how much his daughter felt unseen and unloved by him and might be in a ditch somewhere because of it.

Tom set the bottle down on the island, and for a moment, I wondered if he was going to throw it against the wall or at me. I waited for the wrath to come, for him to take out all his frustration on me. Instead, he walked around the island, his jaw pulsing dangerously. "I'll take care of it," was all he said. Just like that, he scooped his keys into his hand and marched toward the door.

"What do you mean, you'll take care of it? Where are you even going?" I slipped off my stool and stood there, shocked.

He slammed the door behind him so hard the art shook on the walls. I didn't understand why *he* got to be so angry. This was his child, and he'd missed all the signs. And now it might be too late. I studied Lily's phone again, combing back through the texts to see if anyone had replied. Nothing.

I felt like I was going out of my mind, crawling out of my skin with worry. A thousand worst-case scenarios launched through my brain all at once until I felt faint.

I tried to call Tom, but he didn't answer. Not wanting to stay at home, I rushed out the door and ran to Ryan's house.

He opened the door, surprised. "Hey, neighbor."

I launched myself into his arms before I could stop myself. I screamed, cried, and wailed, all my fears pressing into his capable body. He held me tightly as my legs crumpled, and I slipped toward the floor.

"I'm right here," he murmured into my hair, never letting me go. "I've got you."

23

I scrambled to stand, my heart in my throat.

I rushed to the door and opened it. Detective Ellis stood with two cops behind her, and for one fleeting moment, I thought they were going to arrest me.

"May we come in?"

"Sure." I opened the door wider. Ryan sat on a chair, scrolling through his phone, looking like the poster child of calm.

Detective Ellis motioned to the couch, and I took a seat while the three of them stood. "We got a call about one of your neighbors, Cassie Flannigan?"

I nodded, feigning innocence. "Okay."

"When's the last time you spoke to Cassie?"

"I saw her this morning, when she admitted to having an affair with Tom." The words gushed into the room before I could stop them, and Ryan looked at me sharply. I knew that would insinuate a motive, but I wanted to be honest. "I got a text from her to come over a little while ago. But I didn't." The lie left my lips as easily as the truth. "I don't want to talk to her. I have nothing more to say."

The detective studied my face, then gave one of the officers a small nod. "Well, we went to check on Cassie just now." Her eyes roamed over my face. "She's dead."

"What?" I sat up straighter, attempting to force myself to act surprised. "What do you mean? How?"

"Homicide." She glanced back at one of the officers again and jerked her head. "She had this in her hand." The shorter officer walked over and held something up in a bag. I squinted to make out whatever was in there. When I realized what it was, I involuntarily gasped. It was a crumpled mug shot of my mother, from the case file Daisy had pulled, the case file I'd shredded.

"She had a key." I realized it just as these words left my lips. "From when she decorated our house."

Detective Ellis waited for me to continue.

"She must have dug it up somewhere."

"Regardless of how she got it, Ruby, what I want to know is why. Why was she clutching this?"

"I honestly have no idea."

Detective Ellis already knew part of my secret, that my mother had been arrested for my father's murder. But what did that have to do with Cassie? The thoughts tumbled in my head like clothes in a dryer. Why was someone after me?

"Ruby, I'm having a real hard time here. Can you see that? All of these disappearances and deaths seem to have just one person in common."

I steeled my gaze. "Then you're obviously not doing your job, because that's what the killer *wants* you to think. I don't have anything to do with any of this." I stood up and walked to the front door. "And unless you're here to arrest me, I think I'm done answering questions."

The detective paused on the way out. "We're definitely going to need to bring you in for further questioning."

I rolled my eyes. "Then you can call my lawyer."

When they were gone, I collapsed back against the door. Ryan was by my side in two seconds flat. "What was that? In the bag?"

"Something from my past." I brushed him off and shot Greg a frantic text. "Someone is trying to set me up, Ryan, and I have no idea why."

I cycled through all of it: Who could have been in my house? Who had I foolishly trusted that could be involved in all this? Just as I turned, my eyes snagged on Ryan. Ryan, who had approached me at the pool. Ryan, who'd pumped me for personal information. Ryan, one of the first people I met in Cottage Grove.

"Is it you?"

Ryan turned, genuine surprise flashing in his eyes. "Is what me?"

"This? All of this? Are you trying to set me up?" I took a few steps back toward the kitchen, wondering if Ryan was one of those murderers who had to screw his victims before chopping them into tiny pieces. What in God's name had I been *thinking* inviting him in? I scanned my surroundings for a weapon. If I could get to the kitchen, then at least I could grab a knife.

"Ruby, what are you talking about? Of course not. I'm here for you. I've always been here for you."

Did I really know that? "I need you to go," I whispered.

He simply stared at me with a tortured look, and I waited for the inevitable attack. Why in God's name had I never learned self-defense?

Instead, Ryan sighed and let himself out the front door. My shoulders sagged as I thought about what I'd just accused him of. I still didn't want to stay in this house alone. I wasn't sure it was safe, even if the detective thought the only dangerous person was me.

I locked all the doors, took a shaky breath, poured myself a glass of wine, and decided to take a bath. I filled the bath to the top with bubbles and Epsom salts. My mind was racing, and I just needed to calm it back down. I wasn't sure what was true and what wasn't, but I knew if I was going to problem-solve, I had to be in a calmer headspace first.

Just as I started to relax, I heard footsteps again and shot up in the bath. I grabbed my robe, once again scrambling for a weapon. I snagged one of the heavy lamps in our bedroom and wrapped the cord tightly around my hand.

I moved toward the sound down the hall, tired of being intimidated, tired of feeling like I was on a wild-goose chase, tired of feeling like a damn suspect. I stopped right outside Lily's room.

I waited, and as if on cue, I heard movement again. Taking a deep breath, I kicked open the door and nearly fell to my knees.

There, sitting on the bed, was my missing teenage daughter.

24

I startled awake and checked the time on my kitty alarm clock.

Its white eyes stared back at me in the dark as I strained to see the numbers. Midnight. I'd learned time superfast because my parents left a lot, and I needed to know when to eat, take a bath, and go to sleep. I was only ten, but I was learning when I had to take care of myself.

When it was time to hide.

The voices of my mother and father rumbled down the hallway. Though my room was on the opposite end of the house, when I stuck my ear to the vent in the floor, I could hear every single word. Sometimes, when the air was on, the stale, cool breeze tickled my ear and made their words muffled.

I rushed from my daybed and stuck my ear to the grate. My father's words were slurred, mean. *Whore. Bitch. Tramp.* His awful words punctuated the weighty silences in between. My mother's voice was steady and strong in response. *Drunk. Loser. Deadbeat.*

Everything went silent for a moment. I pulled back, then repositioned myself closer to the vent, the cold grate pressed against the soft flesh of my cheek.

What sounded like a clap thundered through the vent; then something heavy hit the floor. *A body.* I crawled away from the vent, grabbed my favorite Care Bear, and dashed inside my walk-in closet, deep into the back, behind the long coats and snow pants, where he couldn't find me.

My mother had taught me what to do when I heard certain sounds. Though my father had never hurt me, he hurt my mother all the time, which was basically the same thing. I hurt when she hurt. Plus, I was the one to take care of her boo-boos when he disappeared for days at a time. I was getting old enough to understand that what he was doing was something called *abuse*, and I didn't understand why my mother didn't just leave. I would never let a man touch me that way. I would never get married at all, I'd decided. Men hurt women, and I didn't want to be hurt by anyone.

"Penny!" My father's voice ripped down the hallway, and I let out a tiny gasp and squeezed my eyes shut as I clutched my Care Bear to my chest. I was hidden behind a row of long coats that trailed to the ground, and I'd trained myself to be still as a statue so he couldn't see me.

My father's heavy footsteps thumped to a stop outside my door. He jiggled the knob, which was locked. I'd positioned a chair just under the knob to be extra safe. His fat fist pounded against the wood.

"Penny Elaine Richter! Let me in right this instant—do you hear me, young lady?" His words all clumped together, so it sounded like one never-ending word. It was so quiet for a moment I thought he'd gone away, but then I heard wood cracking. Shards scattered across my room, the chair went skittering, and I felt a swell of anger override the fear. He'd kicked my door in! My door was the only thing separating me from *them*.

I held my breath, something I did to stay still and small. I was up to forty-five seconds, though my heart felt like it might explode. I closed my eyes even tighter, but the fabric of my winter wool coat hanging in front of me tickled my nose. I prayed that I wouldn't sneeze and give away my hiding spot.

He kicked his way through my room, spraying Legos, dolls, and toys across the room like bullets. If he touched my dollhouse . . . again, the rage built. He was ruining my things. He was hurting them, just like he hurt Mama.

I didn't know where my mother was, if she was too injured to move. Even at ten, I realized if he kept doing this, he would kill her someday. Suddenly, my closet door creaked open, and I clamped a hand over my mouth to keep from screaming.

"Penny! I know you're in here!" He immediately lowered his voice to a whisper. "Just come talk to Daddy, baby. I just want to talk. I promise."

He never wanted to talk. He wanted to hit. He wanted to yell. He wanted to scream. He was a liar, and I hated him. I hated him so much it hurt.

"Daddy would never hurt you, sweetheart. You know that, don't you?"

It was true. He'd never laid a hand on me, but I didn't trust myself to be around him when he was having one of his drunken fits. He pulled a few clothes off the hangers, and then, as he stopped to listen, my mother moaned from down the hallway.

"Ronald! Please . . ."

My mother's voice was hoarse and weak. At that moment, I hated her too, hated her for calling to him when he was the one who had hurt her. But I also knew she was doing it to get him away from me. She always sacrificed herself, even when I told her I could handle it. Yes, I was a child, but I would take some of the punishment if it meant he didn't hurt my mom.

"Oh, Lenny, my love, what have I done?" My dad retreated and jogged back down the hallway, just as he always did. The remorse was consuming and swift, even bigger than his rage. He would spend the next day or two on his best behavior. He would baby her, love her, kiss her. He would make us all stew, build fires, and bring home fresh fish from the river. He would pretend to be a good father, not a fraud.

I still sat in the same spot, too afraid to move. I had to figure out how to convince my mother that it was time to leave. It wasn't safe here anymore. She had to choose: me or him. Stay or go.

As I curled up on a blanket I had stored for this very occasion and tried to rest, sleep wouldn't come. The floor was too hard. I didn't have my pillow. My room was ruined. I closed my eyes anyway and strained to hear, which was hard without the vent.

I wondered if Mama was okay or if he'd broken a bone like last time. *What an awful man,* I thought. *What an awful, terrible man.*

I knew he was my father, but I couldn't ever trust a person who could hurt someone I loved so much. I didn't understand how she could love him back, how she could even stand to be around him. She used to tell me stories of when they'd first met, of what a good man he was. *Honorable* was the word she used.

But all I saw was a coward. I knew what that word meant because I had heard her call him a coward, and then I'd looked it up in my dictionary. *Coward: a person who lacks the courage to endure dangerous or unpleasant things.* My father was a coward. Could he endure the same kind of pain?

I clenched my Care Bear tighter to my chest and shivered in the cold depths of the closet. Tomorrow. Tomorrow, I would make her choose. Me or him. Stay or go.

My eyes popped open as I imagined sitting her down, staring at her assortment of bumps and bandages. I would look directly into her eyes, and I would ask. I could picture it even now. Her big brown eyes going wide. The way she would look at the table, then back up to me. The excuses she would make. The words she would say.

Yes, I was her daughter, the supposed love of her life, but part of me knew if I made her choose between him and me, she would choose him every time.

25

My knees buckled as I fell against the door. *"Lily?"*

She exploded from the bed and burst into tears as she hugged me. I gripped her so tightly I feared she might break. But here she was, in my arms after all this time. I kissed every inch of her head and her cheeks and cupped her face in my hands as I pulled back to look in her eyes. Her color was good. She'd changed and grown. Her red hair had been chopped and dyed dark but was still wild.

"*Where* have you been?"

There was nothing Lily could say that would make sense. I knew that. You didn't just disappear and suddenly show up again months later with a logical excuse.

She sighed and wiped her eyes as she sat heavily on the bed. "Ugh, Mom. It's complicated."

I followed, not trusting my legs to keep me upright. I wanted to be close to her. I didn't want to ever let her out of my sight again. "I don't understand," I said. "You were *gone*. I thought you were . . ." I couldn't bring myself to say the word *dead*.

She shook her head and clenched her fists in her lap. "I know. I'm so sorry." A shuddered breath racked her body, and finally, she looked into my eyes. "Especially after everything you did for me after . . . you know."

She didn't have to finish the sentence. I did know, and I was just glad she was safe.

"Dad found me." Her voice was flat as she said it. "He checked me out of my facility."

The shock nearly bowled me over, but I reached for the bedpost to keep me upright. *I am here. This is happening. It isn't a dream.* I attempted to keep my voice calm. "Lily, I need you to tell me exactly what you mean."

After I'd confronted Tom about Lily and her meds, he'd disappeared for a few days, presumably to search for Lily and file a police report. That's when Lily had come home and told me everything. Where she'd been. What had happened. What she'd done. And then I'd decided to help her clean it all up, another secret to keep from Tom.

"I can't." Lily chewed on her bottom lip. "I promised Dad I wouldn't."

A white-hot rage consumed me so completely I nearly jumped off the bed. *Tom found her. He knew Lily was alive and getting treatment. He withheld her as a way to punish me.* "The police think he's dead, Lily."

"What?" Genuine shock tore across her face, and with those wide terrified eyes, I still recognized the child in her.

I placed my hand on her knee. "I know this is a lot right now, but I need you to tell me what happened."

She shot up and gathered her hair in a tiny knot before gnawing on her cuticles. "He checked me out. He was furious. I thought we would take some time to cool off and then come back. But we just kept moving."

"Moving where? Where have you been all this time?"

"Mom, look." She stopped in the center of her room. "I told Dad. About Andrew. About what I did."

I pulled back slightly. *Why would she do that?* My mind worked over-time, trying to put the pieces together. "Just start from the beginning."

Right then, my phone buzzed. I glanced at it. It was from Greg. They rushed DNA results. Meet me at the station.

No. I couldn't leave Lily here, not with a potential murderer on the loose. "Lily, I want nothing more than to hear what you have to say, but I have to go to the police station first."

She wrinkled her nose. "What? Why?"

"It's complicated." I used her own words. I couldn't bring her with me, couldn't risk Detective Ellis seeing her and opening a brand-new can of worms. Not until I knew all the facts first. I texted Daisy an urgent message, and she immediately replied.

WTAF (WHAT THE ACTUAL FUCK?????) YES, BRING HER HERE!

I typed back a hasty thanks. "I'm going to drop you at Daisy's."

Lily smiled. "I missed that weirdo."

"Hey, be nice. She's not a weirdo." It was insane how instantly I reverted back to Mom mode, as if there had been no gap in between. No endless, lonely nights. No crushing guilt or paralyzing worry. All that wiped clean with her sitting next to me on the bed. "I need you to stay with her while I'm gone."

She looked around. "Why can't I just stay here?"

I had so many questions. If Tom had released her from the facility, where had they gone? Had she been off her meds this whole time? Wouldn't they have called me to confirm? Then, I realized: she was now eighteen. Perhaps she could have simply signed herself out. I shoved all the questions away and thought of how to answer in a way that wouldn't worry her more than necessary. "Just trust me, okay? And then you can tell me everything when I get back."

I stood and pulled her into a hug again, too shocked for tears to fall. "I can't believe you're home. I thought I'd lost you. I love you so much."

"I love you too. I'm so sorry, Mom." She squeezed me tightly, her head stopping almost evenly with my chin. "I missed you."

"I missed you more."

I grabbed my wallet and keys and dropped Lily off with Daisy, who knew better than to ask questions. "So you're not dead! That's great," she said as a way of greeting, opening the door wide. "You still need a job?"

I rolled my eyes as Lily gave her a high five and stepped inside. "Thanks for this." When Lily was out of earshot, I leaned in. "DNA results are in."

"How's that possible? It's only been a few days."

I shrugged. "No clue."

She looked up as if thinking deeply about something. "They must have done fast forensic testing. It's rare, but it happens."

"Whatever they did, it's the moment of truth." I let out a giant breath and stared into the living room, where Lily collapsed on the couch and crossed her arms. "I'm either going to come back and tell Lily that her father is dead or that he abandoned us both."

"Well, either way, he's a dick," Daisy said. "DNA won't change that."

She has no idea. I squeezed her shoulder. "I'll be back soon."

For what felt like the millionth time, I got in my car and headed to the police station. I knew I should be solely focused on results, with who had killed Cassie and what Ryan's intentions really were. Instead, all I could think about was the fact that my daughter was back.

She was alive.

She was finally home.

26

When I returned back to the house from my morning row, Tom's car was gone.

He usually had a pickup basketball game on Saturdays followed by drinks with his friends, but he hadn't attended since Lily went missing. It was the first time he'd been social in months. He spent every spare second trying to locate Lily. So far, nothing had worked. She'd officially been gone for ninety days and counting. He kept a calendar in his office and morbidly checked off each day she didn't return.

I made myself a pot of coffee, showered, and walked to Tom's office. A light shone from under his door. He knew one of my pet peeves was leaving lights on, an aftereffect of growing up poor. The door was locked. Tom was always private about his cases, for legal reasons, obviously, but he never locked the door.

I vacillated between letting it drop and picking the lock, a skill I'd learned as a kid in foster care. Taking a breath, I grabbed a bobby pin from my hair, maneuvered it into the groove, and popped the lock. The space was open and airy, full of light modern furniture instead of the typical dark wood of most masculine spaces. Cassie's influences were everywhere.

I ran my fingers over his desk and turned in a circle. Nothing looked out of place. Maybe he'd locked it accidentally? On my way out, I stopped. The edge of his safe was visible from the end of his desk, and I could see the door was slightly ajar. My heart skipped a beat. Tom wouldn't leave his safe open.

I knew Tom had a safe, of course, but I'd never seen what was inside. Part of me wondered if he could have as many dark secrets as I did; I'd destroyed Daisy's file, but I'd kept other things from my past: little keepsakes from my mother and the truth shared between us. What was in Tom's past?

I strained to hear if Tom had suddenly come home, but I knew he'd be away for most of the afternoon. Creeping quietly, I crouched down and pulled the door open, staring inside. It contained only a few files and several stacks of cash. Hurriedly, I flipped through the files, but they all pertained to work.

I stood and assessed the layout of his office, wondering where I would stash something I didn't want found. Why not the safe? I didn't have the code . . . maybe it wasn't me he wanted to hide things from? I turned in a circle and then carefully checked every nook and cranny, sliding my hands behind art, his bookshelves, and even under his desk. Nothing. About to give up, I stopped at his office closet, where he kept his printer and larger filing cabinet, which was always locked too. I opened the closet door and scanned the inside. My eyes snagged on the floorboards near the back. I remembered so many nights hiding in the back of a closet just like this. Dropping to my hands and knees, I smoothed my hands over the wide planks of wood, stopping at the edge of a corner piece that was bowed up, almost like a tiny handle.

After checking to make sure I was still alone, I ran my finger along the edge and then wedged it under the lifted corner and tugged. It popped free easily in my hand. I hesitated, part of me wanting to know what was down there and the other part wanting to ignore it.

I stuffed my hand into the tiny space and felt the sharp edge of a folder. Sliding onto my belly, I reached in farther, feeling for something more, but it was just a single file. Carefully, I pulled it out, knocking a bit of dust from the top. The manila was stuffed thick with papers and photographs. I flipped through, in shock at what I was seeing, before snapping photos of everything and then placing the file just as I'd found it beneath the floorboard. I tiptoed quietly from the room and relocked the door, getting as far away from his office as possible. Halfway down the stairs, I paused. What if he'd installed a camera? I repicked the lock and examined every inch of the room but saw nothing suspicious.

I missed Lily at that moment, so much that it stopped me in my tracks. Of course, true to his word, Tom had filed a police report and attempted to "take care of it" once I'd confronted him, but after a few months of searching for her, the cops had transitioned Lily's case to a cold one. Despite all his money and combined resources—which had resulted in search parties, an investigation, and even hiring a PI when the cops failed to produce any results—she was nowhere, a ghost.

And that *not* knowing—if Lily was alive, if she was okay—was enough to undo him. The world continued with its same robotic pace, but his child could still be out there, and no matter how hard he looked, he couldn't seem to find her. At least now he was distracting himself by getting back to some semblance of normal life.

My phone dinged with a reminder: I had the Murderlings tonight. I didn't feel like being social, but I didn't want to be with Tom tonight either. I shot him a quick text, and he replied that he was going to get dinner with the guys.

For just a moment, I remembered the way things used to be when we'd first met. He'd been my patient after a minor fender bender where he'd whacked his nose hard when the airbag deployed. I was overworked, chronically single, and completely oblivious to romantic advances.

I had my bungalow in East Nashville; my cat, Mr. Gatti; and my job. Because I'd never been able to rely on family, I avoided getting too entangled with men. I dated, I slept with people, and then I moved on.

When he hit on me, I was oblivious, too busy making the rounds with my patients. But when he checked out, he left a note:

You took such good care of me. Please let me return the
favor. Meet me at Lockeland Table tonight at 8?

No phone number so that I could politely decline. Plus, the restaurant was literally down the street from where I lived. I sighed, pocketed the note, and completed my shift.

By six that night, I was hungry, but I didn't eat. Instead, I took another shower, put on something nice, and, at 7:45, walked down the street to the restaurant. It was a warm summer night, thick with humidity, and I knew my hair was going to frizz. The cicadas, crickets, and frogs drowned my nerves. I'd already had a couple of glasses of wine to take the edge off, but I was still jittery. Over the years, I'd seen endless shrinks, and they'd always said the same thing: at my core, I simply didn't trust men.

I didn't need to pay $125/hour for that bit of knowledge. For some reason, I decided tonight, I would act like a normal woman; not someone riddled with a secret so horrendous no one would love me if they knew.

I was the first to arrive, but he'd made a reservation under his name. I was led to a table in the corner, with a clear view of Woodland Street. This part of town was becoming more desirable, and yet it still had its trouble spots, which I didn't mind. I didn't trust places without crime, because anyone, when put to the test, could do the wrong thing.

Tom showed up a few minutes before eight and smiled as he took his seat across from me. He was handsome, even with his swollen nose. His eyes were fiercely green. Even in the dim light, I could see the

154

outline of a body kept in shape with weight training or running. He was well groomed and well spoken.

The entire night, he was attentive. He listened as I talked, though I kept the conversation turned mostly on him. There weren't any fireworks, really, but I didn't trust fireworks. At that stage in my life, if I wasn't alone, I wanted something solid. Tom seemed solid. And after that night, he pursued me with a fervor no one ever had.

I bought into it hook, line, and sinker, not realizing I'd chosen someone who was terrible for me. I'd vowed to never be with a man like my father, and yet, somehow, that was who I'd found. Tom was stable and safe; he had a good side. He was a saint before we were married, but after, there were tiny explosions that morphed into something darker. But every time he hurt me, I didn't remember. It was a game I played with myself, wondering what was real and what wasn't.

And now, I'd found his ultimate secret, his own sordid past he'd never wanted revealed. Finally, I had something to hold over his head, an easier way out. I responded to his text, telling him to enjoy his night. A huge weight sloughed from my shoulders as I decided to enjoy the rest of the evening too, despite what I'd found in his safe. Not wanting to stay at home even one second longer than I had to, I left a little early for Daisy's. She and I had gotten closer since Lily had vanished, all that tension dissolving between us as if it had never existed. Daisy opened the door wide and ushered me in. "Wine time?"

"You know me so well," I said.

During the months since Lily's disappearance, Daisy had attempted to help, even doing a few podcasts to try and gain some traction. She'd suffered from Lily's absence on a professional level, and though she didn't say it, I think she'd grown quite fond of her. No one could make sense of what had happened or where she could have gone, and it ate at Daisy, as she was so good at solving puzzles. It was literally like Lily had been plucked from thin air, and she talked about it constantly.

"Where's the old ball and chain?" Daisy asked, filling my goblet up to the brim with a cabernet.

I took a small sip. "With his buddies."

Daisy filled up her own glass and took a healthy sip. "I didn't know assholes had friends."

Despite the fact that she was talking about my husband, I laughed. Her feelings about Tom had never changed, and it was one of the things I liked about her. "Oh yes. Lawyer friends."

"Gross." She set out some snacks on a tray, and I helped her carry them to the table. My secret hovered on my lips. I'd thought about telling Daisy so many times, because if anyone understood, I felt it could be her, but despite it all, I still didn't know if I could really trust her with something so big. Instead, I focused on what I'd found in Tom's safe.

"Speaking of lawyers," I said, "do you know any divorce attorneys?"

Her eyes sparkled as she wiped her hands on her apron, her full cleavage bouncing in her tight dress. "Please tell me this means what I think it means."

I cocked a shoulder, dropped it. "It does." I tried on the sentence. How did that feel? My whole life, I'd tried to avoid abandonment. If I divorced Tom, that would mean I would be left with nothing and no one. But that would also mean he could never hurt me.

"I've got you covered. She's Latinx, she's queer, she's a shark. She'll eat Tom alive."

I moved back to the island, slid on a barstool, and tapped my nails on the granite. "Good."

The doorbell rang, breaking my train of thought. As neighbors spilled in, all of them telling me hello, I tried to push Tom from my mind. I was sure he'd show up late, probably drunk, and maybe we'd have a fight about where he'd been. Or maybe not. But now that I knew what he'd done, for once, I had the upper hand.

I was the one with power.

I sat at the end of the table and tried to concentrate on the "murder" at hand. Ryan wasn't here tonight; he was in New York, showing his latest collection at a gallery. Suddenly, I envied his life, his budding career, the simplicity of having his art, his home, and his friends.

He had nothing at stake, nothing to lose, really. Nothing that was life or death.

I downed my wine until the edges of the room softened and then filled my cup again. I didn't want to think tonight—or worry.

I just wanted to numb myself to the possibility of anything else bad happening.

I wasn't sure I could survive it.

27

My mind was spinning as I waited with Greg in the same stuffy room.

I was dying to tell him that Lily was back. I hadn't even fully comprehended what this meant. My phone buzzed, and I glanced at it, nervous that it might be Daisy telling me Lily had escaped again, that she was gone, or that I'd imagined her return. It wasn't. It was Ryan.

Really worried about you, Ruby. Please call me when you can.

I pocketed the phone. I fidgeted in my seat as Greg thumbed through texts.

Finally, Detective Ellis sauntered in and slapped a folder on the table. "Thanks for coming in. As you know, results are in."

I waited for her to bake up some more lies, to concoct a story about who this stranger in the water really was. She could apologize; then we could all go back to our lives. They could find out who killed Cassie. I could get back to Lily. Life could finally move on.

She flipped open the folder and stabbed a line on the piece of paper. "Results are conclusive that the John Doe is, in fact, Tom Anthony Winslow."

I sucked in so fast I choked and began to cough. Greg clapped me on the back, which made it worse. My eyes watered, and I cleared my throat. "That's not possible," I croaked. "It can't be him." My heart thumped madly beneath my sweater as my eyes blurred.

"And yet here we are." She spread her arms and let them drop, her expensive watch clipping the edge of the table. The clang reverberated through the room as I attempted to process what she'd just said. She adjusted her watch and finally leaned forward. "I'm not sure whatever game you're playing here, Ruby, but it's enough now."

Her voice was quiet, but the intent was clear. I leveled her with a stare. "It's not a game. I don't recognize him. It doesn't *look* like Tom. Why would I make that up?"

"Because maybe you don't want anyone to dig into how he got there?"

A sticky silence filled the room, pungent with insinuation.

I crossed my hands on the table to match hers and opened my mouth to speak, just as Greg butted in. "Do you have a murder weapon? Evidence linking my client to the crime?" He blinked at her, knowing she didn't. Greg yanked the file toward him and read the fine print.

"I must say, for a woman who just found out her husband has been murdered, you don't seem that torn up about it."

She obviously did not know me well. How I could turn off tragedy, how I could disassociate from things I didn't want to remember. It had been part of my job, but it had also been part of my childhood. Normal people might be crying or hysterical. But I wasn't normal. "I'm in shock."

"And you are also officially under investigation for the murder of your husband, Ruby. This is serious."

"I thought I was already under investigation." I opened my arms, my coat rustling in the silence. "I have nothing to hide. Search away."

She smiled this time, revealing a crooked incisor. "Oh, we will. Trust me."

I listened as Greg took over, spewing out a bunch of legal jargon I couldn't make sense of. They bantered back and forth until I interrupted and said I needed to go to the bathroom.

I didn't need to go to the bathroom, but I would use any excuse to leave this room, leave this police station, and hopefully never come back. I stood on wobbly legs, overcome from Lily's sudden reappearance and this shocking news of Tom's death. She'd just returned, and I had to deliver the news her father was dead. My thoughts spun and jumbled in my head. The room tilted, and I realized I was holding my breath. Greg shot out an arm as I capsized to the left.

"Are you okay?"

What a ridiculous question. I searched for words and finally nodded. "I'll be right back."

When I closed the door, their voices faded. I pressed a hand to my chest and closed my eyes. *Tom is dead. Tom is dead. Tom is dead.*

The neighbors had been right. *Everyone* had been right. Which meant they knew something I didn't—that they recognized something I couldn't, or wouldn't, see. I kept my hand in contact with the painted brick as I walked toward a bench. Lily was home. Tom was dead.

I dropped my head in my hands, thoughts still spinning. What would happen now that this was an actual murder investigation? Just as Greg had said, my life would be flipped upside down. My marriage. My home. My past. Everything cracked wide open for the world to see.

My head shot up so fast my neck popped. *No.* They could not dig into my past. If they found out the truth . . .

Then there would be nothing to prove I *wasn't* guilty. I closed my eyes, trying to remember right before Tom had left. The fight we'd had came whipping back so fast it sent an electric jolt through my whole body. *How did I forget about that fight?*

I slumped against the wall, buying time. After a few minutes, Greg opened the door and stuck his head out, surprised to see me leaning against the wall. "Ruby. We need you."

The hefty groan of the door and Greg's clipped tone made me cringe. This was all beginning, and I couldn't stop it.

I was part of an investigation now, a *murder investigation*.

Tom was dead. Cassie was dead.

And everyone thought I had killed him. Did everyone think I had killed her too? I prepared myself as I walked back into the office and sank into my seat. They could investigate me all they wanted, but I would never tell them about the last time I'd seen Tom alive.

If I did, I would hand them over a motive on a silver platter.

28

Tom stumbled in the door at six on the dot.

I sliced the pot roast I had been cooking all day. We hadn't had dinner together in what felt like months. Ever since Lily had disappeared, every facade I'd built had come crumbling down. I wasn't a successful nurse; I'd been fired. I wasn't in a healthy relationship; I was in an abusive one. I wasn't a mother; my child was gone. I wasn't a good wife; secretly, I detested my husband.

I'd messaged Tom that we needed to talk. Earlier, I'd sent him divorce papers, in an effort to issue a clear message. Talking hadn't worked. *Not* talking hadn't worked. This was my final ultimatum. *I wanted out and there was nothing he could do to stop me.*

He pushed through the door and slammed it shut. "Ruby!" His voice was erratic, thunderous. He found me in the kitchen, in a bloodred apron, with a glass of wine in hand. The picture-perfect wife before she became the ex-wife.

"What is this?" He waved the packet of papers in his hand and slapped them on the island. "You want a divorce?"

I sipped my wine and took my time to respond. "Yes, Tom. I want a divorce."

He glanced around, as if a hidden camera crew were going to jump out and tell him this was all a joke. "You can't divorce me."

I walked over to the credenza and produced my own file to slap on the table. "Yes, I can."

Tom's dirty secret lay between us. He'd been married before me to a woman named Trish. When we'd met, he'd told me he was a widow, that she had died tragically of cancer. It was one of the reasons I had been drawn to him, because I had felt sorry for him.

But it had all been a lie.

Trish Brinkley wasn't dead; she was an addict. He hadn't helped her get treatment. Instead, he'd paid her off to keep quiet, annulling their marriage and sending her somewhere to live off the grid. *Did he hurt her too?*

"What's that?" He stared with disinterest at the file.

"One of my reasons," I said. "Let me walk you through it. Wine?" Before he could answer, I poured him a massive glass.

He slid the folder over and flipped through it. When he saw what it was, he sighed and closed the file. "Ruby, this isn't what it looks like."

I laughed. "Oh? You mean that you didn't lie about your first wife being dead? That you didn't throw her away like garbage? The only thing I can't figure out is why you'd leave a paper trail. I thought you were smarter than that."

He slid the wine closer and took a massive gulp. A dark-red line dribbled down his chin. He roughly wiped it away. "You're one to talk."

"Meaning?" I lifted my chin.

"Meaning nothing." His eyes softened, and there was real pain there. "I didn't toss Trish aside. I did what I had to do." He stabbed the file with his finger. "I made a sacrifice in order to move on, to do what was best for—"

I moved around to the other side of the island. "What was best for you, right? All you care about is yourself. You ignored your daughter, who has a mental illness. You threw away your ex-wife, who had a drug problem. You ignore what's not convenient or what you can't buy off. But you can't buy my silence, Tom. Not even with divorce."

He reared back, as if I'd slapped him. "What's that supposed to mean?"

"It means I'm done keeping your dirty little secret about who you really are . . . what you're capable of." These were the same words I'd always wanted to tell my father, right to his face. Now, here was another man who'd abused his power in a different way. A man who'd abused *me*. My father's words from all that time ago came roaring back. *Don't ever let a man hurt you*, he'd once said. I couldn't even keep that promise.

"I'm done being hurt by you." What I couldn't say, but what we both knew, was that all this time, I had stayed for Lily. She'd been the ultimate Band-Aid for our marriage. Now that she was gone, I could see clearly.

That muscle in his jaw twitched. "This is about Ryan, isn't it?"

"What?" I shook my head. "This has nothing to do with Ryan."

He smoothed down his emerald tie. "He'll grow bored with you in two seconds. Guys like him always do."

"I just said this isn't about Ryan. It's about you."

The sad cracks in our marriage hung between us, this big beautiful facade of a life in this shiny house crumbling at our feet like dust. Everything we'd worked so hard for was imploding. I had no daughter, no job, and this big old house. What had I let my life become?

"You don't even know how to be alone anymore."

I laughed and tossed back the rest of my wine. "You have no idea how alone I've been in my life, Tom. Or in this marriage."

"Yes, I do." He motioned to the file. "You think that's it? Those are all my secrets? Well, I know your big secret, Ruby. I've known for a very long time."

My heart stuttered in my chest. *Is he bluffing?* I sorted through all the ways he could find out the truth, but he couldn't. Still, I played dumb. "Why don't you enlighten me?"

"I don't have to enlighten you. You know what you did. And I love you anyway."

I stepped within inches of him, chest heaving. "Love? You don't love me. You *hurt* me."

"I do love you. I have always loved you."

"I guess I have the scars to prove it, huh?"

A storm passed across his face but just as quickly vanished. He swirled his wine, as if we were having a casual conversation. "Well, I know you got fired—that you didn't quit."

Relief coursed through my veins like blood. "Because I was protecting your daughter."

To my surprise, he smirked. "You know, I could have you arrested for medicating her without my permission." His eyes danced across my face as he taunted me. "In fact, that sounds like a great idea. Let's see what the cops have to say." He fished in his pocket for his phone. How many times had I threatened to call the cops on him? To turn him in for the piece of shit he truly was? To finally be done?

Before I could think about it, I reared back and struck Tom as hard as I could. His phone skittered across the island and landed on the floor. I'd never hit anyone, especially not after watching my father beat my mother all those years, but suddenly, my rage cracked wide open. I hit him once and then again and again, until, instead of fighting back like I'd assumed he would, he cowered under my spray of slaps and punches, something in me coming completely undone. I thrashed and latched on to his shoulder, biting him as hard as I could.

"What the fuck!" He pushed me back, hard, and I stumbled into the dining room table, catching the edge of my back against a sharp edge. He looked at me, bleeding and wide eyed, then dabbed at his nose with the palm of his hand. "You broke my nose."

"Get out of this house, and never come back," I said.

He stared at me, panting and bleeding. "This is my house," he said simply.

The fury still coursed through me, wild and unexplored. I was horrified and, at the same time, curious. It had felt powerful to strike him, all my own pent-up anger unspooling and growing, like a beast. I felt unstoppable. "If you ever step foot in this house again, I will turn you in to the police. I have taken photos and written detailed accounts of every single moment of your abuse." His eyes shot up to mine. "It's all documented. And I bet if I find Trish," I added, "she'd have a few things to say to back me up too, yes?"

Before he could respond, the doorbell rang. We both turned, caught. I had my husband's skin under my fingernails. He was bleeding. This didn't look good.

The doorbell rang again, followed by a round of insistent knocks.

"Don't answer that, Ruby," he said, even as I rushed past him, hurrying to air our dirty laundry, to expose who we really were to whoever stood on the other side of that door. I yanked it open. On the other side stood Ryan. I balked in surprise.

"It's not really a good time."

He eyed me worriedly, then glanced past me and saw Tom dabbing at his wounds. He stiffened. "Did he hurt you?"

"No." I was already coming down from my adrenaline surge, already regretting how I'd behaved. All that time trying to outrun my past and my genes, and in a fit of rage, I'd done the same thing my father had done to my mother. The same thing Tom had done to me.

Who is the monster now?

"What do you need, Ryan?"

He sighed and stuffed his hands into the pockets of his painter's overalls. "I've just been worried about you. You haven't returned any of my calls."

It was true. I'd stopped innocently flirting, painting, or hanging out since Lily had disappeared. Part of me felt guilty for paying so much attention to Ryan and not enough to Lily. Maybe if I had, she'd be here now.

"I'm trying to get my life together," I said, in a way of explanation.

He glanced behind me again and lowered his voice. "What happened?"

"Nothing," I said. "Listen." I stepped onto the porch, shutting Tom on the other side of the door. "Please don't tell anyone about this. Tom and I . . . I'm filing for divorce, and he's not taking it well." I stopped talking, steeling myself for what awaited me inside. "I just need some time, okay?"

He placed a hand on my lower back, and my body tingled beneath his touch. "I'm here for you, Ruby, okay? Whatever you need."

"Thanks." I leaned into his hand and curled into a hug. I let his strong fingers run up and down my spine. Here was a man who'd been here for me since the beginning, never crossing a line, even when I'd wanted him to. Finally, I pulled back. "I'll call you, okay?"

I waved goodbye, and when he was safely on his way, I stepped back inside.

"Perfect timing. Did you and your boyfriend plan that?" Tom pressed a wet paper towel to his nose.

"You have no idea what you're talking about."

"Sure I do," he said, following behind me as I hurriedly climbed the stairs, goading me. "He just wants to fuck you, Ruby. You know that, right? And like I said, the moment he does, he'll lose interest."

At the top of the landing, I whirled around so fast he nearly fell backward. "That might be you, Tom, but it's not him. I'm going to take a bath."

"No, we're not done talking." He grabbed my elbow, wrenching his fingers deep into my flesh and twisting, like an Indian burn.

"You're hurting me. Let go." My voice was calm, but that same feeling was building, the feelings that I'd kept buried my whole life.

"Or what?" His face was battered, but his eyes were cruel. In them, I saw my father; all his taunting, his ridicule, his meanness. The way he'd bullied, and cajoled, and played with my mother's emotions, batting at them like a cat toy. He'd robbed me of having a mother and a father, all because he couldn't control his drinking or his temper. As a result, I'd had to raise myself.

Time seemed to freeze as I contemplated my next move. I could strike out, I could scream, I could hurt him even more. But I didn't want to hurt anyone because it only ended up hurting myself. Instead, I twisted my arm down and yanked with such force it sent Tom reeling backward.

I watched it all in slow motion: the twirling arms, the clawing grasp for air, the desperation for some sort of solid purchase. I could have stepped forward, offered him a hand, but I didn't. Instead, I stood silently as my husband tumbled backward down the stairs, without much thought or feeling.

It was only when he landed with a sickening crunch that I turned, continued to the bathroom, and filled the tub for a bath.

29

I pulled into my driveway, bumping too hard over the edge of the curb in my haste to park.

I rushed over to Daisy's house and panicked when I didn't see Lily on the couch. Daisy told me she was upstairs in the guest room, asleep. I resisted the urge to check on her, to gather her in my arms. I didn't know what her life had been like this past year, what she'd been through. I wanted her to tell me everything, but I realized that would be on her terms, not mine.

Daisy jerked her head for me to follow her onto the back patio. When we were outside, she crossed her arms. "So?"

I wanted to ask how Lily was, if she'd been talking, if she seemed okay. But I knew that wasn't what Daisy wanted to talk about. I sighed. "It's him. It's Tom."

She blew out a breath to match my own and shook her head. "Okay, well then. It's time to find the killer."

I glanced behind me to make sure Lily wasn't suddenly within earshot. "Listen, I was wondering . . . would the Murderlings think about digging into Tom's case?" I realized how silly it all seemed, to include people in the neighborhood who thought I was guilty.

"Are you up for that?"

I nodded. "I am now." I knew I shouldn't tell her about Cassie, but it was vital. "Cassie's dead too."

She took a shaky step back. "What? When?"

I explained that I'd received a text, gone to visit, and found her in her bed with her throat slit, the same as Tom. "The detective is trying to pin them both on me." My mother flashed through my mind. "I can't go to prison, Daisy. I *can't.*"

"Hey, we'll find out who did this, okay? We will." She patted my arm lightly.

I wanted to believe Daisy. She did this for a living, after all. But there was so much at stake suddenly; if I could come out of this unscathed, that meant I got to be a mother again. I would receive my second chance. But I had to lead the detective away from me and figure out who'd done this. What their motives were.

"Can you gather everyone tonight?"

She cocked her head and smiled. "For you? Always. Coffee?"

"No thanks." I wanted to wake Lily up. I wanted to hide her in my house. I needed to tell Greg that she was back. I needed to do a lot of things. Ryan flashed through my mind again, and I realized I'd never gotten to hear what he'd wanted to tell me about Tom, why he wanted to talk in the first place.

I excused myself to Daisy's front porch and called Greg to fill him in on Lily's return.

"Ruby, listen. Things are going to get intense." He was silent for a few moments. "If the detective comes around, do not answer questions—do you understand me? Just call me. I'll figure out legally what we do with Lily, since technically, she's still a missing person."

"I don't want her to have to give a bunch of statements or be dragged through the press. Can you just make it go away, Greg? I don't care how much it costs."

"I'll see what I can do. Talk soon."

I stepped back inside to find Lily stretching her arms and yawning, walking slowly down the stairs. She smiled when she saw me. My heart seized. We had so much to figure out, so much to discuss.

"Ready to go home?"

She nodded. I told Daisy we were leaving.

"I'll text you about tonight."

We let ourselves out. Lily walked sleepily down Daisy's porch stairs and over to ours. "What's tonight?"

"One of Daisy's infamous Murderlings nights."

Lily rolled her eyes. "I guess some things never change, huh?"

I didn't know how to tell her that this night was more important than most. I didn't want her to be a part of it, but where else could she go? I didn't want to let her out of my sight ever again.

Inside, I strained to make sure I couldn't hear any strange noises. "Why don't you take a shower, I'll make us some food, and then we can talk, okay?"

"Okay."

I watched her disappear upstairs and threw together some food from the fridge: crackers, cheese, olives, fruit. I made a big batch of the tea she loved—rooibos with a heaping spoonful of raw honey—and arranged everything on the island, just like old times. She would soon sit across from me, and we could talk about everything.

Just as my nervous system started to settle, an earsplitting scream erupted from upstairs. I froze for one imperceptible moment, grabbed a butcher knife, and sprinted up the stairs.

30

After my bath, I calmed myself enough to deal with the aftermath of what I'd done.

I knew, when I walked down those stairs, I would see the crumpled form of my husband. The husband I was going to divorce. The husband I was going to leave. The husband who had done horrible things to the women he loved. The husband who had abandoned his first wife, who had let his kid disappear. The husband who didn't truly know what his current wife was capable of.

I popped a couple of pills from my medicine cabinet, just to take the edge off, and slowly padded back down the stairs. A snapshot of Lily flew to mind—when I'd found her drunk and nearly catatonic. And now, this was where I'd find her father, dead.

As the stairs curved to the right, I froze in my tracks.

He was gone.

"Tom?"

I rushed down the steps and listened for sounds. I knew what happened when someone injured hid in the shadows. They could attack when you least expected it. They could surprise you. They could *hurt* you. A smear of blood stretched from the bottom of the stairs and then evaporated like smoke. No tracks. No errant drops. I spun around.

Where did he go?

His phone was gone, as were his keys. My first thought was that he'd gone to the police. I would be arrested for domestic violence, though Tom falling down the stairs was not entirely my fault. I began to get my story straight, as my father so often had when I'd called the cops on him, desperate for them to see the monster he truly was—and yet, every time, he would simply talk his way out of being hauled away in handcuffs. I'd listened from behind closed doors as he'd joked around and found common ground with the cops. He'd tell them I had a vivid imagination, that he and my mother were madly in love and just argued sometimes. He'd never lay a hand on her. She was just clumsy. On and on he went, and they ate it up like pie.

I grabbed my still-full glass of wine and drained it in two gulps. I filled it to the brim again and sat in the dark in the keeping room, waiting, plotting. The art played tricks on my eyes and morphed into haunted, shadowy beings with gaping mouths.

As the hours passed and Tom didn't return, I wondered if he had gone somewhere to just sleep it off. Regardless, I made myself move.

I mopped up the blood, ensuring there were no remnants. The divorce papers still sat on the island. I scooped up the file, went upstairs, and shredded them in Tom's office. I placed the file about Trish in my own safe spot, one he'd never find. If he came home, if he accused me, it would be his word against mine.

Sleep did not come, and by five the next morning, he still hadn't returned. I showered, made myself a strong pot of coffee, and vacillated with what to do. Over the course of our marriage, there had definitely been fights. Not every fight had ended up with me being physically hurt. Yet sometimes, I'd sleep at my East Nashville house for a few nights, and he'd stay at his. The distance had been good for us so we could clear our heads and create space.

I thought of that now, how we no longer had that option.

My phone buzzed, and I jumped to check it. It was from Ryan.

Still thinking of you after last night. You good?

I deleted it and weighed my options. Maybe Tom wouldn't come home as long as he knew I was here. I went online, found a cute local inn, and booked it for a couple of nights. I packed a quick bag, locked up, and sent Tom a text on the way.

Going to a hotel for a few days to cool off. The house is yours.

I waited for the read receipt, but nothing came. It sat there for hours, unread. When I checked in at the inn, I stared at my small clean room and flipped on the gas fireplace in the corner. I made myself a pot of tea with the electric kettle, curled up in a rocking chair, and plucked one of the five novels they had stacked on a little shelf.

As I tried to relax, our fight kept coming back. Was that how it had started between my parents? One day, my father just lost his temper and then, from there, became addicted to it? The power I'd felt, the absolutely blinding, white-hot rage . . . that hadn't been about Tom. It had felt like it was embedded in my DNA.

A sickening thought occurred to me: What if my father's rage hadn't been about my mother either but about something, or someone, else? I knew my father's own childhood was tough, that his father had hurt him too. What if he was taking out all his old demons on her?

I cleared all thoughts of that man from my head and retrained my focus on Tom. Now that I knew the truth about Trish, maybe he was going to simply leave. I thought of his words to me: *I know what you did, and I love you anyway.*

In the back of my brain, just like with my father, I wondered what Tom's definition of *love* could possibly be. How could you love someone and hurt them repeatedly? Every time my father would leave, I wondered when he'd walk back through that door, bigger and angrier than before. I wondered when he'd make promises and break them. I wondered when he'd surprise me, or us. I wondered what wrath would unfurl every time he stepped in the door after a long day, what price my mother would inevitably pay.

Though Tom wasn't like my father, he was close enough. And if and when he did return, I'd be ready.

31

At the top of the stairs, Lily was hyperventilating and pointing to my bathroom with a trembling hand.

She always preferred my bathroom because we had a massive steam shower. With the knife aimed, I kept her behind me and crept toward where she was pointing. Splayed in my bathtub, with his throat slit, was Ryan.

"Oh my God." I dropped the knife, sank to my knees, and yelled at Lily. "Call 911." I thrust my phone at her, then searched for a pulse, even though I knew he was dead. I tried to catch my breath, but everything began to blur.

I stood on shaky legs and turned in a circle, reclaiming the knife. Was the killer still in my house? I could hear Lily shaking out fragmented words on my cell. After she hung up, I reached for my phone and called Detective Ellis myself.

"To what do I owe the pleasure, Ruby?"

"I just came upstairs to my bathroom, and there's a dead body in it."

She was silent. "Who?"

"My neighbor, Ryan Fisher." My voice broke. Ryan had just been in my house because he wanted to tell me something, and I'd turned on him in an instant, thinking he was the killer. I realized my DNA would be all over him, as well as in my bathroom. "Get someone over here now."

I stood over him, knife in hand, then let it clang to the floor. *What happened here?* I had to get Lily out of here. I thought about going back to Daisy's, but I didn't know if her place was safe either. I vacillated between who to call, where to go. Who could we trust?

Ralph.

I texted Ralph and asked him to come over. I knew I could not just flee a crime scene, and while I didn't want to drag Ralph into this mess, he already knew one of my biggest secrets. He was already complicit. If we stayed outside, we'd be fine until the police arrived. He texted back immediately that he'd be right there.

"Lily, let's go out back."

I guided her out to the patio and scooped a tumbler and bottle of scotch from the sideboard. She sank into an Adirondack, and I gathered wood to start a fire. When the flames were gently crackling, I poured myself a drink. My fingers ached from the cold glass, and the liquid burned my throat.

Ralph walked up a few minutes later, blowing warm air into his large hands. He stopped short when he saw Lily, glancing at me and then back to her.

"Well, this is quite the surprise."

"So is the dead body in my bathtub," I said, offering him my glass of scotch.

Without a word, he tossed the entire shot back and extended it for a refill. I didn't know where to start, and I wasn't sure how honest I should be in front of Lily, but I was so tired of lying. I was tired of keeping my stories straight, from then to now. I honestly didn't know what was going on, and it was time to get clear about what I'd done versus what other people thought I'd done.

I told him about Tom. My eyes flicked toward Lily when I said it. Her face contorted as she stared into the fire and wiped at a few tears that carved a trail down her cheeks. But she stayed quiet and listened. I told him about Cassie and Ryan, the sounds I'd heard in my house, and then finding Ryan upstairs. The newspaper clipping Cassie was holding in her hand, alluding to something from my past. I hesitated, not yet ready to give up that truth.

"They think I did it, Ralph. They think I killed Tom. And probably Cassie and Ryan too."

He clapped a large hand on my shoulder. "Ruby, you may be many things, but you're not a serial killer."

"The detective thinks I am."

As if on cue, the doorbell rang, and I excused myself to let her in. Detective Ellis had a team and nodded for them to enter before I'd even opened the door wide enough. I knew the drill. I'd be taken into the station, photographed, and swabbed, my clothes probably checked for DNA. I knew my house would become a crime scene and that they would search for any evidence of who had done this, starting with me.

"You okay?" she asked, eyeing me up and down.

"No." I shut the door behind her. "We're out back. My friend Ralph is over. I didn't feel safe here alone."

"You're going to have to come down to the station."

"I know that."

"Stay put, and I'll come get you shortly."

I left Detective Ellis alone in my house, part of me wondering if she was the type of detective to plant evidence just to nab a suspect and move on. But something told me she was more honorable than that, and even if she did have it out for me, she seemed like the type of woman who was after the truth, not just a convenient story to make her case.

Out back, Lily was talking to Ralph, and they both stopped once I returned. Lily settled back into her chair, gnawing once again at her cuticles. I glanced between the two of them. "Don't stop talking on my account."

Ralph cleared his throat and looked at Lily. "Sweetheart, I think it's time you told your mom the truth."

My heart seized. *The truth?* What was he talking about?

She offered a shaky sigh and sat upright, clenching her cold hands between her jeans before extending them toward the roaring fire. The last time I'd seen her, before I'd admitted her to a psychological rehabilitation facility, she'd been completely unglued. After hiding out after Leonard's party, she'd finally come home when Tom was gone and revealed what had happened. She'd left the party and accidentally hit someone on the way home: Andrew Tarver. He'd been wearing all black, walking down the road. She was drunk and hadn't seen him.

I knew if I told Tom, it would ruin his career; it would ruin everything. It might even turn his rage toward her. So I had gone to Ralph. Ralph, who had ignored all his principles and morals to help keep my daughter out of jail. He'd made a deal to get her the help she needed. She'd stayed in the facility for months, getting better. She'd never been missing, and I hated to admit that I'd derived a small bit of pleasure at seeing how unglued Tom had become at thinking she was gone. But then, she'd actually disappeared, and I couldn't find her. It hadn't taken much for me to realize Tom had most likely gotten to her thanks to his fancy PI and that he was keeping her from me on purpose. But in all this time, I'd never figured out how he'd found her. I'd covered my tracks so well, unless . . . I looked at Ralph.

"Did he come to you?" I asked.

Ralph sat stonily before learning forward and warming his big hands by the fire. "He bribed me, Ruby. He had something on one of my cases, so I had to help him, or he said he'd have me disbarred, professionally ruined. I'm so sorry." He sat back heavily in his chair, and I jumped back, as if burned by a popping ember.

"Are you kidding?" My fists shook in my lap. "You saw me devastated when she *actually* disappeared, and you knew where she was this entire time, and you didn't tell me?" My mind couldn't compute what he was saying.

"No, I didn't know where they went," Ralph said. "I never heard from him after that."

It seemed both of us had been watching our backs for different reasons, waiting for Tom to return and air all our dirty laundry. So who had killed Tom? My eyes raked over Ralph again, but he would never hurt anyone. Would he?

Before he could explain further, the detective approached the patio. Her eyes landed on Lily, then shot back to me. "Ruby, may I speak with you?"

I walked on shaky legs back inside. I didn't think my brain could handle any more surprising information. I could feel myself shutting down, closing off, coping in order to move forward.

Detective Ellis cocked her head toward the patio. "Who is that?"

I sighed and leveled with her. "My missing daughter. Apparently, Tom took her." The halftruth hit the air, sharp and hard.

Detective Ellis's mouth formed a soft O of surprise before she snapped it shut. "We'll have to talk about that later, but, Ruby . . ." She motioned upstairs. "We've secured the area and contained the scene, but whoever did this knows what they're doing. The scene is clean. Same as Cassie's. It's like the suspect had time to stage all of this, right under your nose."

My nerves were shot, and so was my patience. "Look, if you're insinuating *I* planned all of this, just like you think I magically had time to kill and dump my husband in our lake, then you're mistaken. I didn't *do* any of this. I have no clue what's going on or why someone is targeting me, okay? I swear I had nothing to do with any of these murders."

It sounded so ridiculous coming out of my mouth, like a thriller novel or a movie. But this wasn't fiction. This was my life, and if I wasn't careful, I could have three murders pinned on me because there was no evidence pointing to anyone else.

"If it wasn't you, Ruby, then it's someone who has access to your house, who knows their way around."

She glanced back outside, right at Lily and Ralph.

I laughed. "Don't be ridiculous."

"Why is that ridiculous? Because you trust them?" She crossed her arms, the fabric of her tight blazer stretching. I noticed one of the seams at her cuff was popped.

"Because they aren't murderers."

"And neither are you, right?"

My skin erupted into chills. I didn't have the energy to fight anymore. I was so tired—so tired of being questioned, so tired of this insane game.

"You all can't be here now. It's a crime scene. We need you down at the station. I can escort you there myself."

Right then, two paramedics brought Ryan down on a stretcher. His body was covered, only the lumps of his features distinguishable beneath the sheet. My heart ached for another life lost. Though Ryan didn't know all my secrets, he'd seen some of the darker parts of my marriage and tried to be there for me. Now he was dead because of me.

Once she was down the porch steps, she turned and stared at my house from the driveway. "You should have considered security cameras, by the way."

"What?" I stepped farther out onto the porch.

"Your house. It's the only one without an alarm or any of those fancy cameras. Except Cassie's was conveniently turned off." She opened her car door. "You coming?"

I texted Ralph that I would be back and asked that he watch Lily while the crime lab did what they needed to do. He insisted on driving to the station and told me he'd call Greg to meet us there shortly. I stared at the other houses on the street, sets of eyes peeking from behind parted curtains. I wondered what they were all thinking. That I was a murderer? That they were next?

Suddenly, every emotion burst out of me in a flood. I spread my arms wide and screamed, "The show's over! I'm not a murderer!" I slammed the passenger door in Detective Ellis's car, closed my eyes, and, for the first time in a long time, cried.

COTTAGE GROVE FORUM

crystallover: DID YOU GUYS JUST SEE RUBY
MELT DOWN???

lettucehead4life: we did! we were at shianna's! we
were watching through the window! Did she just
get arrested?
crystallover: wow, thanks for the invite.
hippiemama23: Did you see them bring out another
body on a stretcher??? YOU GUYS, THIS IS EPIC.
WHO ELSE DIED???????
dahmernotjeffrey: looks like we have a serial killer
among us
crystallover: OMG, OMG, OMG, OMG
lettucehead4life: @nashvegasart, where are you?
We need your quippy responses.
crackersmp: what if he's the one who died??????
shianna: @lettucehead4life certainly wished it on
him enough. Maybe it finally came true!
dahmernotjeffrey: words have power
shianna: #truth
crystallover: you guys. Who was on that stretcher?
This is so intense.

hippiemama23: We have to get to the bottom of this, ASAP. we r going on vacation in a couple of days, so we need to know.

nashvegasart has joined the conversation

shianna: Thank God! We thought you were dead!

nashvegasart: no, just late to the party. what did i miss?

hippiemama23: Ruby just had a PUBLIC meltdown and they just rolled A BODY out on a stretcher.

nashvegasart: do we know who?

lettucehead4life: not yet.

shianna: uh, this is weird. where are the jokes @ nashvegasart?

lettucehead4life: yeah, @nashvegasart, what gives?

nashvegasart: what do you mean?

crackersmp: okay, this is definitely weird. maybe someone is PRETENDING to be @nashvegasart, because he was the body on that stretcher?!?! And this person is posing as him trying to pump us for info.

dahmernotjeffrey: you realize he is right here.

lettucehead4life: is he tho? @nashvegasart that's when you make some sick joke about standing behind us or telling us to go eat a dick or something.

nashvegasart: why would i tell you to eat a dick?

crackersmp: oh helll nawwww that ain't him, y'all! I'm telling you!

lettucehead4life: I don't like this. Something is off.

crystallover: Should we log off???

hippiemama23: Let's stay focused. We have to figure out who is on that stretcher! @nashvegasart any
ideas??? You've been right so far.
nashvegasart has left the conversation
lettucehead4life: holy shit. that definitely wasn't
THE REAL him.

32

THEN

I knocked on the door and waited.

The trailer was in disrepair, though the land around it was spectacular. Fields of wheat as far as the eye could see stretched high toward the sky, outlining bald, jagged mountains. Protective pines enclosed this tiny space from the rest of the natural world. I always marveled at how some of the most jaw-dropping land was spotted with trailers or folks who could barely afford the basic necessities, and yet they woke up to such natural beauty every day for free. Seemed like the joke was on us.

The door was unlocked when I tried it. Slowly, I stuck my head inside. "Trish? Trisha?" Beer cans littered the floor. Used needles were stacked on a small laminate table by the window. Dirty clothes, unwashed dishes, and the smell of rot everywhere. No one was here. I stepped back outside, gulping clean air, and glanced at the sole lawn chair with gaping holes in the seat. An old grill sat beside it, a spatula dangling from the side. There was no car, no signs of other life. This wasn't a trailer park; it was simply a trailer on remote land in the Blue Ridge Mountains.

My body ached from the drive, but I was desperate. Lily was no longer in the psych facility, Tom had vanished, and I'd discovered this bombshell that his ex-wife was still alive. I wanted answers. I wanted *intel.*

I plopped into the lawn chair and decided to wait. When Tom had talked about his ex-wife, I could see the pain on his face. But I had thought that pain was from her death, not from him sending her away.

The sharp crunch of gravel and a crooked blast of headlights made me bolt upright. Patsy Cline crooned from an old Cadillac. The engine cut, and a door creaked open, but it was too bright to see who was behind the wheel. Panic set in. What if this wasn't Trish's trailer? What if someone else lived here?

"You're trespassing." The slurred words of a woman I'd never met bounced across the small expanse of land.

I stood and inched my way closer until my eyes adjusted to the halflight. She looked a decade older than she probably was. Her light, frizzy hair erupted in a halo around her head. Before the sun drained from the sky, I glimpsed her startling eyes and once-pretty face. When she opened her mouth to speak, I saw yawning black gaps where teeth should be. Wrinkles cut into the flesh around her mouth and eyes. Her skin puckered in sections, as if she'd picked at it.

She was grotesquely thin and white as milk. "What do you want?" she spat. Her eyes were unfocused. She was high; that much I could tell.

I tried to find my voice. "I'm Tom's wife."

The woman's eyes widened slightly, and then she looked away. "Sucks for you."

To my surprise, I laughed. "You could say that."

I could see her trying to get her bearings, trying to come down from the high long enough to have this conversation.

"That's not why I'm here. It's about Lily." It was such a shock to see how much Lily resembled this woman, and my eyes filled with tears as I realized I might never get to see my daughter again.

Her eyes focused in an instant. "What about her?"

I grabbed a photo from my back pocket to show her. "She's missing." I didn't know how much to tell her—that she'd committed a crime I had wiped clean, that I'd stashed her away like a secret, in hopes to get better. But now, she was really gone, and I had a pretty good idea that Tom was to blame.

Trish's hard eyes softened as she traced the photo with such tenderness it almost brought me to my knees. What kind of mother could this woman have been if she'd gotten help? It dawned on me for the first time that Tom, with all his money and resources, could have helped her. Instead, he'd sliced her out of his life—and Lily's. Why hadn't he given her another chance?

"This is my baby?" Her voice was hoarse. "My baby girl?" Tears dripped freely down her face and splashed onto the photo. She clutched it so tightly the edges bent. "She's gorgeous."

"Smart too. Wants to be an engineer." The pride swelled in my voice as I realized we'd been able to give Lily a good life. And yet she still had problems. She'd still made a monumental mistake. She still might be gone for good.

Trish handed the photo back, but I told her to keep it. She smoothed the wrinkles and stuffed it into her jeans pocket, then motioned for me to follow her inside. She cleared a space off one of the chairs by the window. I sat, staring directly at a used needle. She was wearing long sleeves, probably to cover the tracks.

"What happened?" She popped a beer and offered me one, but I shook my head.

I sighed. "She just disappeared. No one has been able to find her." I clenched my hands in my lap. "I thought maybe she'd come here."

Trish laughed, a croupy smoker's laugh. "Why in the world would she come here? Tom made sure to keep her as far away from me as possible. The bastard," she added under her breath.

"It's the only other place I could think of."

"Does she even know about me?"

I hesitated. "I didn't even know about you until recently. He told me you were dead."

Despite her tough exterior, the hurt was evident. "Sounds about right." She eyed me up and down. "He bang you up too?"

I thought about lying, but this woman had been through enough. I nodded. "He has, yes."

She sighed and dropped into the seat across from me. "I threatened to kill him if he ever touched me again. The last time was when I was pregnant with Lily . . . he pushed me down the stairs. I thought we'd lose the baby. I told him I was going to call the cops, but he said it would be his word against mine."

Tom pushed her down the stairs when she was pregnant?

I thought about his fall down the stairs, then his disappearance. "How did he take her from you?"

She rolled her eyes. "Money, honey." She took a healthy sip of her beer and sighed. "He got me addicted to pills, you know."

I blanched. "What?"

"After that fall, I was on bed rest. The moment I had Lily, my back never got better. He got me the prescription, convinced me to take them. Said they wouldn't be addictive. I trusted him, so . . ."

Icy shock coursed through my veins as she continued.

"When the prescription ran out, I was desperate. Started finding different ways to make the pain stop. I . . . I forgot about Lily. Just once, in the car. I'd fallen asleep inside, and I'd left her. It wasn't hot or nothing, but that was it. Tom filed for divorce and custody all in the same day. I was too messed up to even put up a fight." She lit a cigarette and blew the smoke into the air. "I got clean after that. Stayed sober for a year, wanted to prove myself to him. Showed up at his office one day because I wanted my second chance, I wanted to be in Lily's life, but he had me escorted out by the cops." She looked up at me, glassy eyed. "Wouldn't even give me a chance to see her. I tried to fight the courts, but it was like I didn't even exist." She flicked ash onto the table. "He treated me like trash." She smiled, revealing the gaps in her teeth. "So here I am, living like trash."

Anger rippled through my chest. How could Tom have just thrown her away, never given her a chance to prove herself to Lily? To let Lily get to know her own mother? "I never knew about any of this, Trish. I'm so sorry. That must have been so hard."

She eyed me suspiciously. "He send you here or something?"

"No. He took off, and all I care about is finding Lily." I plucked a card from my back pocket. It was one of Tom's, but I scribbled my cell on the back. "Will you call me? If you hear anything at all? I know it's unlikely, but . . ." *But I need to find her, even if he doesn't want me to.*

As I stood to go, she stopped me. "How'd you even find me?"

"Tom has a file on you. I read it."

She nodded as she stubbed out the cigarette on the table. "Figures. I sure hope that prick gets what's coming to him one day."

I turned at the door. "And what is that?"

"Death," she said, staring me straight in the eye. "Or slow, painful torture. Whichever comes first." She smirked; then her eyes softened. "Please find my baby girl."

"I will," I said as I let myself out the door. It didn't feel like a promise I could keep, but I was going to try.

I was going to try to find our girl . . . for us both.

33

Once I was done being swabbed and questioned at the precinct, Detective Ellis dropped me off back home but told me not to enter the house.

As the crime lab people were still working upstairs, Ralph, Lily, and I resumed our place out back. I poured myself another scotch, understanding that it was just a matter of time before they arrested me, before they had enough to charge me with multiple murders. Quite frankly, I was shocked I hadn't been hauled away in handcuffs yet. That was what Greg was for, I guessed.

"Okay, let's get it all out on the table." I slammed the amber bottle on the glass coffee table. "No more lies." I sniffed, exhausted from crying. I hadn't fully let myself go in so long, instead storing everything inside. I sat down, glassy eyed, and stared into the fire. *And where did that get me?*

I took a shot, repoured, and took another.

"Maybe you should slow down, Ruby."

"Maybe you should start talking, Ralph." My voice was harsh, and I readjusted in my chair. "I'm sorry, but I just can't understand how you could lie to me." I stared between them. "Regardless of whatever

Tom had hanging over you, Lily is my daughter too. You should have come to me."

"I kept him away from you," Lily suddenly blurted out. She pulled the cuffs of her sweatshirt over her fingers and blew into them. "I told him I wanted to live with him, that we could start over. I just wanted to keep him away." She looked deep into my eyes. "I wanted to keep you safe."

An entire lifetime of conversations with my mother just like this one flashed through my head. Hadn't I done the same—and more—to protect my mother? If I could have possibly convinced my father to leave with me, I would have. I would have done anything to keep her safe. But as I looked at Lily now, so young and vulnerable, I realized it wasn't a daughter's job to protect her mother. It was the other way around.

I massaged my temples and sighed. "So what happened, then? He just left you? That doesn't sound like him."

She chewed on her bottom lip. "Not at first." Lily sat up and shook her head. "We kept moving from place to place. He was completely unhinged. I think he was building a case against you somehow. I'm not sure. But then one day, he said he had to run some errands and just didn't come back. I waited for a week." Her eyes brimmed with tears. "I didn't know what to do. So I came back here."

I tried to understand what she was telling me, but some of it didn't add up. I'd had a private PI looking for Lily ever since she left her facility. And he hadn't been able to find her.

"I called Ralph right away. I didn't know what else to do, Mom. I'm so sorry." Her sprinkle of freckles seemed to dance on her face in the firelight.

"Why didn't you call me or just find a way to reach out and let me know you were okay?"

"Because I was afraid of what he'd do if he found out."

Silence buzzed between the three of us, all the messy truths swerving into focus. How naive to think for a second that Lily didn't know exactly what her father was capable of all these years.

"I told Lily she needed to tell you everything," Ralph said. "I'm sorry I didn't tell you the truth sooner."

His words weren't much of a consolation now, but at least she'd finally come home. "Lily, did Tom ever hurt you?"

Her face twisted, confused. "No. Never."

I sighed, placated for the moment at least. The day's events rooted me in place. First Lily, then the precinct, then Ryan, and now this confession. "So Tom disappears without a trace. Who killed him, then?" My voice was blunt, and I realized I should be softer around Lily. This was her father, after all. It was still a loss.

Ralph gripped his knees and sighed. "Now that, I don't know."

I tapped my fingers against my chair, thinking about our fight, about how I'd physically assaulted him, about how I'd watched, so emotionally detached, as he had fallen down the stairs. "I wonder if a disgruntled client did it." Even as I said it, bits of his corpse flashed through my mind. The bloated, blue pallor. The tarp. The puckered skin. The slit throat. The decomposing feet. And I was still wondering the exact same thing as everyone else: Why hadn't I recognized my husband?

You know why.

"I'm sure the police will find the killer," Ralph said.

"And if they don't? I take the fall."

Ralph looked at me, genuinely concerned. "You don't know that."

"Ralph, there are three dead bodies, all pointing to me. My husband, Cassie, and my . . ." My voice snagged. What was Ryan to me? He was my friend. He could have been a good friend if I'd let him be. "And Ryan. But all three are connected to me. And I covered up a crime for my own daughter. No matter how you look at it, I'm going away for something."

Lily looked worried, but she stayed silent.

"I'm sorry. I shouldn't be talking about this now." I wanted to tell Lily to go inside, but she couldn't. It was still a crime scene. I checked the time just as I heard a "yoo-hoo!" from next door. Daisy looped her arms over my fence and waved. Five other neighbors stood behind her, short, tall, bundled, and underdressed. Daisy wore her signature tight dress with a fuzzy sweater on top. I realized that she'd probably been out back or in her dining room and hadn't seen the crime vans pour in.

She motioned to the bag slung over her shoulder, a bottle of tequila in hand.

"Ready for some murder?"

For some reason, that struck me as hilarious. Maybe I was drunk or delirious from the events of the day, but once I started laughing, I couldn't seem to stop. In between gasps, I told her that we couldn't have murder night here because an actual murder had just taken place upstairs. Her face fell when I told her who it was.

"Ryan?" She lowered the bottle of tequila and stared at the second story. A collective gasp rose behind her as the news sank in.

Daisy composed herself in a second, snapping to attention. "Okay, this ends tonight. We're going to your house, Ralph. We're getting to the bottom of this. No more questions."

I perked up. *Yes, no more questions.* This was exactly what I needed. *Answers.* No more dead bodies. No more insinuations. No more pointing fingers. I looked at Ralph, hopeful.

He rolled his eyes. "Don't you dare think I'm going to say no and become the next victim. Let's go."

People piled into cars as Ralph gave them his address. I told him Lily and I would walk. I hadn't had more than a few seconds alone with her since she'd reappeared.

We walked side by side, our breath coming out in tiny puffs. "Do you hate me?" she finally asked.

I stopped on the sidewalk. "Oh, honey, of course I don't hate you." I searched for what to say, what I would want to hear in her shoes. "I'm sorry for what you went through. I'm sorry you felt you had to stay with Tom to keep me safe, but I understand exactly why you did it. More than you know." I gripped her coat and looked deeply into her bright-green eyes. I had so many questions. Had she been off her meds all this time? How had Tom just made her disappear? How had he kept the facility from calling to alert me that Lily had checked out? I guess none of that mattered, but now that he was dead, I worried she could still go to prison. Or that she would be scarred for life from everything she'd been through. Instead of bombarding her with questions, I released her coat. "I'm just glad you're home safe."

"Me too."

I thought about how Tom had found out the truth when he'd put two and two together. Even though he was dead, part of me still didn't believe he couldn't somehow figure out how to hurt me, even from beyond the grave. We stopped at the edge of Ralph's house. The lake glittered beyond, placid and calm despite what had unfolded here. What would have happened if Tom's body hadn't resurfaced? Would Cassie and Ryan still be alive? Would Lily have ever returned?

My heart pinched as I thought about Cassie and Ryan. It hadn't sunk in yet, those losses, and I still felt solely responsible. All this had to do with me, and I needed to find out why.

Inside, I could hear the gang gathering around Ralph's long dark wooden table, buffed to perfection with Pine-Sol. Ralph was nothing if not traditional. A few people clutched cigars and were already drinking bourbon. Daisy was arranging facts and photos of Tom, Cassie, and now Ryan on the gleaming table's surface. When everything was in place, she gripped the table and eyed the crowd, her bloodred lips parting into a smirk.

"Okay, Murderlings. Let's do our thing."

34

THEN

"Like this?"

I clutched the boning knife in my hand and struggled with the slippery fish. Once it was steady, I slid the sharp blade along the seam of its belly and folded it open like a book.

My father inspected it. "That's right, Pen. A natural." He winked at me, and I broke into a grin.

I hated that I craved his approval, especially knowing what he was capable of. But it had been weeks since he'd hurt Mama, and I thought maybe he'd changed. He showed me how to bleed the fish, remove all the entrails, identify the anus, and cut a notch or V shape into it.

"Now, here's a little secret." He showed me his own fish, digging his thumbnail around its backbone. "Some fish have a kidney right here." He dipped his dirty fingernail against the flexible spine and scraped out something small and dark. "Now you check."

I moved my fingers along the backbone of mine until I found a tiny little knot. I gripped it and pulled, pinching the spongy kidney between my fingers.

"That's right. Good girl. Now, we wash."

He showed me how to dip the fish in water until it was clean, then scale it, which was my favorite part. There was something satisfying about seeing all those glittery scales fly through the air like confetti. When I was done, I wasn't confident I could remember all the steps.

"Again," I said.

He winked. "That's my girl."

I shivered at the words. That's what he always said to my mother, right before he pounded her face in. *I love you, my girl. You're my girl. Such a good girl.*

But we were here now, and I was learning something. He wasn't drunk, at least, and as I sliced into a new fish, I gathered the words I wanted to ask, mulling them over before finally spitting them out like bad food.

"How come you hurt Mama?"

He stopped the race of his knife against the fish and took a shuddering breath. "Penny." There was sorrow in the way he said my name, enough to make me want to apologize, but I didn't.

"I just don't understand," I continued. I looked up at my big burly father who was so much larger than me. "Don't you love her?"

He dropped the fish. It slapped juicily against the rock while his knife clanged and slipped into the dirt. He was nearly bowled over, as if he'd been gut punched. "Oh, sweet baby girl, yes." He reached out, gripping my shoulder, the stink of fish all over him. "Yes, I love her. I love you both more than anything."

"So why do you hurt her, then? You don't hurt me."

His features twisted into the saddest arrangement I'd ever seen as tears poured down his cheeks. He wiped at them with his fingers full of guts. Little bits of fish flesh clung to his cheeks and beard. "Because I'm sick, Penny. I'm so sick, and I really want to get help. I'm going to get help."

I'd been reading about men like him, and they were usually so mean because the same thing had happened to them as a child. Had my mother ever asked him? I figured there was no harm in trying now. "Did your daddy hit you?"

His lower lip buckled in on itself, and he cried silently, just like my mother. That was one thing that could be said in my house: no one hid their emotions. They were big. Anger was big. Joy was big. Fear was big. Because of it, I stayed small.

When the tears had stopped, he looked at me with vacant, bloodshot eyes. "He did, Penny. He wasn't a good man."

I lowered my own knife and rinsed my hands in the bucket of river water next to me. I placed my hand on his. "I think you're still a good man. You just do bad things sometimes."

I didn't know if I believed that he was still a good man, but I wanted him to stop hurting Mama. I wanted him to stop more than anything, and maybe this—here, today—could be the day he changed forever.

"I'm going to stop, Penny. I swear it. I've been doing better, haven't I?" He opened his arms, and I fell into them. I hadn't been hugged by him in so long. He smelled like sweat, fish, and fire smoke, and I folded against his flannel shirt as he held me so tightly I could barely breathe.

"You're a good girl, Penny." He kissed my hair and rocked me back and forth. "Don't ever give yourself to a man who doesn't deserve it— you hear me? You stand up for yourself. You fight if you have to." He craned back to look at me. "Men can hurt you, even if they love you. If that ever happens, promise me you will stand up for yourself, Penny. Or you just run. Run as far and as fast as you can."

I was so confused by his words. Why was he telling me this? Why couldn't he take his own advice? Instead, I moved away and began fiddling with my fish again, dying to get it just right.

"I will, Daddy," I finally said. "I promise."

35

Two hours later, I felt like we'd been going in circles.

I glanced around Ralph's living room, my eyes glazed from too many drinks and staring at the whiteboard he'd wheeled in from his study. A few of the most veteran Murderlings were already arguing about who the killer could be. I watched them with an almost detached fascination, as if this wasn't my life at stake.

Unsurprisingly, Daisy had started with me as the prime suspect: my motives and whereabouts. Daisy didn't know about what had happened on those stairs, how I'd thought I had accidentally killed Tom, and how that fact had haunted me for months. What we did tell her, however, were the basics around Lily— not that she'd hit a boy but that she'd gotten treatment and Tom had found out and taken her from me. What had happened next was anyone's guess.

I quickly realized, laying it all out, that I could understand how Detective Ellis was looking almost exclusively at me for these crimes. Deep down, I hated Tom for so many reasons. Besides myself as the prime suspect, we were exploring Cassie's husband, Charlie, but he'd been out of town at the time of his wife's murder and Ryan's. We kept circling back to enemies of Tom's, but that had nothing to do with Cassie and Ryan. Or maybe someone had separately killed Tom and was now messing with me by picking off my friends. What no one could figure out was why.

Daisy fiddled with the dry-erase marker in her hand. "What if. . ." She crossed out my name and moved Tom's photo to the top. "Okay, let's say someone had it in for Tom because of a case, right? Are there any connections between Cassie and Ryan, in terms of what he was working on?"

I perked up, shuffling back through memories of case files. Had Cassie or Ryan ever come up? Had they ever used his legal services?

"That's good, Daisy." Ralph nodded as he rocked in his recliner and puffed on a pipe. "Though I don't ever recall Ryan or Cassie seeking his counsel, I'm sure someone could get ahold of his case files if we needed to check."

The notion felt flimsy at best. I sat up. "What about if Cassie heard about one of his cases or found out something she shouldn't have? You know she has a huge mouth. What if someone offed her to keep her quiet because Tom's body resurfaced?"

"But what would Ryan have to do with that?"

"Maybe Ryan was poking around, looking where he shouldn't," Patrick, one of the neighbors, said.

I thought about Ryan lurking outside my home. Had he been conducting his own investigation, trying to get to the bottom of who killed Tom? "The last time I saw Ryan, he said he had to tell me something about Tom." I sat up straighter. "What if he'd made some sort of discovery?"

"If any of that were true, there would have to be *one* culprit," Lionel, the local piano teacher, said. "*One* person at the center of all of this. But who?"

"Or maybe there's more than one killer."

Everyone's head swiveled toward Lily, who was sitting cross-legged on the couch. Her fuzzy socks drooped at the ends, and she pulled the ends of her hoodie sleeves over her hands, embarrassed, as everyone stared at her. "What about if the killer had help?"

"Oh, I get you," Zoe, a hairstylist for celebrity country singers, said. "Like in *Scream*, right? Double-team."

"Exactly," Lily confirmed.

"This isn't some dumb movie," Beth snapped. "This is real life."

Lily caved in a little. "Sorry, I was just trying to help."

Chills traversed my skin once again. Did whoever did this have help? I stared at my neighbors, whom I'd gotten to know over the last year: Lionel, Zoe, Beth, Katy, Patrick. But how well did I really know them? Who was to say it wasn't one of them? In fact, how could I even trust anyone outside of Daisy and Ralph? My stomach dropped as my eyes rested on Lily. Maybe this had been a terrible idea.

"I'm going cross-eyed," Daisy said. "Let's take a snack break. Get some fresh air. Meet back here in fifteen?"

Everyone dispersed, and I sat, nursing another scotch. Everything was blurry, my thoughts were too malleable, and I realized I needed to sober up if I had any chance of thinking clearly. "I'm going to go splash some water on my face."

It felt good to stretch my legs. I walked down the hall to Ralph's powder room, which was really no larger than a small closet. There was a window that overlooked the lake. I wondered how long it would be before I would row again without thinking of Tom's body bobbing to the surface. Before my life had once again gone to shit.

As I was washing my hands, two of the neighbors, Beth and Lionel, stepped onto Ralph's patio and spoke in hushed tones, casting looks back to the house. My hackles went up, and my suspicions were confirmed. I *didn't* trust these people, and I didn't want to discuss theories with them. This was too personal, too private, with too much at stake. I didn't know what I'd been thinking. How did I truly know it wasn't one of them?

I flipped off the light and reentered the kitchen, where Lily was helping herself to snacks. I smiled at her and stepped out on Ralph's patio to get some fresh air. Beth and Lionel were no longer there. I tipped my head to the sky. The stars were infinite. I reveled in the beauty above us, in how complicated we made it all seem. Sometimes, in my darkest moments, I often longed for the moment when all the pain of being human would evaporate and I could finally rest in eternal peace.

"Mom?"

I jumped and turned to find Lily shuffling from foot to foot.

"You okay, sweetie?"

"I'm really tired. Will we be able to go home tonight?"

The detective had called to tell me we still couldn't return home. "Not tonight," I said. "I'll see if we can stay here with Ralph."

"Okay." She looked like she wanted to say more but turned to head back inside.

I couldn't even imagine what she'd been through these last six months: First in treatment, with such a huge secret. Then, on the run with Tom, all because she'd feared he would hurt me. I didn't even want to think about how this might ruin her college experience. Instead of being here, facing all this scandal and death, she should be enjoying her first semester at MIT. Even though he was dead, I was still furious with Tom for putting this on her shoulders.

I stood outside for a few more minutes, rewriting my feelings about Tom, which wasn't hard. The affair, the lies, the ultimate betrayal with Lily, the abuse; it made it easier to let him go completely. As I turned to head back inside, a commotion swelled on the other side of the screen door. Breaking glass. A scream.

"Oh God." I bolted toward the kitchen, immediately thinking of Lily. It seemed every time I stepped away, something bad happened. Would the universe take her away from me again, just when I'd gotten her back? I entered the kitchen, expecting to see another dead body, but it was just Beth, standing on her bare tiptoes, a shattered glass of wine around her.

"Sorry! It just slipped from my hands."

Ralph moved around her, delicately pinching shards of glass between his large fingers. I searched for a towel and mopped up the red stain on the floor until she hopped to safety. My nerves were frayed. I threw the rag in the wash and then pulled Daisy to the side.

"I don't want these people here."

She studied me. "Got it." She turned to the neighbors and, in a flat tone, stated, "Time to pack it up, guys. Thanks for coming."

I sagged in relief. That was what I loved about Daisy. She didn't ask unnecessary questions. She took what you said at face value. She studied people. And she seemed to understand me, even with all my withholding.

"Thank you."

"Do you want to keep taking a crack at it, or are you fried?"

I nodded. "I want to keep trying."

"Cool. I'll make sure these losers get out of here." She winked at me, and I helped Ralph open a fresh garbage bag to dispose of the fragments of glass.

"They're like wild animals," he said.

I laughed. "Well, they're mostly millennials. Or xennials. Or whatever the term is now."

"Exactly my point."

I secured the garbage bag. "Thanks for being here, Ralph. Even if you did keep such a big secret."

He sighed and took the bag from my hands. "You've been more of a friend than Tom ever was." He looked down at the bag. "I should have come to you. I'm so sorry that I didn't."

Once the last neighbor was gone, Daisy clapped her hands. "We gonna do this thing, or what?"

I could tell Lily was warming up to Daisy again. We all gathered around the whiteboard, and Lily said out loud what I'd been thinking.

"Could it be anyone else in the neighborhood? Even one of those people?"

Daisy tapped the marker against her chin. "Doubtful."

"Why?" Lily perked up.

"Because they lack the necessary skills or clear motive. You see, my dear girl, there's always a motive, and it usually boils down to one of three things: revenge, money, or sex. If Cassie was sleeping with Tom, there would be motive to take both of them out . . . but where does Ryan fit in? Where's the motive for all three? One murder months ago and then the other two back to back. The threads don't connect."

I sat up a little straighter. "They don't, do they? Unless *I'm* the thread?"

Daisy looked at me and then the board. "But even so, you'd have to know something or have some giant secret someone was trying to reveal. And even then, what do Ryan, Cassie, and Tom have to do with it?"

None of them knew my secret, even though Daisy had a vague idea and Tom said he did. I rubbed my eyes, which were dry and gritty. "Can they really pin this on me, Daisy?"

She snorted, clicking the cap back on her dry-erase marker. "Not with anything substantial, but they can certainly try. But without a murder weapon or evidence, it's all just circumstantial."

"Well, we won't let it happen, will we?" Ralph was back in his chair. We all looked at him, and Lily and Daisy shook their heads.

"We won't. We've got your back, dude." Daisy smiled at me. She had lipstick on her front tooth. I stared at Lily, whose knees were now inside her hoodie. She offered me a tentative smile.

I didn't have much, but I had three people who cared about me. A judge, a neighbor, and my daughter. For the moment, that had to be enough.

COTTAGE GROVE FORUM

hippiemama23: Are you guys there? Did you hear? RYAN, that hot painter, was the other person who died!!!!!

crystallover: OMG, HE WAS SO HOT.
lettucehead4life: That's terrible. He was like getting super famous or something.
shianna: his work will sell for way more now tho.
lettucehead4life: Has anyone heard from @ nashvegasart?
crackersmp: nada
dahmernotjeffrey: nope
lettucehead4life: i'm starting to think he WAS Ryan. That makes sense right, with his handle and everything? God, I feel so bad now.
crystallover: Is that true?????
hippiemama23: I think she's right. He never came out with us or came to our meetups. And we all know each other's real names on here, right?
shianna: um, duh. It's my handle!

lettucehead4life: I feel strangely sad about it. But also, WHO was that the other day? If it wasn't him????

dahmernotjeffrey: prolly THE KILLER

lettucehead4life: you think???

crackersmp: i mean, it would totally fit the profile, right? especially if the killer broke into his computer. god, this is creepy.

hippiemama23: Do you think we should start a new thread???

lettucehead4life: UGH, that's so much work.

crackersmp: I mean, I guess it's fine?!?

crystallover: what r u guys up to this weekend?

hippiemama23: HOPEFULLY NOT GETTING MURDERED.

dahmernotjeffrey: heres hoping

lettucehead4life: you have to admit it though. It's all strangely thrilling, right?

shianna: OH TOTALLY. It's fun.

nashvegasart has joined the conversation

nashvegasart: it's all fun and games until you bitches get your throats slit too.

shianna has left the conversation

crystallover has left the conversation

hippiemama23 has left the conversation

lettucehead4life: is it really you?

nashvegasart: want to meet and find out?

lettucehead4life: what's in it for me?

nashvegasart: 4222 lanyard row, 20 minutes. i'll be waiting.

36

I bolted upright from the floor.

My head pounded, and my back was sore. Why was I on the floor? Outside, I heard a car door slam and the squeal of tires. I blinked hard and oriented myself. I was in my home in East Nashville. Tom had dropped Lily off. So where was Lily?

"Lily?" My throat was dry and parched. I grabbed the island to help me stand. My head thumped, as if it had a heartbeat. Had I slipped?

"Mommy, you're taking forever! Come find me!"

I glanced around and saw a smear of water on the floor. I must have slipped while playing hide-and-seek. I searched for the memory, but there was nothing. Only a void. I usually didn't lose chunks of time unless I'd done something bad or something bad was being done to me.

"Okay, sweetie! I'm coming!" I tried to orient myself to the here and now and walked toward Lily's voice. She always hid in unique places, and sometimes it took me a long time to find her. I stepped into my bedroom, flipped on the light, and called out, "Now where oh where could my Lily be?"

Tom had a late case and had dropped her with me for the day. Never mind that I was just coming off of a twelve-hour shift at the hospital. From the moment we'd become a couple, Tom had passed the parenting baton to me. In the four years we'd been together, I had been shocked to see how hands-off he was with his daughter. He could do drop-offs and pickups, but I made every social plan and handled all her schoolwork, doctor's visits, field trips, and extracurricular activities. I bit my tongue constantly, not wanting to give Tom more ammunition to hurl back at me, but I didn't understand how he could just hand off all the parenting responsibilities to someone who wasn't actually related to his daughter.

Of course, I loved her as my own, but juggling a demanding job, two separate houses (my idea due to my insane work schedule), and my role as stepmother was wearing me down. But secretly, I loved when it was just the two of us. Tom hid his violent behavior from Lily, but she was a smart girl, always watching, always observing. Sometimes I wondered if she knew.

I fingered the small lump at the back of my head, still wondering what had happened. "Is she here?" I searched under the bed, which made my head pound even harder, then walked over to the closet. My hand froze on the doorknob. I closed my eyes, took a sharp, deep breath. I could still hear my father's voice on the other side of my childhood closet door, burning into my ears.

I opened it and saw my long dresses and coats rustle, followed by a tiny giggle. I was caught between then and now, my own past and Lily's present. I smeared the image from my mind, dropped down to my knees, and reached into the empty darkness, my fingers swiping at my clothes. "Could she be . . . here?" I thrust deeply behind the dresses, making contact with her tiny ribs. Lily screamed in delight.

"You found me, Mommy!" she said, popping her head out. "Now it's your turn to hide."

I knew the drill. We would keep going back and forth until Lily wanted to play another game. We walked back to the living room couch, which was home base, and she began counting. I rushed to the opposite end of the house and decided I would hide in the guest-bathroom shower. It was a small tub that had seen better days, but I hadn't gotten around to retiling it. I pulled back the curtain, carefully stepping into the empty bowl of the tub. Down the hall, I could hear Lily yell, "Ready or not, here I come!"

I held my breath, though my head was still pounding from waking up on the floor. I tried to remember, but there was nothing there, just a soft black void where memory should be. I could hear Lily opening and closing doors; then she ran to the bathroom and shouted, "Got ya!" before throwing her arms my way and tickling me.

"Okay, break time," I said, stepping out of the tub. I made Lily a snack and then searched for Mr. Gatti, my cat. He wasn't in his usual spot, a soft bed on top of his cat tree. After a thorough search, I looked at Lily. "Do you know where Mr. Gatti is?"

Lily scratched her nose and popped a strawberry in her mouth. "Daddy let him out, remember?"

"What?" I turned to her. "When?"

"When he came back after he dropped me off. He said he forgot to give you something, remember?" Her lips were stained pink, and her words jumbled in my sore head. I didn't remember. I shook my head no. Mr. Gatti had been with me for almost fifteen years. He was the only animal I had ever had. He was my closest companion, and I never let him out, no matter what.

"Should we look for him?"

I nodded, and we both crept outside, calling his name. I felt sick. He was old and wouldn't last five minutes with all the stray dogs running around. I searched the street, afraid I'd see his smashed body along the pavement, but there was nothing.

We searched the tiny yard, calling his name, but he didn't show up.

Inside, Lily settled onto the couch with a book, but she could see how troubled I was. "Why did Daddy let him out if he's not supposed to?"

My spine stiffened. "I don't know." An icy warning tapped its fingers against my spine as I looked at her earnest face. I didn't black out unless I was made to black out. When had Tom come back, and why would he let out my cat?

She lowered her book. "Maybe because he's allergic? He says as long as you have this house, you have a cat."

Her words landed like a slap, and I was too stunned to speak. Would Tom purposefully let my cat out just so I would finally move in full time with him?

"Well, I'm sure he'll show up," I said, though I didn't know that at all. Maybe Lily was mistaken, as I couldn't fathom that Tom would do something like this.

I searched the yard again, and we walked up and down the street until my voice was hoarse and my head throbbed even worse. Back inside, I collapsed on the couch, trying to stay calm while Lily created a Missing flyer.

"Do you want me to run you a bath, Mommy?"

My eyes filled with tears, and I scooted in beside her. I felt like I was stuck. Tom and I weren't married yet, and I could walk away at any time, but we both knew I wouldn't leave Lily. I didn't trust Tom with his own daughter, didn't trust that he wouldn't eventually hurt her too.

I breathed her in and kissed the top of her head. "No thank you, sweetie."

I didn't need a bath, no. What I needed was a way out of this relationship without losing Lily.

37

I woke up with a crick in my neck and groaned.

I blinked in the early-morning light, momentarily confused. Surrounded by plaid, I realized I was in Ralph's guest room. I rolled over, happy to find Lily still sleeping soundly. I smiled and pushed a few hairs from her face. Her mouth was open, and she was snoring softly. She'd always slept harder than anyone. It had been so long since I'd watched her sleep.

I followed the rise and fall of her breath and marveled at how peaceful she looked. Regardless of the lies I'd told and what Tom had done, it was the ultimate gift to have her back. No matter what it had cost me to think she was gone, all that pain was worth this moment.

Even with a killer on the loose.

I shivered at the thought, maneuvered out of bed as quietly as I could, and freshened up in the bathroom before entering the kitchen to the smell of freshly brewed coffee. Ralph was sitting at his kitchen table, reading the paper and sipping from a Harvard 1990 mug. Just the sight of this strong, sturdy man who shared one of my secrets somehow put me at ease.

"Morning."

He lowered the paper and smiled. "Morning. How'd you sleep?"

"Like the dead." I winced at my own choice of words, but it was true. I'd slept better here than I ever had at my house. "May I?" I pointed to the coffeepot.

"Help yourself. Cream's right beside it."

I poured a healthy dash of cream into a mug and filled it to the brim with coffee. As I sipped, some of the fog lifted. I sat down across from him. "Did you sleep?"

He looked at me over his spectacles. "I did. Strange times, huh?"

"That's putting it mildly."

We sipped in silence as the events of the last few days shuffled into place: the confirmation of Tom's murder, then Cassie, and then Ryan. Lily's return. The cops. I was feeling a desperately sinking sensation that I wasn't going to be able to crawl my way out of this hole—that one way or another, I was going to be blamed.

I'd never told anyone what had happened that night with Tom on the stairs. Ryan was the only one who knew about our fight. *Ryan.* At the mere thought of him, a surge of grief took hold, but I shoved it back down. I didn't know why I hadn't been honest with Detective Ellis about the last time I'd seen Tom. That we'd fought. That I'd found out he'd lied to me. That he had been abusive. That I'd watched him fall down the stairs. That he'd been injured and then disappeared. That he'd found Lily and kept her from me.

None of that seemed to matter now. He was dead, and someone *else* had decided to take his life. That seemed way bigger than our altercation. I sat up straighter suddenly, realizing that when he'd left Lily, someone must have killed him soon after, because Tom would never have left town for good without erecting some sort of revenge on me, despite my threats of what I'd do if he returned. I knew Tom. He could never let me have the last word. *Why didn't I think of that?*

It *had* to be someone in Cottage Grove, someone with a personal or professional beef with Tom. Someone who knew who he really was, what he'd done, what he was capable of.

Someone like me.

"Ruby, I wanted to talk to you about something." Ralph interrupted my reverie and folded his hands over the paper.

Right as he was about to speak, the doorbell rang, startling us both. A knot formed in the pit of my stomach. We both walked to the door, and Detective Ellis stood on the other side. She looked surprised to see me.

"Have you been here the whole night?" Detective Ellis skipped the formalities and got right to business.

I nodded. "Why?"

She sighed. "There's been another one. A neighbor." She glanced at her notes. "Beth Waterson. You know her?"

I looked at Ralph. "She was here last night," we both said in unison.

"But she left around ten, with the others," I jumped in. "That can be confirmed."

"The others?" Detective Ellis flipped to a fresh page on her notepad and let out a weary sigh. "Start from the beginning."

We filled her in on the gathering last night: who had been here and who'd left when. Apparently, this was much like the others: throat slit, body positioned just so. It seemed someone was literally picking us off, one by one. I realized instantly that it was time to get out of this neighborhood, maybe even out of this state. Lily and I could go somewhere new, start over, even though I'd done that once before. And trouble still seemed to find me, all these years later. Maybe it was karma.

"Does this mean I'm not a person of interest in this one?"

"No, not just because you claimed to be here, Ruby. I need someone to confirm your whereabouts."

"I can, because I was here with her, up the entire night," Ralph boomed. "This woman is not a killer."

My consciousness snagged on the word *killer.*

"That's my job to determine," she snapped. "Not yours."

Ralph squeezed the bridge of his nose beneath his spectacles. I'd seen him do the same thing in court. He was running out of patience. "Now, look. I understand that a killer is on the loose and keeps murdering innocent people right under your nose, and *you* can't seem to do your job and catch them. So I would suggest to you, young lady, that you stop pointing fingers at Ruby and start looking at other suspects."

We were all struck silent by his bold tone. Luckily, Detective Ellis let the words roll right off. "I'll be sure and keep that in mind, Judge." She hustled down the steps and then turned. "We still need you to bring in your daughter for questioning, Ruby. Or should I say stepdaughter?" She paused, then cocked a half wave and left.

I realized that was her way of revealing she knew more than I was telling her—that there were other secrets, other halftruths she'd probably found.

Ralph closed the door and shook his head. "Is this really happening?"

It seemed too sensational to be real, like something out of a movie. How were these people getting picked off so easily with the cops literally watching? I gripped Ralph's elbow. "Who do you think is doing this?"

"I literally have no idea." He poured himself some more coffee and sat heavily in his chair. "It could be anyone."

He was right. So many people in this neighborhood were running away from something: a city, a past, a career. Most of us wanted to keep to ourselves, and yet we all seemed to converge around murder, either in the fictional nights Daisy assembled or now, in real life. But why?

Something suddenly struck me, and I sat up, my chair legs scraping loudly across the floor. I winced as I adjusted. "Every victim has their throat slit."

He cleaned his spectacles and rocked gently in his chair. "Is that a question?"

"No, just an observation. The killer is obviously trying to send a message." Even as I said it, I knew what message they were trying to send. It was a message directly for me, though I wasn't sure exactly what it meant yet. They were talking *to* me but weren't trying to kill me. I just didn't know why.

"Morning." Lily yawned as she entered the room and poured herself a cup of coffee. Her short hair was wild and tangled, and she rubbed sleep out of her eyes as she sat at the table. She glanced between us. "Jesus, who died?"

There was so much of Lily that wasn't a child anymore. She'd been through hard things: having her mother taken away, mental instability, the accident with Andrew, rehab, lying to the ones she loved, being stashed away by her father. Now Tom was dead, and yet here she was, alive and resilient.

Ralph glanced at me, and Lily clocked the change in the air. She lowered her coffee cup and stared at me, wide eyed. "I was kidding. Did someone else . . ."

I nodded. "A neighbor. Beth. She was here last night."

Lily chewed on her bottom lip nervously, a trait she'd picked up from me. "So there really is a serial killer on the loose."

Is there? Who was sick and twisted enough to murder innocent people one by one just to toy with me? I knew it was time to end this one way or another before one more person was murdered. I needed to send a message to the killer somehow that I was game to listen, that I would sacrifice myself if it meant no one else got hurt.

I just didn't know how to do that. It seemed like whoever was doing this was always one step ahead, had their pulse on what everyone was doing when.

"Is there a public forum or anything for this neighborhood?" I asked suddenly.

Lily rolled her eyes. "Oh my God, it's the worst. I got on when we first moved here, but it's just a bunch of ancient neighbors talking crap about each other. They're worse than teenagers."

My heart rate ratcheted up a notch. "Can you show me, Lily?" I didn't want to tell her yet that she was going to have to go to the police station and be questioned—that Detective Ellis was going to upend her life, just like she had with mine, and that it was important she tell the truth . . . at least the important parts. Despite all my efforts, Lily was becoming subject to the same invasions of privacy that I'd worked so hard to keep her away from. I'd wanted to give her the right education, the right neighborhood, the right opportunities. And yet, she was turning out more like me than I could have ever imagined, even though we weren't related by blood.

Ralph loaned us his laptop, and she pulled it up.

"See?" She cranked the screen toward me. "Everything that's been going on, you hear about it here first." Once I was in, Lily grabbed her phone—a phone I assumed Tom bought her—and lost herself to a sea of scrolling and texts.

I scanned the page. She was right. "Ralph, did you know about this?"

He stared down the length of his nose over his spectacles. "Do I look like I join forums?"

I shook my head and scrolled back to the very beginning, reading and absorbing all that I could. While most of it was fluff, once Tom's body had surfaced, the conversation turned shockingly toward me. I read the awful things they'd said about me but paused when @nashvegasart seemed to disappear. Ryan. Was this Ryan?

I copied down some notes and then created my own handle, @morethanyouthink. I typed out my first message and waited with bated breath. If the killer was someone in the neighborhood, chances were they'd easily be able to hide out right here.

I was going to find them and put an end to this . . . one way or another. I'd done it before, and I would do it again.

COTTAGE GROVE FORUM

crystallover: You guys!!!!!! @lettucehead4life is DEAD!!!!! That detective was going door to door this morning.

shianna: NO WAY
crystallover: yes way
shianna: i'm scared
crackersmp: we all should be
dahmernotjeffrey: okay this is getting strange
hippiemama23: Someone is picking off all of us, one by one! WHY? And who's next?
shianna: i just saw @lettucehead4life she was so nice she made the best margaritas
crackersmp: WAS being the operative word
hippiemama23: We have to get serious and stop whoever is doing this once and for all.
crystallover: How do you suggest we do that?
hippiemama23: an eye for an eye, right? I know self-defense.
crystallover: somehow, i don't think self-defense is going to keep your throat from being slit. what's

up with that, do you think? why kill someone like that???

dahmernotjeffrey: why not?

morethanyouthink has joined the conversation

shianna: WHO THE FUCK IS THIS???? IT COULD BE THE KILLER, Y'ALL!

morethanyouthink: I'm not the killer

shianna: spoken like a killer

crystallover: who are you and what do you want?

morethanyouthink: I just want to talk to whoever is doing this.

shianna: i don't think they are interested in talking

morethanyouthink: They might be to me.

crackersmp: um, and why is that?

morethanyouthink: Because I know something they don't

hippiemama23: And what is that????? That YOUR A PSYCHO?

shianna: let them talk, jesus

hippiemama23: *YOU'RE

crystallover: this is totes the killer, ya'll

shianna: quit saying y'all

morethanyouthink: I have a little riddle for the killer

shianna: oh, hell noooooo

crystallover: NOPE

hippiemama23: shhhhh, let them type!

morethanyouthink: you think you know where to go, but I have proof of what you've done; meet me where i find my peace, make sure to come alone

shianna: WHHHHHHATTTTT THE FUCK?

crystallover: this is insane

morethanyouthink has left the conversation

38

I waited patiently in the visiting room for my mother.

She had been convicted after a short trial and was now housed in a maximum-security prison. I was allowed to see her once a week, thanks to my foster parents, who drove me out here. I glanced around at the other visitors, none of which were kids.

The giant metal door buzzed, and in poured a group of prisoners in their bright-orange jumpsuits. My mother looked frail and tired, but it was the first time in so long I'd seen her without bruises or cuts from my father. Her entire face brightened when she saw me.

She sat across from me, reaching her fingers to brush the tips of mine. We weren't allowed to hug or touch, though every part of me wanted to throw myself in her arms. I missed her so much I couldn't think straight. Despite her best efforts, they'd still found my father's body before we could start over, and she'd been arrested and convicted. She hadn't even put up a fight.

"You look well, sweetheart," she said. "Fed. Rested."

I nodded. My foster parents were nice, but I knew they were biding their time until someone adopted me. But I didn't want to go to a bunch of different homes or have new parents. I just wanted my mother.

"You look well too, Mama." My birthday was last week. I'd turned eleven, and it was the first time in my whole life my mother hadn't made a cake or sung me a song. My eyes teared up as I thought about it now—how I'd spent my special day all alone. I hadn't reminded my foster parents, hadn't wanted to bother them.

She laughed and rolled her eyes. "Penny Elaine, do not lie to your mother." She grinned, and I grinned back. I wanted to ask her so many things: how she felt without my father, if she could sleep, if she'd made any friends, what she did all day.

"Look, baby. I have a friend. He's a cop." She glanced behind her and then back at me. "He's going to get your name changed, help you with a new identity. He thinks he knows a nice couple who might want to adopt you. So you won't be tainted by this, won't grow up with this stain on your back."

My brain spun with her words. *Change my name? Adoption?* I racked my brain, thinking of any distant relatives I could stay with instead. My father's family was just as mean as he was and lived in Arkansas. And my mother didn't have anyone.

"I don't want to change my name," I said simply. "I love my name." My mother had told me the story of why she'd named me Penny a million times, but I almost asked her to repeat it now. She'd had a feeling she was pregnant, and when she'd placed her hand on her stomach, she'd glanced down at that exact moment to see a shiny penny by her shoe. She'd kept it with her the entire pregnancy. She called it her good luck coin. And she'd made a promise that if she had a little girl, she'd name her Penny.

"Sweetheart, I know, but . . ." I knew what she was trying to say. No one wanted to adopt the daughter of a murderer.

I didn't want to argue with my mother, so I nodded. "Okay, Mama, if it will help, I will." I wondered if I'd get to pick my own name or if it would just be handed to me, like an assignment.

"Good girl."

The words made me think of my father. It haunted me, thinking that maybe if he was still alive, then we could have left on our own. That maybe he *wouldn't* have followed us. That maybe we *could* have gotten away. Even now, he was ruining my life, taking away the only person I'd ever truly loved.

"Do you know anything about the couple?" I couldn't imagine living with someone else, calling them Mom or Dad. It all seemed like a nightmare—like any minute, my mother would be released, and we could finally start our lives together.

She shook her head. "I think they live in Utah. You've always wanted to ski—right, baby?"

Utah. We'd never been to too many places outside of Wyoming. I needed to start reading about it. "Yes," I said now. *But only with you,* I almost added.

She asked me about my schoolwork and if my foster parents were taking good care of me. Before I knew it, our time was up, and as I stood, I asked the question that I shouldn't have.

"Do you hate me?" My voice was small, but I needed to know. I needed to know if I'd done the wrong thing. By protecting her, I'd ruined her life. And possibly mine.

"Oh, my sweet girl." She leaned forward and took my hand when the guard wasn't looking. "I could never hate you. I love you more than anything in this whole messy world, and I don't regret anything, okay? You go out there, and you live the most beautiful life you can. Find something you love to do. Remember to play. Have fun. Keep learning. Find a good partner if that's what you choose to do one day." She squeezed my hand again and let it drop. She started to walk away, then turned. "Just promise me you'll live your life for you, Penny. Don't worry about me. Follow your dreams. Promise me?"

I opened my mouth to respond, but then she was gone. The only dream I had was for her to come home and be with me. As she disappeared in a sea of orange, I choked on a sob. Those words felt like a warning, not a request. I left feeling sad, but my foster parents didn't ask any questions on the way home. That night, I couldn't sleep. Something felt off, and I wasn't sure how to articulate it. I just had a feeling—a feeling like when my father's mood had shifted or when I could feel an actual storm rolling in. The smell of the rain coming. The way my hairline would tingle when it thundered.

The next morning, I helped myself to breakfast, and my foster mom sat at the pocked wooden table, a Kleenex clutched in her fist. Her eyes were red and swollen, and my first thought was that something had happened to her husband, Phil.

"Penny, come sit down for a second."

I worried that I was in trouble or that it was already time for me to leave. I hoped I hadn't been too difficult or too loud; I'd tried to listen, tried to make myself invisible to stay out of the way. I waited for Pam to continue.

"Penny, I'm afraid I have some bad news." She sniffed and wiped her nose. "It's about your mother."

A pit spread so wide in my stomach I was afraid it would consume me completely. I groped the table, and tears sprang to my eyes so fast they burned. I swallowed, not wanting to know.

"I'm afraid . . ." Her voice drifted, and I wanted to scream for her to just tell me. "Well, Penny, I'm afraid she died. I'm so sorry."

I sat there, numb, blinking at the table. Finally, I lifted my head. "How?" I didn't want to know, not really, but I had to.

"Oh, sweetheart, I'm not sure that's important."

"It's important to me," I said. "Please tell me." My chest heaved, and I was afraid I was going to be sick.

"She slit her own throat." Her hands flew to her mouth, as if she couldn't believe she'd just said that to an eleven-year-old.

I closed my eyes, wondering how she'd gotten a weapon but mostly wondering why she would have done that to herself. Why now? Why like that? And why would she do that to *me*? Had she done it so I wouldn't think about her anymore? If so, that had been a terrible thing to do. Of course I would think about her. I would blame myself. Hadn't she known that? I would never be able to live my life now, not without her. My heart splintered, and I clutched my chest, as if it were actually breaking in two.

"Honey, I'm so sorry. I know how much you loved her."

She didn't know. She couldn't. My father was gone, and now it really was all for nothing. Maybe it would have been better to let him destroy her slowly, let him destroy us. At least then, maybe she'd still be alive. I closed my eyes as tears slipped down my cheeks. "May I be excused?"

Before she could answer, I ran back upstairs and threw myself on my bed. I gathered my stuffed animals in my arms and cried until my throat was raw and aching.

For the first time in my life, I had no one. No one to watch me grow up. No one to love me.

No one to love.

39

NOW

I looked at the riddle I'd typed out, pretty sure that someone on that thread could be the killer.

I was putting an end to this tonight, even if it meant placing myself in danger. I shut the computer. "Hey, honey, can I talk to Ralph for a second?"

"Sure. I'm going to take a shower."

Ralph told her where the guest towels were, and once she was out of earshot, I leveled with him. "I need you to watch Lily tonight."

He knit his brows together. "And where will you be?"

"Here."

"Ruby, spill it." He lowered his paper and crossed his legs, waiting.

"I told the killer to meet me tonight. On the lake."

Ralph tossed the paper back to the table "Ruby, sometimes I think you forget that life is not a horror movie."

"But isn't it? Isn't that exactly what this is?"

"Why are you telling me this?"

I swallowed. "In case it doesn't go my way. In case someone needs to care for Lily. I trust you, and if anything happens . . ."

He lifted a meaty hand. "Stop right there. Number one, how do you even know whoever is doing this is on that forum?"

"It's the only thing that makes sense. Ryan was on the forum. Cassie was, too, and so was Beth. The killer is picking these people off, one by one. That can't be a coincidence."

He sighed. "You need to tell the detective what you're doing."

I nodded. "I will." *I will not.* I knew Detective Ellis didn't trust me, especially if she'd been digging into my past.

I'd blocked so much of those years: all those horrible moments with my father, what we'd done to get out of that life. And then, after my mother and I had been granted the opportunity to start over, she'd basically turned herself in. We'd been given a second chance, and she'd chosen an impossible way out. I still missed her, still wished there could have been a different outcome.

I cleared away those haunting memories and focused only on the task at hand: luring the killer to the lake. It was strange that I was more curious than scared. Someone in this community was killing people, and it was time to find out who had started all this with Tom.

If I made it out of this alive, Lily and I would move from this community. I'd find a new line of work, begin helping people again. Maybe I could even take Lily to meet Trish. We could finally live our lives free of the past.

After Lily emerged from the shower, I informed her Greg was going to come take her to the station; then she was going to stay with Ralph for a bit. I hesitated before pulling her into a hug.

"I love you, Lily. I'm so glad you're home."

She squeezed me back. "Me too, Mom."

I bundled up in my coat and left the house quietly to walk back to my own. Technically, it was still part of a crime scene. I had been cleared to enter but instructed to stay away from the bathroom.

I fished for my keys but saw the door was already ajar. Heart in my throat, I toed it all the way open.

"Hello?"

I listened for voices or noises, but all was quiet. I wondered if forensics had forgotten to lock up, but something told me it wasn't them. I sorted through all the things that someone could search for in here and then gasped as I raced for the stairs.

I flew to my own hiding spot in the attic, but everything was gone. "No, no, no." My mother's mementos. The file on Trish. Gone. I climbed down the ladder and whipped around, suddenly furious. Was this the police or someone else?

I closed my eyes, trying to think. I thought of my dad, always so friendly with the cops but a horror show behind closed doors. And I thought of what those papers insinuated about Tom, throwing his ex-wife to the wolves. I thought of his body in the lake again, how easily I'd blocked it because it had reminded me so much of my father, of what had happened to him. I'd dissociated from the truth, unable to remember.

I walked to Tom's office and studied it with fresh eyes. Had someone been searching for my secrets . . . or something else?

I'd been through the filing cabinets a million times. The same with his desk. I slid my hands underneath the surface again, tapped on the walls to make sure there were no false surfaces or hidden compartments beyond the loose floorboard in his office closet. If Tom had wanted to keep something secret, he wouldn't have hidden it here.

Something nagged at the back of my brain as I walked to our bedroom. I stared at it as an observer might until I glimpsed my nightstand drawer.

I rushed over and opened it. Tom's book that had been at Cassie's caught my eye. *The War of Art.* I flipped it open and scanned all his notes. What I'd assumed was just commentary about the book quickly revealed itself as fragments of something else . . . coded messages, perhaps?

As I read through the notes, I wondered if whoever had killed Cassie had come looking for this book. Had Tom stashed it over there to keep the book safe?

After I'd flipped through the whole thing, I closed my eyes and summoned Tom's thought process, a common refrain he'd used when he would work on cases: things aren't always what they seem.

I scanned the book again, and phrases in the margins popped out at me. *Cold-blooded murder. Sick. Premeditated.*

I hesitated. Words like these could be used to describe any of his clients. But Tom would never write about his clients here.

What if he was writing about me?

I didn't have time to decipher his words now, but I threw the book into my bag and began gathering supplies for tonight. Despite everything I'd been through, I rarely carried a gun, but tonight was life or death. I grabbed my Glock 19 from the back of my closet, a gift I'd bought myself once Tom had disappeared, and stuffed it in a duffel, along with a few other items.

On the way out, I stopped at the entrance to the bathroom, which had been sectioned off with crime scene tape. I didn't dare walk in, didn't stare into the tub. I closed my eyes, wondering if Ryan had known something I hadn't. Was that why he'd been slinking around my house? Had he known who the killer was?

Moving past the bathroom, I realized I wanted nothing more to do with this house. I'd worked so hard for so long to build a stable life for myself. And then Tom had come in and blown it all up. He'd convinced me I needed a big fancy house with expensive things in a good neighborhood to tell me that I was somehow a decent person. That bad deeds could be forgotten. I was trying to outrun who I'd been, but I couldn't. I never would.

Whatever happened tonight, some sort of truth would be revealed. Maybe I'd make it out alive, and maybe I wouldn't. But either way, I wasn't running anymore.

It was time to face who I was and what I'd done.

Even if it cost me my life.

* * *

When Cottage Grove was soundly asleep, I pulled my boat into the water.

There were still patrol cars on the end of every block, but no one was by the lake. I silently rowed until I was out of sight and began to relax as my limbs shook awake.

There was only one invisible spot on the water as you rounded a curve and came to a tiny slice of land, its own little self-erected island, before it opened into a cavernous forest. Whoever was doing this had been watching me, maybe for some time. They would know my habits, understand from the clues that this was where I came after a long row. This was my peaceful spot, my safe haven. I assumed that whoever I was meeting would be clever enough to figure out my riddle on the forum and already be there, waiting.

My muscles ached from the lack of movement the past few days. I'd been plagued by adrenaline, fatigue, and fear, but not anymore. Now, I was just pissed. I wanted my life back, a life without secrets, a life without this place.

I picked up my pace as I pushed back with my legs and pulled with my arms. It was bitterly cold, but my lungs adjusted. I rounded the corner, searching for other boats in the water but seeing nothing. I was the first to the island. I tied up my boat and stepped out, my legs shaky from the sudden late-night exertion.

I checked behind me in the clump of trees, wondering if someone would suddenly appear and just end all of this. No fighting chance. No explanation. Just swift and clean.

I breathed into my palms, bouncing on my toes to stay warm. I waited for an hour, but no one came. The adrenaline surge had left me depleted, and I was antsy to get back to Lily.

If I made it back at all.

I shook away the grim thoughts, always the pessimist. Now that Lily was back, I had something to live for. It was my job to make sure she had the type of life she deserved. And I would do whatever it took to give it to her.

Just as I was about to give up and row back, I heard something beyond the trees, edging up from the left. I checked my watch: it was nearly one in the morning. I steeled myself, tapping the icy gun in my pocket.

This is it.

Suddenly, I heard someone curse as they bumped close to shore and then groan as they heaved themselves out of a canoe. I peered into the darkness and visibly relaxed when I saw Daisy.

"What are you doing here?" I hissed.

"What do you think?" She straightened, clearly out of breath. "I'm *crackersmp*. I figured out your little riddle."

My blood turned cold. "You?"

She lifted her hands, as if in surrender. "It's not what you think."

I snorted. "When, in the history of the world, has that sentence ever been true?"

"I'm here to help you figure out the truth, Ruby, not kill you."

I didn't want her to twist words or distract me. Before I could think about it, I took the gun from my pocket and aimed it at her. "Get in the boat."

"Come on, Ruby. We need to talk privately. We need—" Her eyes fell to the gun. "Really? You know me. Think about it."

"I'm not listening to anything you say. Get in your boat."

She grumbled but obeyed. I didn't want to leave my boat here, but I wanted to get off this island and back to where people could see us.

"Now row."

"Are you serious? It about killed me getting out here to meet you. I'm not a freaking Olympic athlete."

"Row!" My voice thundered between us, and she closed her mouth, took the oars, and began to row. Her form was sloppy, and she was so out of breath I almost thought about taking over, but instead, I kept the gun trained on her.

"I'm not the killer, Ruby."

"Spoken like every killer in history." As we rowed closer to shore, it all came together in my head. "Of course it's you. Your job. Your special skills. You're obsessed with murder."

She huffed. "Obsession is different from being a psychopath. I didn't kill anyone."

I pointed the gun right between her eyes. "How could I possibly know that?"

Daisy stopped for a moment, still gasping for breath. "Because I like to research murder, not *actually* murder people."

"You hated Tom."

She gave me a pointed look. "So did you."

I didn't want to talk more until I could record our conversation. The dock came into view, and I coached her on how to bring the boat in safely. "When we get out, do not make a run for it, or I will shoot you. Do you understand? We are going to my house, where we are going to talk, and you are going to tell me the truth."

"Understood." She stood on wobbly legs, and I worried for a moment that she was going to pass out. I stuck the gun in my pocket, still aimed at her back as she walked a few paces ahead.

We stayed silent until we reached my house. I gave her the keys and then told her to sit on my couch. I sat on the sofa across from her, placed my phone on the end table, and aimed the gun at her chest.

"It isn't me, Ruby. Think about it."

I thought about it. She was the only person who was obsessed with murder, who could hack into phones, who seemed to know everything about everyone.

"You pretended to be my friend."

"I am your friend." She sighed again, blowing her bangs into the air. "What would be my motive?"

That I couldn't answer. "Ratings?"

She opened her mouth but then shrugged. "Well, yeah, actually. That would be one way to get them, but it's *not* me. I swear."

"Fine. It's not you." I rummaged in my duffel with my free hand and tossed the book with Tom's notes onto the coffee table. "Then help me find out who."

"By reading Steven Pressfield?"

"Tom kept notes in there that aren't about the book and most definitely aren't about work. I found the book at Cassie's, so maybe there's a connection. Maybe Cassie figured out who was after him. If there are any clues or answers in there, I haven't had time to figure them out."

She nodded, always up for a task, even with her life in danger. I threw her my pad of paper and a pen and watched her work. As she did, I wondered if I did have it wrong, if it wasn't Daisy after all.

After a while, she looked up at me. "Does 'wasn't innocent hit-and-run' and 'failed Glencoe psych eval' mean anything to you? They're lumped together, but I'm not sure what goes where."

I opened my mouth to say no, then froze. Every hair on my neck stood up as a few of the puzzle pieces shifted together. I lowered the gun. "Oh my God," I said.

She offered me a pained smile. "Are you getting it now?"

"Wait, you know who it is?"

"I have a very strong hunch."

"Well, well, look who finally figured it out."

We were sitting in the shadows, but Daisy and I both jumped in surprise as a figure emerged from the hallway, a butcher knife poised in the air like a sword. "Are you surprised?"

I looked straight into my daughter's eyes and nodded. "Yes, Lily. I am very surprised."

40

Lily came into my life when she was only six.

I was petrified of becoming a mother for so many reasons. I didn't trust any parents, and I most certainly didn't trust myself to become one. I didn't know how to tell Tom that I shouldn't be his first choice to take care of his daughter, but I loved him, which meant loving her too. I was overwhelmed by his faith in me, that he'd want me to step in as a mother figure for his child.

There were so many things I wanted to tell him before we got serious: about my own childhood, about what had happened once my mom had gone to prison and then died by suicide. I'd seen things and blocked things and sometimes scared myself as I mixed up reality with what happened in my head.

The first day I met Lily, I went to Tom's house. I brought her a stuffed penguin because Tom told me that was her favorite animal. When I arrived, she was on her swing set out back. My heart kicked. She had unruly red curls and was wearing a purple dress. She was barefoot, and as I approached, I could see a smear of dirt across her cheek.

"Hello," she said. Her eyes were bright and curious. "I found a dead bird. Do you want to see?"

I was shocked by her discovery, but I nodded, forgetting about the stuffed animal in my bag. Tom stood behind us, hands thrust in his pockets, as he observed the two of us. I was nervous about him judging me. I wanted to be what *he* wanted me to be, and I was afraid if I spoke, I might say the wrong thing. She brought me over to a little play table, where a bird lay, one of its wings snapped like a twig. I tried to keep my face passive as she started telling me facts about birds.

"What happened to its wing, I wonder?" I finally asked, my first words to my boyfriend's daughter. *What happened, what happened, what happened.* Something in me burned hot as an ember, but I focused on what Lily had to say.

She shrugged her tiny shoulders and squinted into the summer sun. "I don't know," was all she said.

I rummaged in my oversize bag for the gift. "I'm Ruby, by the way."

She scratched her freckled nose. "I know."

"Close your eyes," I said. "I have a surprise for you."

Her little lips quivered as she held out her dirt-streaked palms. I set the penguin softly in her hands and told her to open her eyes.

She bounced up and down and smiled, revealing a missing front tooth. "I love penguins! Daddy, look!" She wagged the stuffed bird back and forth and then set off with imaginary banter between the dead bird and the penguin. I took that as my cue to let her play.

Tom slung an arm around my shoulders as I joined him. "See? A natural," he said, kissing my temple.

But I wasn't a natural. I couldn't fill his dead wife's shoes, and I certainly didn't have a role model for what a perfect parent should be. The only good parents I knew were ones I saw on TV, ones I pretended were mine. I'd seen so many horrible things during my own childhood, things I'd buried deep inside. So instead, I pretended. I pretended I'd had a happy childhood; I pretended I was a stable adult; I pretended, now, that I could handle becoming a mother seemingly overnight. But this was all too *awesome* of a responsibility, I realized, and every part of me wanted to run.

That night, Tom cooked us all dinner, and I struggled to make conversation with Lily. But she was eager to show me her room after and invited me to play Legos. "Not dolls," she said. "Dolls are for babies." I couldn't believe how sure of herself she was, even so young. I knew that trait would carry her far, and I almost told her so, but something stopped me. She'd just met me. She didn't need life lessons from a stranger. We talked about books and friends, and as I stood up to leave, I noticed the stuffed animal I'd given her on her bed, but its head was missing.

"Lily," I said, scooping up the black-and-white body. "What happened?"

Her eyes lit up. "I did surgery!" She reached under her bed and produced the stuffed-animal head, the cotton oozing out of its neck like blood. "See?"

"But why?" I asked. "Didn't you like the penguin?"

She smiled at me with her whole face, the space of her missing tooth an inky block. "I like it like this," she said, tossing the head up and down in her small palm. "Don't you?"

I offered her a smile and told her good night, something traveling up my spine like a ghost.

Tom stopped me on the way out, his eyes warm, the skin around them crinkled and tan. "You did great today," he said, almost as if I'd passed a test. "Maybe we can try a sleepover next?"

I kissed him in response, but inside, I was itching to get back to the safety of my house, away from the little girl who had looked at me with something dark in her eyes.

I recognized that darkness because I'd felt it too . . . I'd been running from it my whole life.

41

Lily tapped the edge of the butcher knife against her open palm.

Her eyes were wild and unfocused, and I knew immediately she was having an episode.

"What are you doing, Lily? Put down the knife. You're not a killer."

"Aren't I?" Her tone was sharp and biting, her face twisted into a disgusted scowl. "Like mother, like daughter—isn't that right?"

"You hit a boy by accident. That doesn't make you a murderer."

"You don't really believe that, do you?"

I opened my mouth to protest, then hesitated. Did I believe that? I'd always *wanted* to assume that she'd hit Andrew by accident. When she'd come to me, she had been hysterical. She'd left Andrew at the scene, and I'd taken her account of the story at face value.

We'd ditched her car and made sure she was nowhere to be found when the news broke that he'd been part of a hit-and-run. I knew that boy had hurt her, but I didn't know the extent of the circumstances, did I? Instead, I'd just been willing to cover up what she'd done and lock her away for her own protection, just as my mother had. I tried to keep my voice calm and steady, tried not to look at Daisy. "Why don't you tell me what really happened?"

She sighed and lowered the knife briefly. "I did hit him," she said. "But at Leonard's party, he . . ." She swallowed and shook her head, her eyes finally landing on mine. "He tried to rape me. I got away, ran to my car, but he came after me. He was enraged. He was banging on the glass so hard I thought he'd break it. I backed up, and he was just standing there, so I . . . I hit him. I didn't know what else to do. I didn't mean to. It just happened."

My heart broke for her, and even though she was holding a knife, I almost wrapped her in a hug. "Why didn't you tell me the truth?"

"Because I didn't want to believe it. I wanted to believe it was an accident."

Didn't I know that story all too well.

"What I *didn't* know was that afterward, it's all I could think about. I just kept seeing his face, how shocked he was at that exact moment of impact, the sound his body made under the tires." She knocked a few tears away. The blade glinted under the artificial light. "When Dad came to get me and I got off my meds again, I just . . . I had that urge. I wanted everyone who'd hurt you or me to pay. And he sensed it. He was finally seeing who I was. And he wrote everything down in that little book." She motioned to the book on Daisy's lap.

"What did you do, Lily?" My voice was hushed. Part of me wanted to know, and part of me didn't.

"When I called Ralph and came back, Cassie had Dad's book. He'd told her his fears about me, so she confronted me about what I'd done to Andrew. Dad knew it wasn't an accident, and he knew you covered it up. Cassie said she was going to go to the cops. I couldn't let her get you into trouble . . . or me. She had a copy of the file about your case, so I took it. But she must have ripped away that mug shot of your mom at the last second to leave as some sort of clue for the detective." She blinked her eyes and shook her head. "I didn't mean to."

I studied Lily. She didn't look remorseful; she looked unhinged. I glanced at the book still clutched in Daisy's fist. So Tom had figured it out, had seen straight through to what Lily had actually done. Why hadn't I? "And Ryan?"

She clenched her jaw and sighed. "If he was in the picture, it could never just be the two of us. It should have always just been the two of us, right?" She tightened her grip on the knife, and Daisy flinched on the couch.

I thought about Lily's genuine shock when she had seen Ryan in the bathtub. How had she done all that alone? When had she become such a good actor?

"Mom, I know how hard you tried to make me better. The meds worked for a while, but the moment I came off them, I felt like myself again. I felt . . ." She glanced up and searched for the perfect word. "*Powerful.* Did you feel powerful when you killed your father?"

I knew I shouldn't buy into her tricks, but I played along. "I didn't kill my father, Lily."

"Yes, you did!" she shrieked. "It's all in the details!" She bounced excitedly from foot to foot, manic. Daisy shifted uncomfortably again with Lily at her back, scooting to the edge of the couch to create some distance. "That night at the Murderlings when we did that case. It was your case. I started to look into it after and put it all together. I just couldn't believe you were the kid of a murderer, and you'd never told me. I found some of the reports. The angle of the knife suggested someone taller than your father. Your mother was much shorter. She could have never overpowered him, and even if she'd snuck up behind him, the angle of the knife would have been tilted up, not down. The angle of *your* blade was from above, which made me think you climbed up on a chair—am I right?"

My mouth went dry. *How could she possibly know that?* No one did. Not even Daisy. "Your mother must have really loved you to turn herself in. I should know. You basically did the same thing for me." Her eyes were full of love and pain. "When Dad found out what I'd done and what *you'd* done to keep me safe, he started seeing what you've seen all these years." She leaned forward. "Deep down, he knew. He knew what I was." She rolled her shoulders and sighed. "He brought me home, you know, but you weren't here. I thought if we could all just talk and finally be honest, then everything would be fine." She sniffed and looked at her shoes.

I racked my brain to think about where I would have been and then remembered that I'd checked myself into a hotel after our fight. Was that when he'd come back? Or later?

"When we got here, he rushed to his office and hid something in his closet," she continued. "He went to make some calls, and I found the loose floorboard. I realized he'd been lying to me about my mother for my whole life." Her eyes teared up again as she looked at me.

"Did you know about Trish?"

"No." Her voice wobbled as she answered. "I didn't."

"Why did you kill your father, Lily?"

"Why?" Her voice ricocheted off the walls. "Because he was horrible! I slit his throat for doing to you what your father did to your mother. We're the same, you and me. I did it for you."

I tried to keep my face passive as I calculated her every move. She kept pacing behind Daisy, who was now sitting as still as a statue. The gun twitched in my fingers, but I would not shoot my child. "So where have you been all this time if you killed Tom? And why did you come back if you got away with it?"

"I knew the combination to his safe, so I grabbed all his cash, packed a bag to make it look like he took off on his own. But once I was low on money and found out the body had resurfaced thanks to the forum, I called Ralph. I was tired of being a ghost, tired of sleeping on couches. I don't know how his body floated to the surface, and I was worried it would be traced back to me. Or you. But then Cassie and Ryan happened, and Beth pissed me off the other night, so . . ."

Something clicked. "You're @dahmernotjeffrey," I said. "On the forum."

239

"Ding, ding, ding!" She scratched her head with the blade. "You know, I really think Jeffrey was misunderstood. All he wanted was for someone to love him, someone to *stay* with him. I know just how that feels."

"I never left you, Lily. I was always there for you."

She shook her head until it was bobbing obsessively. "I know. You've always been there for me, which is why you're still alive."

She braced her hands on the couch, the blade coming within inches of Daisy's throat. "Don't you see, Mom? I'm just like you. We're the same."

"Why did you kill them all the same way?"

She stabbed the knife my way as a few tears fell down her cheeks. "I wanted to make you remember."

A vision surfaced of my tiny body on a chair, holding a razor. Something so horrific that had, in fact, been so easy. And I had gotten away with it too.

"But why?"

"Because you're not *honest* about who you are and what you've done, Mom. You saved your mother's life by slaying a monster, and you hid that? Why? You let Dad abuse you and kept all your emotions inside? Why? Aren't you stronger than that?"

My heart felt like it was being ripped in two. I'd tried so hard not to be like my mother, to numb myself, to ignore what was going on, and now here I was, setting the same exact example for Lily. I'd failed in every possible way, but I still had a chance to make things right.

"Lily, drop the knife. We can figure this out. Get you out of this."

I could tell I'd genuinely shocked her. "What did you just say?"

"I won't tell anyone what you've done. We can just leave, start over, like you said. Just you and me."

Her intense gaze faltered, and for a moment, I still saw a glimpse of that girl I'd raised: the one who loved Legos and animals and games.

But taking someone's life changed you forever. I didn't want that for her—didn't want for her to disappear completely.

"We're the same, just like you said." My voice was low and even. "I won't tell anyone. I promise."

She lowered the knife by her side, as if the entire weight of the world was on her shoulders. "You won't?" Her voice was small, a little girl's.

"I won't," I said, reassuring her. "I promise. And neither will Daisy, right?"

"I won't say a word," Daisy said, turning. "I promise."

Just when I thought she'd drop the knife, Detective Ellis silently stepped behind Lily and placed a gun to her temple. I flinched, even though I knew she wouldn't fire.

"A word to the wise," Daisy said, staring up at Lily from her place on the couch. "Make sure your victims are as good as dead before you confess all your crimes."

Detective Ellis slapped handcuffs onto Lily's thin wrists, forcing her to drop the knife. "We've got it from here, Ruby." Her eyes were softer, apologetic. "Smart play with the phone." I stabbed the "End call" button. I'd called her right when we'd walked in the door and placed it on speaker.

"You liar!" Lily shrieked, her whole body bucking to life. "You promised!"

My heart ached as I looked at her. "I didn't break my promise, Lily," I said, suddenly exhausted. "I didn't tell anyone what you've done. You did."

42

"Get in your closet."

My mother's breath smelled like alcohol. It was warm and tickled my cheek. I rolled over and checked my kitty alarm clock. It was three in the morning. I rubbed my eyes, realizing I was taking up precious seconds that I might need to hide.

"Get in with me." It was the first time I had ever suggested it, and my mother's eyes filled with tears.

"Oh, sweet girl. I can't." She sniffed and ran a hand over my hair. "I can't get in with you. He'd find me."

I sat up. My body felt heavy, and my voice was still thick with sleep. "No, he won't. He's never found me."

She sighed, and in that sigh, I saw how tired she was: tired of hiding from my father, of his short-lived apologies, of the bruising and pain, of stashing me away like some terrible secret. I wanted a different life, a better life for both of us, and it started with getting my father out of the picture.

"I want to leave," I said. "Let's just go." Though my father had made me a promise that day at the river, he had already broken it. I shouldn't have been surprised, but the ease with which he'd turned evil again had crushed me.

"It's not that simple, sweetie." She gnawed on her bottom lip, the skin broken and red. "He'd find us. He'd find us wherever we went."

Those words cemented something I already seemed to know in my brain. I nodded, gathered my favorite stuffed animals, and slung a warm arm around my mother's neck as I leaned in for a hug. "You can fight back, you know."

She began to cry then, hard, dry sobs that racked her whole body. She'd learned to cry silently, to not make too much noise. My father sucked up all the noise in the room, all the noise in our lives. There wasn't room for anyone else's joy or laughter or pain. I was tired of it all.

A door slammed downstairs, and she cut off her cries in an instant, her eyes glassy and wild. "Go. I'll get you after."

I nodded, though I knew she wouldn't. She'd be in too much pain to get me after. Instead, I would wait until he'd left; then I'd find her, crumpled and bleeding, and nurse her wounds. I couldn't tell my mother that I sought some sense of relief in the process of helping her. It was one of the few times I felt useful. I liked putting people back together again, but I wished my mother didn't need me to patch her up.

Slowly, I slid from my bed and opened the closet door, which I kept oiled regularly so as not to creak. My bedroom door still hadn't been fixed since my father had kicked it in, and it was awful hearing the hateful words he spewed at my mother when he was drunk.

"Lenny, get your ass down here now!"

His voice was thick with drink. She nodded once, mouthed *I love you*, and disappeared from view. She was getting ready for another performance, steeling her already battered body for a fight. Instead of getting into my closet, I pulled the straight razor I'd stashed from beneath my pillow. My mother gave my father shaves once a week with a set of straight razors he kept in the bathroom.

I'd watch her sometimes, the way she dipped the razor into the water, tipped his chin back, and scraped the errant hairs clean. I always wondered how he trusted her to do that, when she could easily slice into his skin. But she never did.

I'd been sleeping with the razor beneath my pillow for days, and he hadn't even noticed. I'd practiced cutting things outside, understanding the weight of the blade, the wooden handle comfortable in my hot palm. I'd studied the human body in my encyclopedia, memorized which places were the most dangerous to inflict wounds. Taking a deep breath, I prepared myself just as my mother had and then padded slowly down the stairs.

He was already yelling. A dish exploded against a cabinet, and I stared down at my bare feet. I hadn't accounted for that. How could I have forgotten socks? It was too late to go back. I needed to stay focused. I needed to show my mother that there was another way out.

At the door, I glimpsed his flushed face and his bloodshot eyes. *Crazy eyes.* His mouth was contorted like a monster's, and it reminded me of my favorite Roald Dahl book, *The Witches*, when the little boy stumbled upon all those women in secret, before they all removed their human masks to reveal their truly grotesque identities.

My father was like that: a witch, a monster, flinging off his mask at home because he was too weak to show anyone but us who he really was. He didn't deserve my mother, and despite his broken promises, he didn't deserve me.

"Ronnie, please. Let's just talk."

"I don't want to talk! You fucking *whore!*" He clamped her by the throat, and my mother's face contorted in surprise. Even when she was expecting it, he still found a way to surprise her. I squeezed my eyes shut out of habit but then forced them open. He gripped her so hard her feet lifted off the gummy tile as he slammed her against the refrigerator. Her fingers scraped at his thick hairy forearms, drawing blood. But my father was a towering, hulking man, built from years of construction. His hands were so rough I wondered if the calluses alone would break the smooth, delicate skin of her throat.

Move, Penny.

I entered the room so silently even my mother didn't hear me until I lifted a chair from the breakfast table and set it down gently behind my father. Carefully, I climbed up, catching my balance, just as my mother screamed. He slammed her again and again against the refrigerator, squeezing her throat until it seemed her eyes would pop right out of her head. She was almost purple—such angry, pulsing veins forked along her forehead. I dropped my stuffed animal and looped an arm around my father's neck.

In the next moment, he staggered forward and then turned, his back now to the refrigerator. He looked at me, his only daughter, wild eyed, a river of blood drenching his fingers and clothes. *How did that blood get there?*

I stared down at the razor in my hand, which dripped red. I peered at my mother, who was no longer screaming. Her fingers were still touching her own aggravated throat, a mirror of my dying father. She scrambled to her feet beside me, removing the blade from my unsteady hand. We both stood, watching, as my father reached out for us to help him. We did not. We simply witnessed all that hot anger and spite draining right out of him until he finally slid to the floor in a river of his own blood, dead as a doornail.

I waited for my mother's wrath to pour down on me, but instead, she burst into tears. I could feel anger swirling inside me. How could she be sad for this man? How could she mourn such a monster?

Finally, she grabbed my shoulders and looked at me, tears running down her still beet red cheeks. "I need you to listen to me very carefully, Penny. And do exactly as I say."

There was a light in her eyes I hadn't seen before. *A release.*

The ghost was gone, and now we were free.

"Okay, Mama."

I would do anything she said.

43

NOW

I sat at Ralph's table, nursing a hot tea.

I was done with alcohol. It was time to stop numbing myself to the pain and start healing. That was one thing Lily had been right about.

"I just can't believe Lily killed all those people," I said. Lily had already been booked and processed. Greg was with her now, preparing her defense.

"It's beyond impressive." Daisy whistled and then saw my stricken face. "Sorry. I just mean it's *impressive* that she didn't leave a trace of evidence. For, you know, a kid. But I do feel responsible. I'm sure she learned a lot about crime scenes from working with me."

I dropped my head in my hands. "If anyone's at fault here, it's me. I've known since Lily was six that she was mentally unstable. And I assumed drugs would help. I knew she wanted to get off her meds . . . all those deaths are on me, not you."

"Neither of you are responsible for her actions," Ralph said. He'd let me know that he'd been trying to talk to me about Lily—that he'd had concerns about her well-being for quite some time, though he'd never assumed she was responsible for what police were calling the Cottage Grove Massacre.

"But she's just a kid," I said. "A kid who will spend the rest of her life behind bars."

Daisy rubbed circles along my back, and Ralph refilled my tea. I looked up at these two people who had been here for me in more ways than one.

I thought about my visit to Trish. What would she think if she knew her daughter was a serial killer? It would most likely destroy her.

"I swear, these kids today," Daisy said, sitting back and crossing her arms. "All these infamous serial killers are glorified with their own Netflix shows, and then boom. Life imitates art. It's frightening."

"Spoken by the woman who leads true-crime nights and has a lucrative podcast."

"That's when I knew, by the way," Daisy said, knocking back a shot. "I knew it was Lily when she started chiming in the other night with the Murderlings. My Spidey senses went up."

I knocked away a fresh wave of grief. Just because she'd done horrible things didn't mean I would give up on her. I wanted her to get better. I wanted her to get the help she needed. I wanted her to understand that what she'd done had consequences.

It would be a long life for her behind bars, another life taken.

"What am I supposed to do now?"

Ralph clapped me on the back. "I think it's time you tell your own truth."

I nodded, knowing there was one person I needed to clear the air with. This time, I would leave nothing out. After I had showered and downed some more tea, I drove to the police station.

On the way, I thought about my life over this past year. All the ways I'd changed. All that I'd lost. All that I'd sacrificed. All that I'd missed.

As I shoved the car into park, I took a moment to realize I was no longer a suspect. I could live my life while my daughter spent the rest of hers behind bars. She wouldn't get a second chance, or even a third. Not like me.

Inside, Detective Ellis was waiting for me in her office.

I sank into a chair. "Where should I begin?" I asked.

She twiddled a pen in her hand. "Wherever you want."

"Fine," I sighed. "My name is Penny Elaine Richter, and I killed my father when I was ten . . . though I don't remember it." I'd never uttered those words to anyone, and once I started to talk, the words tumbled out. I told her the whole story—of my upbringing, my father, my mother, my dissociative behavior, my abusive marriage, secretly medicating Lily—and when I was finished, she handed me a tissue.

"That's a long time to hide such a big secret," she finally offered.

I shrugged. "I'm good at hiding." I dabbed my eyes. "My whole life, I've blamed myself for my mother taking her own life. In my young brain, I thought I'd done the right thing, even if that thing was taking another life." I dropped my head in my hands. "I realize now that it was a mistake. I should have turned my father in to the police, forced my mother to get help."

Detective Ellis looked at her pen again, rotating it in her hands. "But you can't force anyone to get help, Ruby. You know that better than anyone."

I thought of myself—how I'd refused to turn Tom in and how I'd thought that by not abandoning Lily, I was somehow doing the right thing. That by getting Lily to pop meds, I was helping her do the right thing. I'd seen what I wanted to see; I hadn't seen the truth. I wiped my nose and sat up straight. "So what now? Will I be arrested too?"

She glanced behind her and then shrugged. "Without a murder weapon or conclusive evidence for your confession, there's not much we can do, I'm afraid."

It couldn't be that simple, could it? My fists relaxed, and I let out an exhale. "And Lily? What's going to happen to her?"

"She's going away for the rest of her life, Ruby. I'm sorry. But you can still be there for her if you choose to."

I thought about Lily, the girl I'd raised as my own. I'd seen all the signs. I'd known what could happen. "I want to be there for her," I said. She would have a long road ahead, and no one should have to travel it alone.

The detective lifted one shoulder, then dropped it. "So be there."

As I went to leave, I stopped at the door. "Can I ask you a question?" She nodded. "Did you really think it was me?"

Detective Ellis sat back and sighed, the pen twirling in her fingers. "At the beginning, yes. And then . . . no. I've never seen crime scenes so wellscrubbed. Not in all my years on the force. No offense, but I didn't think you could pull that off." She straightened her files. "Though I didn't think a kid could either."

I nodded, suddenly overcome with fatigue.

"You take good care of yourself, Ruby."

"You too, Detective."

On the way out, I tipped my face to the sky and breathed in. The cold air invaded my lungs, reminding me that I was still alive, that I was still here.

So much had happened that was out of my control, but I still had a life to live.

If I could just release the past.

If I could just let go of the guilt.

44

I waited until Lily plopped down across from me, the plexiglass smudged.

Her hair had been chopped short, and a long jagged scratch marred her cheek. She stared at me, then picked up the phone.

"That looks infected," I said, pointing to her cheek.

Her fingers reached up to gingerly tap the flesh. Her eyes were glassy, and her gaze hovered somewhere over my shoulder, not directly at me.

"How are you?" The trial had been relatively short, considering she'd murdered five people. Greg had gone for an insanity defense, and though it had merit, ultimately she'd been tried as a sane adult. Now, she would spend the rest of her life in prison, with no chance for early parole. My heart ached for such a horrible loss. Not only for her life but for all the victims and their families. While I had thought I was protecting her, she'd gone on a killing spree.

Her eyes slid back to me, dead and cold. "How am I? Oh, you know, just peachy! We stay up late and tell stories and braid each other's hair. It's just like summer camp but with murderers."

"Lily."

She sighed and dropped her head in her hands. "It's awful," she finally whispered. She raised her eyes. "I just want to come home."

My throat tightened, and it took everything in me not to smash the plexiglass between us and break her out of here. "I know." I pressed my hand to the glass, and after a moment, she lifted hers too.

"I want you to walk me through it, Lily. Starting with Dad." I knew about Andrew, had heard the testimony that he'd tried to rape her at Leonard's party. In a fit of rage, she'd hit him with her car, and while some might say that was still cold-blooded murder, many women I knew would understand that type of retaliation. But to kill her own father as some backward attempt to protect me, and then the others . . . I still couldn't wrap my head around how she'd pulled it all off. Or why she'd felt the need to do it.

I'd learned during the trial that Lily wasn't proud of her murders. She'd said it was a compulsion, a way to channel all that sadness into something that eased the pain. But the moment after she had hurt someone, her own hurt would set in again, deeper and stronger.

But logistically, all of it still didn't make sense. The timing. The skill. The motives. I didn't understand why she'd killed them in the exact way I'd killed my father.

She swallowed too, her eyes full of remorse. "I really wasn't going to kill Dad," she said, fiddling with the beige phone cord. "After he fell down the stairs, he got a call from his PI and then went to Ralph to force his hand. When he discovered I'd been in a psych ward all those months and that you had gone along with the premise I was missing, he was hell bent on getting me out." She scraped her finger against the linoleum in front of her. Finally, she sighed. "He stashed me in a hotel for a few days but then decided to bring me home because he needed to get some things and didn't trust that I wouldn't run if he left me alone. But when we got home, he was irate. I'd never seen him like that. He was going to kill you," she finally whispered.

My blood went cold. "What?"

"You went behind his back. I knew he hurt you sometimes, but when I saw that look in his eye, I believed him. I believed he would do it."

I could barely breathe, but I wanted her to keep talking. I wanted to know the whole truth.

"I didn't know what to do, so I told him I wanted to go for a row to your special spot because I missed you, and then we could go. We could leave. We could start over for good."

This was a surprise. I'd just assumed she'd killed him in the house and then somehow dragged his body into the lake. None of those details had come up in court.

"We rowed out to the island after sunset. I told him I wanted to have a picnic. He was nervous, on edge. I just wanted him to calm down, change his mind about hurting you." She shrugged. "He tried to talk to me about what I'd done, about the psychology evaluations I'd failed. He wanted to get me real help, something other than medication. Suddenly, a whole life of psych wards flashed through my mind, or alternative therapies, and I decided I didn't want that. I didn't want to be sent away or poked and prodded and treated like a patient for the rest of my life. I wouldn't *let* him." She was quiet for a moment. "We had dinner, and when we were getting ready to pack up, I finally asked him if he hurt you." Her eyes filled with tears. "He looked me right in the eye and denied it." She shrugged. "So I just snapped." She tipped her head back and sighed. "Ironic, really, as I did it with the knife he gave me for Christmas."

My mind flashed to the switchblade I'd found in her dresser. Was that the murder weapon? Or one of the blades she'd been trading her meds for?

"I thought I would feel horrible, fall apart. Instead, I felt instant relief." She leveled me with a sympathetic gaze. "You know exactly what I mean, right?"

I held her gaze, but I didn't remember. I didn't remember anything except staring down at my father after the fact, confused. I'd slayed the dragon, all right, but days and weeks and months after, I'd remembered his vow to me that he would change, that he would be better. I'd remembered his tears and his hugs. His promises. I'd remembered riding on his shoulders and being tickled. I had felt shattered after the fact. Not empowered. To placate her, however, I simply nodded. "I do."

"It was over so fast. I left him there, researched what I needed to do to a body to make it never resurface." She laughed. "All that time working with Daisy actually paid off. I sunk his body in a precise location I'd mapped. I knew the water would make it more difficult to ascertain the time of death. I'm not sure how it got free." She leaned forward, her face inches from the glass. "But I did it for you. For us." Her breath fogged the space between us, then disappeared like a ghost. "After, I realized I was free to go. Start over. I wanted to tell you what I'd done, I wanted things to just go back to normal, but I knew they couldn't. I didn't know what to do, so I grabbed Dad's cash and ran. But when I heard what had happened with his body, I came back. I thought what I'd done was just about Andrew, just about Dad." She dug her fingernails into her palms, making instant halfmoons against her flesh. "I wanted it to be because they were bad men, but it wasn't."

"So why hurt all those other innocent people, Lily? They didn't do anything to you."

"Because I could." Spit flew out of her mouth and landed on the glass. She smeared the spit away with her middle finger. Sighing, she sat back.

I couldn't wrap my head around this version of Lily. *Maniacal. Murderous. Monstrous.* I'd raised this person, and here she was, vacillating between remorseful and proud.

"You did some very bad things, Lily," I said. "But you're not a bad person." It was the same speech I'd given my father all those years ago—though in the end, he'd chosen to give in to the darkness. It seemed Lily had done the same.

She bit her bottom lip. "I still need to find a way out of here. Will you help me? If we get a retrial, we can get an insanity defense this time—I just know it. The only reason we didn't is because I didn't have a legitimate prescription. But maybe you can get Dr. Forrester to testify?"

"No, Lily," I finally said. "I won't help you get an insanity defense." I couldn't. I wouldn't let her hurt an innocent person ever again.

Her nostrils flared, a tiny tell, and I didn't know if she was going to scream or laugh. Finally, she motioned for me to come closer, though I chose to stay right where I was. "You should really be careful, then," she said, lowering her voice. "You never know when it could happen again . . . especially if my theory at the Murderlings was correct."

I racked my brain to remember what she'd said.

After giving me one last look, she hung up the phone and called the guards. I watched her walk away, a thousand scenarios clashing for space in my head. *What did she say?* Panic dug a cold, hard fist into my chest as her words exploded to the surface, just like Tom's body had that day on the lake.

Maybe there's more than one killer.

ACKNOWLEDGMENTS

I feel like the incredible team at Thomas & Mercer came into my life when I needed them most. At the time, I was incredibly burned out from running my own business, publishing four books in a row with one of the Big Five, ghostwriting, consulting, homeschooling my daughter, producing a podcast, and trying to keep it all together. I hit a wall, both physically and mentally, and honestly asked myself if I wanted to continue writing fiction.

The answer, as I sat with it, was an emphatic *yes*. Writing fiction is something that has never felt like work to me, so thanks to many healers, sacrifices, and personal and professional shifts along the way, I have learned to streamline other to-dos in my life to make this author journey more of a priority.

Though I've written domestic suspense, *Don't Forget Me* is my first "true" thriller, and I've had so much fun putting this book together. I have been floored by the incredibly supportive editorial team, Jessica Tribble Wells and Angela James, whose organized, streamlined feedback has made this process the most fun I have ever had during dev edits. There are so many behind-the-scenes people who make a book happen, and I am grateful for each and every one of you. [More TK]

I have to say a special thank-you to thriller writers Jennifer Pashley, Vanessa Lillie, and Danielle Girard, for our witchy writer's retreat at Long Rhodes Retreats, which is where I really got to dive into this book and figure out what it could be. Being surrounded by your talent inspires me in so many ways. Thank you to my incredible agent, Rachel Beck, who has been with me from the very start. Thank you to all the thriller writers I read and look up to and all the friends, family, and clients who remind me that getting to use my imagination for a living is the best job in the world. Thank you to my readers. There is no book without you.

And lastly, thank you to my partner, husband, and best friend, Alex. This last year has been utterly transformational for us both. It thrills me that we are showing our daughter what it means to follow our dreams, no matter what.

ABOUT THE AUTHOR

Rea Frey is the award-winning author of several domestic suspense, women's fiction, and nonfiction books. Known as the Book Doula, she helps other authors birth their books into the world. To learn more, visit www.reafrey.com.